The Forgotten Roses

The Forgotten Roses

Deborah J. Doucette

Owl Canyon Press

First Edition, 2014
All Rights Reserved
Library of Congress Cataloging-in-Publication Data

Doucette, Deborah J.
The Forgotten Roses—1st ed.
p. cm.
ISBN: 978-0-9911211-0-6
2014930235

Owl Canyon Press
www.owlcanyonpress.com
Boulder, Colorado

Truths and roses have thorns about them.

Henry David Thoreau

1

Rose

.

"Twisted." That is the word Rebecca's mother, Eva, will use to describe the shoes. It's a word, an image that will drop into Rebecca's memory; a haphazard seed, taking root. "Twisted," Eva will declare wringing her hands as if she were squeezing the life out of a wet washcloth. Rebecca will picture black lace-up oxfords with thick soles and a hard raised heel–prison shoes. In her mind, they are contorted, cartoonishly, into corkscrews.

Rebecca will imagine the girl in the shoes when they were new, shiny. Or, maybe they had been worn by others before her and were beat. Perhaps they were too tight and pinched the girl's toes, or too loose and caused her to shuffle her indignity across the floor Rebecca will ponder. Rebecca will see her in a loose, rough cotton shirtwaist with button tabs where the waistband should be. A dress the color of schoolroom walls, holding areas, of bus station lavatories–numbing and anonymous. Her dark hair spread out stark and alarming against the Vaseline green of the fabric; shocking in its refusal to lie flat and quiet, it coiled and curled wildly, too obvious, dangerous. She will picture the girl as stocky and square and sturdy in her shoes. And angry. Her face, Rebecca will think…her face is…? Familiar.

ॐ

Rebecca's mother stands in front of the white porcelain sink in her new kitchen. The last project Rebecca's father completed before his addiction to nicotine claimed him. The last time her mother would flirtatiously wish for something, the last time Joe would take up the challenge. That was the essence of what they were to each other. Even at the end, Eva was his princess, his damsel in distress, his girl; Joe was her rescuer always, her hero.

The white countertops, cabinets, white tile floor—every surface shiny as a silver dollar—were her mother's idea; he grumbled that the color was impractical. "It'll look like a goddamn hospital." He glowered, menacingly and threw his tools around, kicked an old cabinet door, splintering the dry wood, causing his children to scatter like mice to the four corners of the house. Eva stood by passively, patiently. She cajoled him, babied him, pampered him, and got her way as usual. It was a lot of work for Rebecca's mother, this vision of husbands and wives, this version of marriage. She labored much more strenuously plotting, playacting, and preening than he did at sawing, nailing, and painting. Eva would sigh in the end, smiling like Mona Lisa.

Oh God...*Beauty and the Beast*, Rebecca would think mockingly as her eyes reflexively rolled in their sockets. The beast magically changes into a prince through Belle's saintly patience, simpering affection, and blind love. Rebecca was certain that's the way Eva saw her role, and what prompted these tidbits of advice imparted ever since Rebecca could remember: "Never contradict a boy. Play hard to get. Play dumb. Always let them win." Rebecca ignored the advice. She loved racing the boys at recess when she was a little girl and often won. How the boys felt about it was of no significance to her whatsoever.

Rebecca hated the games her mother played; "I won't do it," she told her mother, once she was old enough to figure out what was going on. After a while, she lost patience with Eva. "That is so insulting! Archaic! Times have changed you know." Eva would shake her head, lifting one shoulder in a half-hearted shrug. "Men never change," she had said. Now, with the way things have gone in her marriage, Rebecca thinks maybe Eva was right.

Eva tips her head back as steam rises, billowing up from the pot of pasta she emptied into a colander. Her short black hair, professionally coifed once a week and carefully maintained in between, is in some danger of wilting. With the back of her hand, she pushes at a few curls that try to relax over her forehead; they won't dare reappear there. She's wearing her house uniform: shapeless worn shift, clean, but irreparably stained, and canvas sneakers with holes frayed through at the toes, the bleached-white laces tied into a tight bow and double knotted. This is what she cooks, cleans, and gardens in. She does laundry in it, mows the grass in it and wears it while carrying on lengthy, involved telephone conversations with her sisters. Over the years, her children have given her designer loungewear, sweat suits, and brand new Keds. No one knows what becomes of them. Throughout Rebecca's childhood, they all thought this getup was the reason she scurried into the bedroom to hide when anyone knocked at the door.

In truth, Eva had no use for neighbors, distrusted strangers. She had her family and that was enough, that was everything. Her Anne Klein's and Ralph Laurens, her silks and linens, her expensive leather pumps and matching handbags wait in dark, perfumed closets for bi-weekly shopping excursions with her sisters, and for lunch at restaurants with invariably disappointing fare, "I make better at home."

She tosses the pasta with the tomato sauce begun early this Sunday morning, simmering for hours with olive oil, garlic, basil, bay leaf, oregano, meatballs, a few sausages. A ritual that keeps the world, for her family, turning on its axis. The kitchen workspace is small, two short steps from the stove on one side to the sink on the other. Stir, taste, lift, pour, tip back, shake the colander, empty contents into the deep bowl, two steps back to the stove, ladle in a little sauce, toss. A ballet as old as generations.

Rebecca Griffin and her mother are talking about Rebecca's latest real estate deal. Rebecca got the listing on a fixer-upper with nine acres on Farpath Road in Havenwood; a coup. She was one of four brokers interviewed by the attorney handling the sale for the owner. Attorney Hanes had been won over with her thorough listing presentation, her record of sales in the area, and partly because of the way she leaned into their conversation, lightly touching his sleeve, speaking directly into his eyes, calling him Noah, as if they were friends. When they shook hands, he held onto hers and placed his other hand on top firmly, lingering a moment; the double-handed shake–a good sign, she'd thought.

Rebecca picks a cucumber slice from the big salad bowl and says while crunching, "I feel so sorry for poor Mr. Deitzhoff, the owner. His wife died a while back and he's like a hermit, drifting around in that old place, a lost soul. I don't know what'll become of him. His attorney's in charge now," she visibly shudders at the thought. "I heard through the grapevine that Harold Deitzhoff was the chief psychologist at the women's prison in Warington a long time ago," she informs her mother.

Eva stops short at the mention of the prison and the man who worked there long ago, wooden spoon raised aloft in mid dip, raining red droplets that splat alarmingly onto the antiseptic white floor. She turns to Rebecca and begins to tell her about those shoes, planting the image that will remain, buried at the back of Rebecca's mind, germinating as if a living thing. Insistent tendrils will work their way through, surfacing when the time is right.

Now, as Eva ladles out the sauce, she serves up the rest of the story along with the ziti. "She was a tough girl, and wild. Remember, this was in the forties in East Boston. Italian parents ruled over their children. Not like now," she huffs, scoffing at these foolish times. "In those days, you did what your father told you. These were very proud people, a little crude, you know, rough, *cafone*. The whole Gabrielli family was rough, but Rose, she had that wild streak."

"She wore a big black leather jacket just like a man. And she smoked, hung around the corner with the boys! Something good girls just didn't do in that neighborhood." the tightly packed, tightly knit Italian immigrant neighborhood of East Boston. Its houses, double and triple-decker boxes packed shoulder-to-shoulder with an occasional sliver of alleyway in between, shrugging their way up and down narrow, cobbled streets that run, eventually, to the sea. And on every accidental spit of land, every meager scrap of dirt on which the sun might shine, a lush garden.

Rebecca remembers the neighborhood, the houses, from sporadic childhood visits to family unable or unwilling to extricate themselves from the pack. And the conversations shared through thin walls, problems floating through windows and landing at the breakfast table next door for enthusiastic consumption; the closeness of the neighbors, the intimate proximity, suffocating as twice breathed air or binding as blood—lack of privacy or cozy confederacy, depending on your point of view.

She recalls stepping out of the car and almost directly onto brick stairs, looking up onto the homely charcoal face of the three-family rising straight up into the fog and the faint urine smell of the foyer with its obligatory, cumbersome navy blue pram parked next to the stairwell. The stairs coiled endlessly upward to the third floor where the Scauzillo's lived, Zia Grace and Zio Louie.

Rebecca is still able to feel the way her shoulders hunched up, her face twisting in distaste as she edged by the closet outside the third floor landing that contained a suspicious looking toilet with a long chain pull dangling overhead. The brightness of the interior of the apartment when she stepped into the kitchen from the dank hallway made her gasp, inhaling the house-smell of food and Bon Ami. The contrast so sharp, she breathed a sigh of relief to have her black patent leather Mary Jane's planted on pale gray linoleum, clean as water and speckled with chips of rainbow colors. She remembers the sunny, smiling kitchen filled with hearty greetings and the happy noise of family, the treacherously listing back porch used only for hanging wash, but an exciting forbidden perch for viewing plane bellies on their slow, impossible, ear-splitting ascent from the nearby airport. Rebecca waited for one of them to fall, with a plop, into the sea.

Children were hugged, kissed, pinched affectionately, boasted about, told they were beautiful—"*Bella! Bellissima bambini!*"—and over fed, but not accommodated in any way. There were no toys, no tv. The children were expected to amuse themselves and be good, so they snuck onto the porch, silently poked each other, played "categories," sometimes smuggling coloring books into the solitude of the seldom used parlor. Kitchen noise floated in, nearly visible, like smoke, like the scent of something familiar and comforting wafting through until they grew heavy with it, tired and restless and slumped to the table leaning against grownups' legs. The children lay their heads in welcoming laps where their backs were rubbed, and patted. Meanwhile, grownups continued hollering, arguing and laughing. Rebecca listened, dozing; occasionally the gist of something extraordinary and strange filtering into her consciousness, making a permanent home there. Some words spoken in Italian only "*mala femmina*" or "*putana*" spat out under stormy eyes. Rebecca never learned to speak much Italian but remains, to this day, fluent in broken English.

"She ran around with men," Rebecca's mother continues. "Older men, married men. Running wild! Shamed her family. So the father, to teach her a lesson, put her in that place. In those days you could do that to bad girls. Straighten them out" Eva says as she straightens her own back sharply to illustrate. "But, she wasn't there long when she was found hanged in her cell!

"The family was devastated, but they never believed she killed herself. Never! They knew how she was, proud like the rest of them, strong as a bull, stubborn, *tough*. When they picked up her belongings, her shoes were mangled, like she'd been dragged and dragged. Struggling.

"The family says she knew something, something terrible. I don't know what, they would never really talk about it. You know, '*non dichia niente*,'" a phrase as familiar to Rebecca as the fragrance of garlic simmering in olive oil. It frequently punctuates family conversations, topping them off with a sprinkle of finality, "say nothing" it means.

"Rose wasn't one to keep her mouth shut," Eva looks across the table squinting, her face still beautiful, cheekbones holding their own in a face fuller and creased with age. Her mother's eyes, usually wide and round under highly arched, well-defined black brows, are narrowed, the brows knitted in warning. "But if you asked them, they'd tell you, 'There was evil in that place.'"

2

Garden

The dish of ziti and meatballs Rebecca's mother packed up, wrapping it first in wax paper then aluminum foil carefully crimped around the edges like a pie crust, is sliding around on the car seat, threatening to ooze onto the tan leather or, even worse, Rebecca's flax colored pants. She steadies it with one hand while turning the wheel with the other to make the ascent up the long driveway to Mr. Dietzhoff's house. Her mother's story swims around in her head, intrusive and unpleasant like background music, tries to find a spot to settle. Eva is full of stories, the three sisters have a million of them for godsake, she tells herself and turns down the volume.

Besides, she's worried about the old man. Rebecca often feels as if she's selling his house out from underneath him. He is an unwilling participant; talked into this by someone. Probably that stone-faced attorney, Noah Hanes. A man too aware of his own good looks with that ridiculous dimpled chin of his, professionally whitened smile– and c'mon –way too bronzed this late in the season. And too sure of what's in poor Harold Deitzhoff's best interest in Rebecca's opinion.

Mr. Deitzhoff was balky and petulant at first and Rebecca worked hard to make him feel at ease. It was shamefully easy really. He was so eager for her attention. She wanted him to feel secure and safe with her, not just for the sake of keeping the sale together, but because she feels responsible for him. For this short time, while they are connected through circumstance, his well-being will be deeply important to her. Rebecca is fairly certain, that he hasn't been cared about by anyone else in a very, very long time. Rebecca stores this information; she takes it to heart but also, she uses it.

Poor Harold, he is clearly in no shape to be living on his own now. He couldn't be eating much, and *what* does he eat? The kitchen is abysmal, its floor layered with years of dirt, the sink and countertops littered with dishes, pots, crusty pans. The kitchen table covered with empty Lipton soup boxes, canned vegetables, a basket of bananas, black and greasy, and jars and jars of jams–opened and unopened, sample size and economy size. Brown paper bags filled with other, folded, brown paper bags, and stacks and stacks of newspapers tied neatly with string piled up; crooked, listing towers. Propped against the wall in one corner is an enormous bag of sunflower seeds that mice have gotten into, its corners open and ragged, spilling mounds of seeds onto the floor leading off to trails of husks and tiny, black crescents of poop. I should look into the refrigerator, Rebecca thinks, I *really* should, she has said to herself every time she visits the mess. It's all so disturbing, she frets, but never opens the door.

Once he called her at home talking gibberish. Rebecca was alarmed and immediately called his attorney as instructed; the icy Mr. Hanes. No, not icy, that would call for an extreme of temperature. Mr. Hanes would shun extremes of any type. Wooden? No, wood is a natural substance. Plastic. The plastic Mr. Hanes–a facsimile of a person. How awful to end up in the hands of Attorney Noah Fax, Rebecca ruminates.

It's sharply sunny and Indian Summer warm, but as soon as Rebecca turns onto the driveway, the stand of pines, thick as a swarm, envelop the car in shadow and the cool, rough scent of pine needles. Rebecca takes off her sunglasses and continues up the hill through the densely forested lot to the rundown brick Cape bringing Mr. Deitzhoff her guilty offering of homemade macaroni and meatballs.

She parks the car in front of the dilapidated garage and looks around, hoping to see Harold outdoors enjoying the sun, soaking up some vitamins through the skin at least. Rebecca loves it, every ray of it. She dreads the coming winter as she does every winter blaming her thin Mediterranean blood. She should be in the Mediterranean instead of this corner of earth that wants to be cold for so damn long, miserly offering its delicious summer treasure and snatching it away just when you get accustomed to the sweet taste of it, the naked feel of it. Spring in New England is a taunt, a promise often unfulfilled; the autumn, its brilliance and lazy sunlight a blessing, but an ending just the same.

How perfect to have a job where you didn't have to work during the summer. I should have been a teacher, Rebecca thinks, I love children. I could still get a teaching degree. She even mentioned it to her friend, Tandy, who manages the office. "Are you kiddin' me Miss Rebecca," she drawled scornfully, "and just what would you do with all that "killer instinct" you got? What a waste!" she snorted out a laugh and turned her back on the notion.

Privately Rebecca concedes the truth in what Tandy said and thinks, she doesn't know the half of it. Rebecca Griffin, the former Rebecca Maria Renzi, is perfectly aware that hidden far below layers of a caring and congenial nature, lies a vein of something dangerously sharp and hard as nails. Relentless. Rebecca sometimes wonders where it comes from, who passed this down to her, what odd combination of genes might have produced this anomaly.

When that vein gets tapped, her irises swell, her breath slows; all the softness leaves her face, and her body tenses as she casts an unyielding gaze, iceberg cold and deep, on her target. Rebecca's normally kind and appeasing demeanor so alters that her opponent is left confused, casting about for blame, feeling duped—or bewitched. But it's no one's fault, just the result of a fatal miscalculation on their part, much like the one made by the captain of the Titanic. They search her eyes, her face where sweetness once resided and finding none, recoil as if she's actually bared her teeth. Caught off guard, aghast–but defeated. Few have seen it; Tandy loves it.

Right now, Rebecca just wants to focus on peaceful retreat. She imagines perfect summer freedom, that "school's out" joy. Without clients to worry about, she could stay up late, listen for the coyote's midnight howl and sleep like the drugged way past the dew point of morning. She could plan great daytrips with her girls: hikes in the woods, long basking days at Singing Beach, maybe take up kayaking, explore some of those cool museums, Isabella Stewart Gardner, or the one at Harvard that has the glass flower collection, and the whale skeleton floating under the ceiling–the girls loved that one when they were little. And blueberry picking; we haven't done that together in such a long time, she realizes. Of course, if she were to suggest such a thing, Dana would ask, "Are you hallucinating?" with a look that would melt dirt, then bolt, as if her mother were a loathsome disease, something oozing, something she might catch. Lilly could be convinced, maybe, but not without some whining and who wants to struggle like that in the summer heat, and would it really be good to spend every day for two months with adolescents? Christ! I've got to get a better fantasy, Rebecca resolves.

She's just dragging her heels. She dreads leaving this sunny spot to go into the suffocating, dank air of the house. It *is* pretty out here, she thinks. The yard must have been a showplace at one time; it still carries the aristocratic look of manicured grounds. Ornamental bushes and flower gardens are overgrown, seedy, with the air of down-on-their-luck dowagers in silks with frayed cuffs. Somehow, the sense of order and design hasn't been totally obliterated by neglect. Rhododendrons and azalea sheltered on the east side, on the west multiple varieties of voluminous hydrangea, and on the south, the remnants of a perennial garden too full of daylilies and wild phlox now, along with a few wispy coral bells that peeked out occasionally this past summer when the breeze was just right. And someone's pride and joy, a generosity of roses, sunbathing like young girls at the beach. An invasion of bittersweet winds around everything it can reach: trees, brush, garage; dropping tiny orange and yellow bits—husks and seeds—soiling the petals below. All are protected by skyscraping pines that stretch for acres and form a ring around the rest; an impenetrable barrier.

She recognized a few rose varieties from her mother's garden: Dainty Bess, Betty Prior, and the old-fashioned ones, like the ones in her grandmother's garden, whose names no one remembers—the forgotten roses. The hardy ones whose petals lacked the delicate detail or range of hue of the new hybrids, but bloomed on heartily in thick, riotous clumps filled with enormous, killer thorns. Nana's roses, the ones with blood red blossoms, deliciously fragrant and as big as your fist with bright yellow stamens, and the tiny tea roses that grew in clusters like grapes whose stems branched out, messily, this way and that. The wildly huge bush filled with ruffled, white flowers next to Nana's back steps were so thick with bees that you had to dodge them on your way down to the yard. Nana arranged over-full bouquets of them, jamming their stems into glass jars until they bent over with the weight of their captive beauty, sighing their scent throughout the house.

Perhaps one of the late Mrs. Dietzhoffs planted the rose garden by the homely little garage; the first one who died a long time ago, or the second one who passed away recently. Whoever did it, made certain that something was blooming from May through October and was hopeful enough to think they could mask something ugly with something beautiful.

Harold Deitzhoff is nowhere to be seen. He does not open the front door to greet his visitor. Rebecca watches the house for signs of life and finds none. She knows he's in there; where else would he be?

The nine acre lot is a long, narrow piece that reaches up the side of a big hill, and is surrounded by conservation land. The house sits on a crest half way up the side, facing the top with its back to the street. The front door looks out onto the lawn and gardens; a flat circular clearing carved out of the forest. Directly in the center is a ledge outcropping, a table-sized rock, its round face turned toward the sky. A butterfly rests there momentarily like an offering on an altar.

This place reminds Rebecca of Stonehenge; something about it feels as old as time. The pines do their job so effectively there is a sense of deep silence that flows like liquid, thick and sweet as honey. It makes the air dense and close as a shroud. Even the labored hover of yellow jackets seems weighted with it. Their nearby drone fills her head as they move among the last of the summer flowers, the ones that linger past their time, a little ragged, but still hopeful.

Rebecca suddenly feels washed out. She's always tired lately and can't understand why. She closes her eyes; the low hum of bees fills her head and she feels a drift, an overwhelming pull towards sleep, as if someone calls to her from a waiting dream. She leans against the car, its heated metal reaches through the fabric of her clothing like an electric blanket, searing and soothing, as if she's swallowed something hot and comforting like the lemon toddy her mother used to make when Rebecca was little and sick. She can taste the lemon and feel the sharp, hot river flowing down her throat, spreading through her body. She has the not unpleasant sensation that her bones have melted and she is smoothly sliding down the side of the car to the pavement below; her eyes snap open with a start.

Rebecca places the backs of her fingers against her cheek as if to soothe a fever and then steps onto the brick walk squaring her shoulders and smoothing the front of her linen blazer. She feels foolish, and horribly embarrassed, praying that Mr. Deitzhoff didn't see her flight to la -la land from behind parted curtains. Mother of *God*, what is wrong with you, Rebecca, she admonishes to herself as she knocks on the door. There is no bell, just two frayed wires poking out of a circular hole next to the doorjamb. She knocks again, more insistently while calling out, "Mr. Deitzhoff…Harold…it's Rebecca? Rebecca Griffin." She waits, listens with her head cocked at the door. Hesitantly, she pushes it open and sticks her head in to call again, "Mr. Deitzhoff?"

Rebecca sees him slowly shuffling around the corner to the living room in the false dusk of pulled-down shades, dust and dinge. He has on a brown chamois shirt, worn and pilly, buttoned high but loose around his scrawny throat, and stained chinos cinched in hard at the waist with a foot of belt trailing down the ballooney fabric over his legs. His slippers make a shoosh-shoosh sound on the wood floors and muffle down to a huh-huh over the old Oriental rug so dark with dirt the pattern is obliterated.

His watery blue eyes blink when he gets to the door. "Hi Mr. Deitzhoff! I have something for you. Have you eaten dinner yet?" She holds out her mother's dish still warm and pungent.

"Oh," he says in a small voice, barely registering surprise. Blinking again as if he's trying to remember the proper reaction. He is a faded man. If there was once fire there, it has been tamped down to gray ash. His frame curves inward, shoulders round, carriage unsteady. Rebecca has seen a picture of him as a younger man. It collects dust on the fireplace mantle along with its companions: a brass bell with a black lacquered handle, a cut-glass vase containing only the brown scum ring of evaporated stem-soaked water, and a cluster of empty prescription medicine containers.

He had lifted the silver-framed photo off the mantel with knobby, spotted fingers and handed it to Rebecca. "My daughter," he announced with neither pride nor anger; it was simply information. She had no idea he had one, she only knew about his wives, both dead, poor guy. Rebecca thought he was all alone.

In the photo, he looked robust, tall with a shock of graying hair and intense blue eyes under thick, protruding eyebrows. He was standing behind a little girl of about eight or nine, his large hands splayed in front of her shoulders holding her in place. He was smiling but intense, casual, and confident in a short canvas jacket and plaid shirt. Rebecca can't recall what the girl looked like. She seemed dwarfed by her father, or diminished. His presence was the focus of the picture, she was barely there; perhaps summoned at the last moment and not wanting to go, an afterthought. At the time, Rebecca had asked him where his daughter lived and he'd turned his back to walk toward the kitchen. She heard "Texas" tossed her way as he disappeared around the corner.

He does it again now, turns around, macaroni dish in hand, and walks away to the kitchen talking to the empty air in front of him. "Have a seat." Rebecca looks around for the only chair she dares sit in, a bentwood side chair with a cane seat. Blessedly free of a cushion. The rest of the sagging seating is upholstered and smells of must and stale urine. There are worn spots and indentations in the cushions as if someone invisible is sitting there. Rebecca washes her face and hands all the way up to the elbows when she comes home from here. Sometimes she showers all over again. She strips off her clothes and holds each article to her nose breathing in deeply, trying to detect any molecule of odor that might have clung to her. She deems everything permanently contaminated and in need of disposal, then quickly flings it all in the hamper instead and slams the lid shut.

Mr. Deitzhoff returns with two cloudy glasses of what looks like ginger ale, one in each hand, held straight out in front of him. He concentrates on them as if they're leading him forward, pulling him like two magnets.

Jesus, Mary, and Joseph, I cannot even *pretend* to drink; I don't want to touch it to my lips, Rebecca groans inwardly; her stomach churns. She takes the glass and says a too bright, "Oh thank you!" hoping to gush away any specks of horror clinging to her face. Not that he'd be capable of noticing subtleties, she reflects. Rebecca holds the glass of bubbly liquid and stares into it trying to detect floaties, weighing the ramifications of a sip against the awful potential of hurting an old man's feelings. When she looks up, Harold is watching her closely, sitting in his easy chair, leaning forward with his twiggy arms resting along the overstuffed, upholstered chair arms, still holding his drink in one hand. He is clearly assessing her behavior. It takes her aback and as she meets his gaze, she sees a beam of clarity, a grain of the observant clinician he once was, crystallized deep at the dark center of each pale blue eye. Rebecca lifts the glass to her lips and drinks one, two, three fizzy gulps in succession while he watches steadily. She places her glass on the small round table next to her and folds her hands in her lap. He sets his glass down, looking satisfied as he slides back further into the easy chair and seems to shrink there. Rebecca realizes she should not underestimate Harold Deitzhoff.

3

Dana

"Would you please, please, please get up now Dana?"

Dana opens one baleful eye facing up like a dead fish from underneath the pillow squashed over her head.

"Didn't you hear your alarm?" It's seven-ten; the high-school bus will be here in twenty minutes. "You absolutely cannot stay home again today. You've missed too much already. Get up. Please. Now." Rebecca is trying to be firm but civil, polite. Reasonable. She practices phrasing, modulation, mentally before each encounter with Dana. Moments before, she stood outside the door and screwed up enough resolve to enter. She tested the script for loopholes, weighed the consequences, applauded the courage of her convictions, re-knotted her bathrobe belt, got a stomach ache and went in.

Rebecca replays her remarks to Dana in her mind. Was that a mealy string of fear that Rebecca hears playing through her words? Did Dana hear it that way? Or could she actually smell it on her?

There is no response from the rumpled pile of scorn that used to be Rebecca's daughter; Dana of the long, tawny gold hair– like that of a lioness–and eyes as big and green as ripe olives. She has the most beautiful eyes on earth. They tilt up at the corners following the curve of her high cheekbones and are fringed with the thickest, black eyelashes under shapely dark brows; all of which Dana despises. She threatens to shave her eyebrows off or dye them blond. "They don't match my hair" and "it looks stupid." Once she dyed her hair black instead, but it didn't take. They had to strip the orangey mess and dye it all over again, but Dana insisted on "nutmeg brown" and she didn't look like herself again until the summer returned and set about putting the sunlight back into her hair once more

At one time, Rebecca worried that Dana was too close to her–clingy. Dana had to be dragged to nursery school and later kindergarten every day, sucking her thumb. She carried her pillow, blanket, and love-worn stuffed Dog–that was his name, still is–into her parent's room to sleep on the floor by Rebecca's side most nights. They held hands when they drove in the car. She wanted to cook by Rebecca's side, followed her while she cleaned, was inconsolable if left with sitters. She was so in love with me, Rebecca remembers.

"*Bitch,*" Dana reaches around her head with one hand and pulls the pillow off flinging it across the room in one smooth motion, hauls herself up and stands in front of Rebecca so close that Rebecca wants to step back, but will not allow herself to.

Dana pushes her face down into Rebecca's. She does this often, brushes by her too close so Rebecca is thrown off balance, or yells at her with her own face an inch from Rebecca's like it is now. Dana is tall, much taller than Rebecca anyway, tall for this family of women. Rebecca's mother, sisters, aunts, barely topped five feet; the older women, those who came over from Italy, never reached that. At five three Rebecca is considered tall on her side. Great Aunt Mary used to fret and wail when she shot up. "How you find a husband? *Povera figlia!* Ooh, so tall, so tall!"

Dana is five eight, wide shouldered, solid–a big girl. At her age, Rebecca weighed ninety-eight pounds and had no hips. She hardly took up any space at all. Dana fills this room with her vitality, her beauty, her contempt.

Rebecca stands her ground, looks up calmly. She hopes it looks that way to Dana who begins picking clothes off the floor, tossing them around looking for an outfit. She showers twice a day, uses three towels—one to step on, one for her hair, one for her body—shampoo, conditioner, shower gel (Aloe Vera only), and prescription facial cleanser, but doesn't hesitate to wear stepped on T-shirts to school. When Dana's in a good mood, she finds some twisted humor in it and jokes with her mother until the tiny dimples at the corners of her mouth wink mischievously. At least, she used to. She would pat the top of Rebecca's head and call her "shrimpy," refer to herself as Amazon woman, strike weight-lifter poses in self-parody. Dana was a great kidder; Rebecca cannot remember the last time they laughed together.

"Would you get out of my room so I can dress!" As Rebecca closes the door, she hears a muttered, "fucking bitch."

She can ignore "bitch." Bitch is the average mean temperature, as common as clouds. Fucking bitch is a call to arms. *Fucking* bitch means a confrontation, a toe-to-toe challenge, a speech, a lecture; punishments meted out and ignored—an ugly, escalating battle. "Fucking bitch" is exhausting—worse, a dead end. Rebecca closes the door and pretends she never heard it.

Lily's at the kitchen table eating Fruitloops and watching Scooby-do. Rebecca leans down to hug her thin shoulders and run a hand over her shiny brown hair. "Almost done, honey?"

"Yup," Lily answers in a cartoon trance, her elbow on the table propping up her head as she brings the drippy spoon of colored circles up to her mouth, chewing slack jawed.

"Come on sweetie pie, it's getting late." Rebecca can still call her that. Lily comes to, and brings her bowl to the sink.

"Isn't Dana going?" Lily asks, her hazel eyes wide with concern. She has milk drips on her chin. At eleven years old, Lily is still all there, still recognizable. When Rebecca looks at Lily, her shoulders relax.

"She'd better," Rebecca tells Lily, straining to hear signs of progress from upstairs. Lily teeters on that fine silvery edge of childhood still. She's a late bloomer and hasn't even looked over to see what's on the other side. Or, maybe she has, and so clings to that fragile post. Dana's behavior frightens and alarms Lily. She vows, "I'll never do that, Mummy. I'll never talk to you that way. I'll never call you those names." Rebecca hears the desperation in her voice, as if she knows, someday soon she just might.

Right now, Lily likes books and basketball. She cracks her knuckles and needs to be reminded to shower. She is small and thin–the boys call her spaghetti arms–and wears delicate wire rimmed glasses that suit her. She has braces and lovely, silky, chin-length, light brown hair that moves in a sheet of shimmer when she bends her head to read. Lily is a bookworm like her father, but unlike him, does not find it amusing that the kids think she's weird because she actually likes reading Shakespeare.

Lily hovers at Rebecca's shoulder to see what she's doing, "What'd you pack me for lunch?"

"I'm sorry honey, all I had was tuna."

She slumps her shoulders, throwing her arms down hard by her sides and opens her mouth in disbelief. "Again! C'm-*on* Mom, I hate tuna sandwiches! They get all soggy and they smell like farts."

"Oh for heaven's sake…"

"They do," she wails. "Samantha's mom gets pocket bread and puts cool stuff like avocado and sprouts and stuff in them. All I ever get is smelly, stinky tuna."

Samantha and her parents are vegetarians. She is Lily's one friend; bookish, like Lily, but doesn't share Lily's interest in sports. She has the pallor of a lopsided life, one that revolves around violin lessons, computer camp and Math club. She doesn't like to "jump around and get sweaty." Sammy is a sweet girl, not a mean bone or a developed muscle in her body. Rebecca worries that Lily will either tire of Sammy's hothouse world and then be left friendless, or become accustomed to it and draw herself down to fit into that confined space.

"You hate avocado!" Rebecca points out.

"Forget it, I'm not bringing my lunch," she announces shoving her books into her backpack. "I'm sick of eating lunch with that bunch of idiots anyway. I'll just go outside and meditate."

"*Lily…*" Her mother warns.

"I mean it mom."

"You're going to make things worse for yourself. Here take this apple, and a granola bar, and buy some milk at least!" Lily puts on her sweatshirt, quickly grabbing for her mother's offerings.

"Wait, I'll make you some peanut butter and jelly, quick," Rebecca turns to get the bread.

"No, *no*," Lily says wearily. As she leaves, Rebecca calls to her, "Don't meditate." When Lily turns around Rebecca blows a kiss to her, she smiles and rubs it into her cheek like always.

Rebecca smells Dana before she sees her, Obsession, for men. It's Corey's cologne, Dana's boyfriend. She flies past in a tight black top, flip -flops, holey jeans with too long, frayed cuffs and Corey's sweatshirt tied around her waist. Her long hair and empty shirt arms wave behind her like defiant flags as she runs for the bus.

4

Drew

Rebecca closes the French doors that Dana left open on her rush out and returns to the sink to finish-up the morning dishes. She feels weighed down, as if her heart has turned to lead, her arms to stone. She mentally walks herself through what she needs to do today and watches herself begin to do it, as if looking at snapshots, candid stills. Oh look, here I am in my robe squirting detergent on a yellow sponge. I'm getting ready to clean up. And here's a picture of me putting cereal boxes back into the kitchen cabinet; I look old in this one don't I? Now, I'm loading dishes into the dishwasher, feeding the cat.

She hears the upstairs shower running. Drew has, again, successfully avoided the morning chaos. He will shower for twelve minutes, shave, floss, brush his teeth dress and come down in a navy blazer, or tweed jacket, chinos, an Oxford-cloth shirt with a button-down collar and whatever tie his hand has landed on. Sometimes it's a bow tie. His hair will be damp. He doesn't blow dry his hair or fuss with it in any way, just runs his fingers through the salt and pepper waves and is done. Any more would imply an investment in his appearance. That would not be in keeping with his image of himself, which is—he would never admit this —quite calculated. That absent minded professor thing he works on, Rebecca observes; the intellectual too absorbed in the lofty to be involved in trivial pursuits like grooming.

He will stroll into the kitchen wordlessly. He will look for the paper and complain to Rebecca if he can't find it, as if she's its keeper. He will drink the coffee she made while reading the paper she located, silently, then neatly fold and tuck the pages snugly under his armpit as he grabs his briefcase. He will turn his round grey eyes, blank as polished stones, to her finally; "I'll be home by six" or, more commonly now, "I won't be home until late." She will look into his face for clues, a map to his interior landscape and find only a surface as smooth and hard as glass. There will be no message for her there. She will not ask for a kiss good-bye, she hasn't done that in years. His cool, thin lips are as inaccessible by Rebecca's choice, as his indifferent heart is by his.

"Was that Dana I heard giving you a hard time this morning?"

"Of course."

He purses his lips, shakes his head. "Don't let her get away with that."

"What do you suggest? If I ground her, she'll go out anyway. I can't wrestle her to the floor, Drew." She hears her voice echo back to her as it bounces off Drew; it sounds like static. "You know I've tried everything. She won't talk to therapists, the school guidance counselors are useless, most of her privileges are gone…her phone, her allowance…," she says this to herself as much as to Drew.

Rebecca is in charge of messes. Drew likes structure; homework after dinner, tennis lessons every Saturday morning, bedtime rituals like baths and the reading of stories. Now, there is this big messy problem of Dana, and Drew wants her to hurry up and deal with it, fix it. He feels it is only a matter of finding the right avenue, the correct tact and this strange, wild thing will be corralled into the docile pet he once knew. It's Rebecca's job. Even Rebecca feels there must be the right words to say but she's incapable of finding them.

"I don't have time for this now," Drew tells her as he draws himself up, straightening his slouch so that he extends to his full six one and she has to look way up to speak with him face to face. He looks down past his nose at her, and sniffs at her inadequacy, pinching his nostrils together. The corners of his mouth turn down; he takes one long look at her before turning on the heels of his tasseled loafers and lopes out the door, all tall angles and aggravation, across the deck and out to the garage. Rebecca watches the tweedy square of his back as he retreats.

Here is a good shot of me standing in the doorway watching Drew leave. Solitude is a relief that pushes a long sigh out into the silence. The house is still, and has stretched with emptiness. The effort to go upstairs, to shower, get dressed, and drive to work seems monumental. She forces herself forward; her legs feel weighted as if quicksand is sucking at her heels. She drags herself through the kitchen, the dining room, reaches up to tap one of the crystal beads hanging from the chandelier Rebecca inherited from her grandmother. It swings back and forth hitting others, setting off a sound like the clinking of glasses—"*cin-cin*"—the sound of knives and forks against china. When Rebecca put up the chandelier here and turned it on, it glowed with her Nana's light. It lent the same familiar warmth to this dining room as had been ever present at Nana's generous table, dinners, and dinners ago. A soft and cloudy, nearly golden light that makes the air appear sparkly as if there are tears in your eyes. Rebecca turns it on now and squints until the candelabra become blurred stars, until the tears leave her eyes, dropping onto the polished table below and her vision clears.

Rebecca loves these rooms, this house, this town. They had come here when Dana was five and Lily was just a baby, for the good schools and the woodsy privacy of farmland long ago reclaimed by nature. This was a farming community years ago, and many house lots are crisscrossed by low rubble-stone walls that the old timers laid down as boundaries. The town fathers had been careful and smart; they did not succumb, like the other towns that circle this one, to promises of lowered taxes by greedy outsiders who wanted to expand the business district, widen Main Street or designate industrial zones.

The Forgotten Roses

Here, the residents maintained the small-town rural flavor by the dry determination of their Yankee will. The town is a pocket of calm in the midst of congested communities and strip mall byways. There are drawbacks; there is no trash pick-up—one hauls to the dump on weekends, a social event. There is no town water, only private wells sunk deep below bedrock to tap into pure aquifers; no public sewer system, just the costly and frustrating prospect of laying in a private septic system by the town's excessively rigorous standards. Still, Havenwood attracts enough determined hopefuls willing to struggle with obstacles like high water tables, strict zoning regulations, conservation wetlands home to endangered salamanders, and impenetrable ledge outcroppings that hide underfoot. All of this has kept the little town tight, insular.

The first couple who owned Rebecca's home had come here over a decade before developers even heard of Havenwood and had chosen this spot because of the long sweep of tall grass and the southern exposure. Driving through one day the couple noticed a pair of red-tail hawks circling over a stand of birch so purely white they stopped the car and got out to get a better look. They walked through meadow and past bittersweet. She stopped to pick some wild aster and Queen Anne's lace as they listened to the hawks call to each other. The warm breeze rippled the dry grass releasing a scent so sweet it startled them and settled them all at once.

He was a mason nearing retirement, thinking Florida might be good. But, now they held hands like teenagers as she reminded him how big the bugs are in Florida and fed him the last of the wild berries right off the branch. He broke off some dry twigs and staked a plot just large enough for a good home, square and true; seven rooms, four bedrooms—for visiting grandchildren—a kitchen with plenty of elbow-room, a porch on the shady side, and windows—big windows—for their new house overlooking the meadow. He was a craftsman and he built this, their final home, with care and methods only the old timers used.

Rebecca loved the oversized windows and the way in which the dormered peaks at the front of the Gambrel roof make the house look wide-eyed, as if surprised to be here. There are three fireplaces, one in the dining room, one in the master bedroom and one in the living room. There is no "family room" because the builder had no idea that family would need a designated area in order to be together.

Double French doors in the kitchen and living room overlook the wide lawn out back that might have been a cornfield in a past life, but now is a fenced two acres with perennial bed on the south side, a stand of paper birch at the front gate and a carpet of princess pine at the forest edge. In back, there is a buffer of blackberry bushes so thick and wild only the rabbits can get through, but if you follow the path around, it clears to a hill just big enough for sledding, topped by a group of forgiving apple trees perfect for climbing up, or picnicking under. When Rebecca swings those French doors open she feels a part of it, connected to the other living things there as if by underground roots.

Rebecca fell in love with this house the moment she walked through the empty, echoing rooms. This was no "starter house," this was a family home, a forever place. After they moved in, she striped off two layers of paper in each of the bedrooms all by herself and thought about the time she wallpapered with Drew in their first home. They put up new paper together. She smoothed on the paste and he draped it over his arms and slid it onto the wall. He was meticulous about getting it even at the seams, fastidiously smoothing out each bubble of air. He was nervous, unsatisfied about the finished product, wished they'd hired professionals.

Rebecca told him earnestly "You did a wonderful job honey!" so pleased that he made the effort, and they accomplished it together. "It looks beautiful!" she had beamed. Drew sighed down at her linking his arm around her waist "I'm a perfectionist," he said running his fingertip along the inside of one corner, as if she didn't know already. "Not a handyman," he added. She felt flustered and embarrassed, as if she'd done an inappropriate thing but wasn't sure what. She had loved that house too, the tiny ranch, their first home. That's where Dana was born, and they were all as new as she.

It would be impossible to leave this house. Rebecca thinks about it more and more, as more and more distance spreads between her and Drew.

❧

Here I am walking up the stairs, passing by the children's portraits hung on the wall, touching each captured baby-face with my fingertips. In this picture I am placing my clothes out on the bed—my new wool blazer, black and brown herringbone with black suede collar, black turtle neck, jeans, and paddock boots; a good house inspection outfit. Good for trooping up to dusty attics and down to damp cellars, for rounding the perimeters of muddy foundations and walking the borders of wooded acres. Now I'm... Oh for chrissake Rebecca, knock it off! Get some medication for godsake...or get a *grip*!

Rebecca slips off her robe and flannel pjs, letting them fall into a soft puddle around her feet, and stands in front of the mirror over the sink. Placing her hands on the vanity, she leans toward the mirror to get a really good look at the circles under her eyes. She regards her face from various angles, heart-shaped with jet black eyebrows she's passed along to her daughters—much to their dismay—and brown eyes, the same shade as her mother's, deeply dark.

At forty-two, she has hardly any wrinkles, the advantages of a Mediterranean complexion she guesses. The crow's feet aren't so bad, she actually thinks they're kind of appealing, those crinkles when you laugh, they look cheerful and sort of kindly. Rebecca frequently, purposefully, crinkles up her eyes and smiles, pouring out sincerity for a client's consumption; a useful feature. Frown lines just barely evident so far, she thinks and rubs the spot as if to erase them. But just look at those pouches, just like her mother's, she can see them forming, the pucker of flesh at the jaw line. When I hold my chin down, way down... see there they are, she thinks, like chicken fat nuggets or twin wattles. She tries pushing on a spot in front of each ear, which doesn't alter the jaw line the way she wants, but makes her lips elongate and flatten. Her reflection is strangely familiar, it's the same one that looked back at her when she was little and brought her face close to a round Christmas ornament; me, but not me–a distorted Rebecca.

She steps back and assesses her breasts, too large for her small frame, soft and pendulous after nursing two children. If she could lose ten more pounds...or fifteen... She puts her hands on her sides, slides them down her rib cage to the deep indent of her waist, still trim, cinching it around with her fingers and sucking in her too fat stomach in as far as it will go. She stands sideways to see the effect, and then slides her hands around to the front, sliding past the Cesarean scar, forcibly pushing her round belly in to see how it would look and holds her breath; not bad. Rebecca lets her breath out finally and her stomach pops out again. Disgusting. Repulsive. It's a good thing no one sees it, she thinks.

After showering, she stands in front of the mirror once more, slowly towels off, but doesn't wipe the steam off the mirror right away. Instead, she remains before the milky surface, brushing her teeth waiting for the fog to clear and her image to take shape, as if looking for her true self to be revealed. She spits into the sink, glances up, but still can't see herself clearly–it's taking too long. She picks the wet towel off the floor impatiently and wipes the mirror down carefully in big arcing strokes until it's totally dry with not a drip or pin dot of dried toothpaste or splash mark left, just the naked truth of her.

She blowdries her hair, recently cut into a short bob. Rebecca couldn't ignore the way her long hair began to drag her face down making the dark smudges under her eyes deeper. Pulling her hair back made her feel like Olive Oyl…she just couldn't pull it off, so she cut it—and now she likes it. She likes the way it frames her face and shows off her long neck; she feels lighter, freed up and, only occasionally, defeated.

Rebecca walks into her bedroom naked, her heels sinking into the new, plush off-white carpeting. Drew had liked the bare polished oak flooring; is bothered by the dusts and fiber in carpet. When he took over the guestroom across the hall, she had this expensive broadloom installed. He was furious, but further away now and his displeasure with her was that little bit more removed. It does not rub up against her like sandpaper all day long the way it used to. Now, it's more like a bad smell blowing in, detectable only now and then when the wind is wrong.

Before they stopped sleeping together, Drew would watch Rebecca with interest, scrutinize her, as she walked by. He would have assessed, then commented on the size of her bottom, the turn of her breasts. "What's that bruise on your arm?" he would ask, not with concern, just the casual notation of a flaw. "That mark on your thigh?" referring to the small, purple spray of spider veins over one knee even though he knew well what it was. She would have felt self-conscious, examined. She would rush to dress or grab a robe and he would needle her about her shyness. He would drawl, "Oh come on, I'm just joking. What, are you embarrassed?" he would say smirking, stretched out on the bed with his hands behind his head, languid, waiting. She would be irritated and angry; he would want sex. She would give in to him to maintain the peace—or not. If she stiffened against him, his mouth would set like cement into two white lines. She would try not to look at the mean in his eyes, the nasty way the muscles in his jaw tightened.

Now things are, if not better, easier. Like any cold war, less confrontational, but no less painful. The ragged anger, the hurt has been replaced with this numb and deadened pall; like that "phantom limb" phenomenon amputees experience. Something huge and important is gone by necessity, but the echoes of its absence remain always.

Sometimes Rebecca tells herself what we have left here, at last, is peace. Other times she thinks it's something else–something that feels like house arrest.

Before she dresses, Rebecca touches a light floral perfume on her wrists, drawing it up the inside of her arms to the crook at the elbow and down her throat all the way to her breasts. Drew hated fragrance of any kind; would sniff the air and claim he could detect the odor of bug spray when it was merely Lily-of-the-Valley or Summer Jasmine. Now, instead of a short furtive spritz in the bathroom, she leisurely splashes away, droplets haphazardly falling onto the sheets and pillowcases. The cat, stretched out on the bed, watches her with knowing eyes.

It's getting late and if she wants to stop for coffee, she'd better get moving. Instead, Rebecca stretches out next to Willow and rubs her hand over Willow's head and down her back. When Rebecca gets down near the tail, Willow raises her haunches shamelessly to meet the caress and purrs, and purrs. The sound comforts Rebecca.

When the girls were little, they were always touching Rebecca, hugging her, their sticky hands holding onto hers, their warm breath on her face. She bathed in their little attentions and demands; floated through days, and years wrapped up in them. She soaked it all up, hungry for it. Only rarely did she feel in danger of drowning, overcome by the press of their needs, the pull of their love, never realizing that it would end, it would end so soon. Never dreaming that some day they would be embarrassed, disgusted almost, by her touch. Those years when she could hold them, kiss them, press her lips to their hot, sweaty foreheads or nuzzle their soft necks, the hollow at the nape–is there anything more delicious–would be gone forever. How did it happen? When? Rebecca can't recall at all when the physical shift away from her began. Sometimes when she thinks about how much she misses the weight of them folded into her arms, how she misses rocking them, her fingertips stroking the baby-fine fuzz at their hairline, murmuring little comforts in their curving, tender ears, inhaling their shampoo sweet fragrance, she feels a loss so deep it gnaws at her throat for release.

"Willow" she breaths into the cat's ear, "Willow."

The sun has come around to this side of the house and is throwing sharp shards of light through the blinds like an alarm. Rebecca heaves herself up, jostling the cat so that she flattens her ears and extends her claws into the down comforter leaving permanent prick marks.

"Bad girl!"

5

The Stop

Overnight there was a frost. The grass has a silvery coating of icy dew that lingers still under the weak early light of morning; it leaves wet marks on Rebecca's shoes. The last of the summer flowers are shriveled, done for. Rebecca passes by the tall pink cosmos that had bloomed so late this year, competing with the fall foliage for admiration. All over the back yard, the morning sun sends the dew off the plants in a barely there, smoky haze that hovers near the ground like an uncertain ghost. In another half hour, the sun will be strong enough to chase the ghost away.

Rebecca's spine shivers as she climbs into her Jeep. The cold has snuck up on her again, catching her off guard and under-dressed. This past summer had seen a drought and the bone-dry conditions made most of the leaves color and fall early in a dehydrated faint. That is why the autumn has seemed so long; drawn out with Indian Summer days that were succulent, overripe with heated color. Glorious heady days to bathe in one after the other until everyone became accustomed to them like spoiled children. Now Rebecca feels cheated at this sudden turn.

Soon winter will be here and the deepening cold will trigger an excessive need for sleep. During long, gray afternoons when the air is dead cold and the only movement across the horizon is the slow flap of big black raven wings cutting across the unwholesome sky, Rebecca's eyelids will grow heavy as iron. At work, she will load up on sugared coffee or chocolate kisses so her eyes won't begin rolling in their sockets with the effort of keeping them open. But if she's home, sometimes she succumbs. On those days, naps overtake her like the vapors, and sleep is always fitful, as rivulets of sweat collect in the tight valley between her breasts. Sometimes she wakes dazed, wondering who she is, how she got here.

She longs for the short, hot, restless nights and long summer days sizzling with excess, to the heavy, bone-cracking oppression of the New England winters. Why couldn't her grandparents have disembarked on the West Coast? Or North Carolina maybe; didn't any Italian immigrants wind up there? Turning the heat in the car up to the max, and the blowers on hi, she slams into first gear, and pulls out too fast up the driveway, scattering gravel and scaring the jays out of the trees.

This is the time of day Rebecca likes best; this small corner that is hers alone, heading toward the day early in the morning, sipping coffee from Sully's. Formerly a barbershop, Sully's Sandwich Stop is the little hangout—every town has one—where everyone goes for coffee, donuts, sandwiches, and information. Sully—Francis Xavier Sullivan—is a gossip, and a damn good one. Brought up in little Havenwood, he knows everyone's business and is generous to a fault about everything including dispensing whatever tidbit he might posses about everyone's business.

"Hey Miz Dale! How's Mikey doing? Hope the cops didn't scare the beejesus out of you when they brought him home from that party down at the Danforth's!"

"Just havin' a bit of fun with the parents away, I guess."

"Yeah…don't worry about it, they're all good kids," he reassures Jeannie Dale. He means it. Sully loves the teenagers, has a special bond with them, which is not so surprising because he looks and acts like one himself. Maybe it's his little silver earring, or his extensive repertoire of Beatles music, and the fact that the kids can always count on Sully for an advance in pay for Prom tickets or a small loan for an emergency car repair—whatever the reasons there is always a waiting list of high-schoolers wanting to work at The Stop.

Sully depends on them. He lets them take over when he decides too much work is making him light-headed and he goes home for a snooze, or when business is slow and excess energy is burning a hole in the soles of his sneakers and he heads off to the golf course. "Don't let Miz Sullivan know," he gives the kids a thumbs-up and they cover for him, though Rebecca is certain his wife is wise to him.

Today Moira must not have checked the weather, because she let him go out in shorts and a short-sleeved shirt. The shorts are so baggy they hang down his long gangly legs, past his knobby knees and nearly meet his hi-tops, which is the way he likes it. His white t-shirt, with Sully's Sandwich Stop printed in Kelly green over the breast pocket, has been ironed. In the colder months, he trades in the shorts for jeans, equally baggy, and his hi-tops for Timberlands. The cold weather version of Sully's uniform includes sweatshirts in appropriate colors; pumpkin and putty in fall, and a special Christmas version, red and green with "Ho-Ho -Hoagie" on the back.

"I'll have a talk with Mikey when he comes in on Saturday," he winks to Jeannie's fretful face. She thanks him and leaves with her bag of bagels clutched tightly in her hand. He watches her walk out. Rebecca catches him looking at Jeannie's bottom but knows it doesn't mean a thing because Sully absolutely adores his wife.

Moira grew up in Havenwood too. But, a few years younger than Sully, they never met until she graduated from Simmons. Anyway, he would never have hung out with honor's Latin, summers in Nantucket, class treasurer Moira Ann McGillvery. It wasn't until years later when he was MC at the battle-of-the-bands on the town common one summer's eve that they crossed paths when he tripped over her blanket with his big feet on his way to the mic. Knowing Sully as she does, Rebecca thinks it a wonder Moira survived the encounter.

Most of the town marvels that the two ever hooked up. Moira's family didn't marvel, they took ill. It was the first unpredictable thing she'd ever done. The bile that rose in her father's throat nearly killed him. To this day he speaks in a whisper, and, when speaking to Moira, only in monosyllables. When Sully's around, Mr. McGillvery's throat constricts to a pinhole, and he just gasps.

Moira reminds Rebecca of a pastel watercolor wash. She is the children's librarian here in Havenwood where she catalogues "The Chipmunk's ABC's" and "The Polar Express" with small white, serious hands that smell of lemon crème. She has long, straight brown hair pulled back at the sides and held with a tortoiseshell barrette, Cinderella style. She is neat and soft-spoken and always kneels down to speak at eye level with the children that come to her with questions. Moira takes their hands in hers and draws them a little nearer so she won't miss a word they say. Long after the children have grown, the scent of lemons will remind them of books and comfort; the mere sight of them, enough to evoke tenderness.

When Rebecca sees Moira with Sully she is reminded of just how dried up her own marriage is and never, ever wonders why those two are together. Moira beams at Sully. Her cheeks color and plump pushing her eyes into happy little half-moons; she is transformed. She has perfect, movie star teeth and her lips spread back like rosy elastics showing everyone of them all the way back to the molars when she smiles. Sully makes her laugh out loud, and in his presence, she is fresh and shined like an apple. In that way of opposites attracting, they are perfect for each other, puzzle pieces that click together snugly. She handles him like laundry; cleans him up, softens him, irons down his cowlicks and bundles him out each day all in order. He makes her sizzle and bubble and adds the paprika to their life together.

The young children that flock to story hours at the library are sweet on Moira, just as the teenagers that hang out and work at The Stop are devoted to Sully. They have no children of their own and so, between the two, have adopted all of Havenwood's young.

This morning Sully's only employee is a young woman from neighboring Warington, Birdie, who works the morning shift while her three kids are in school. Last Christmas, Sully pressed a mustard-stained envelope into her hand with an extra five hundred dollars in it because he'd heard that her husband was laid off. He told her not to tell anyone, but then Sully told Rebecca because she came in right after Birdie had left and Birdie's eyes were misty and so were his. He probably told a whole bunch of other people too because everything that is inside of Sully just has to spill out. And because everything that goes through his head comes out his mouth, and his heart is too big for his skinny chest so it is always falling out onto his sleeve.

As the wooden screen door bangs shut behind Jeannie Dale, Sully begins to sing "Blackbird singin' in the dead of night...," along with Paul McCartney. When he sees Rebecca he shouts, "Howdie Reba!" He needles her, calls her Reba McIntire because he knows she hates Country Western music.

"Hey, *Francis*," she teases back. "Could I have a hazelnut, extra light, no sugar, to go, and one of those low fat blueberry muffins. Tell the truth, are they any good?"

"Ya kiddin' me? Spectacular! Instead of fat they have double the sugar! The mice love 'em." Birdie snickers appreciatively from the back.

"You're a pain. I don't believe you; give me a cranberry instead. I have a house inspection at the old Deitzhoff house on Farpath Road and I need fortification. In fact, put a sugar in the coffee for me."

Sully studies the muffins at great length. That's kind of sweet, he must be choosing the best one, she thinks smiling to herself. He clears his throat, "That house...*sold?*"

"Sure. It's a nice property, rundown, but you know, the potential is there. All that land... the privacy... It's a good deal."

He hands her a muffin and coffee, "And the buyers...they don't mind?"

"Mind? Mind what?"

Just then, Martha Higgins surges in with her twin boys who demand giant chocolate chip cookies and juice boxes. All three, tow heads with identical bowl cuts. The boy's thick hair moves all of a piece, as if on a five-second delay, trying to keep up with the whirligigs underneath. Sully has clammed up.

The little boys hang on Martha's legs, hop up and down, talk non-stop at the same time, and push each other. It's easy to forget what that's like, the same way you forget labor pains. Martha is totally oblivious to the chaos at her feet; the customers at The Stop become instantly exhausted and ask for coffee refills.

Rebecca should be going, but what was Sully talking about? She snaps open the sip spout on her coffee cup and settles down on one of the stools at the window bar pretending to be interested in the Havenwood Press left in front of the plastic stirrers. Sully is busy with Martha and the boys but he keeps giving Rebecca quick, sidelong glances; there is something that looks like discomfort in his eyes. He doesn't banter with Martha. There's no talk about her small part in the local theater production of "Mrs. Merryweather's Legs" billed as a zany farce on the flyers they've distributed. Rebecca can't believe he's not teasing her about it, passing up this easy mark.

"Good choice men," he tells the toddlers and, "help your Mom," as they leave.

Rebecca places the newspaper back exactly where it was before and swivels the stool to face Sully and catch his eye. "So… What did you mean? What is there to 'mind' about the Deitzhoff's?"

He turns away and focuses on wiping down the coffee maker. He examines his dish towel, then comes around to the end of the counter; Rebecca meets him there. Sully leans toward her, bends his head down, and says in a low voice "Lots of rumors about that place, that's all.

Things that supposedly went on there… But that was a long time ago." He glances up finally and then says to a point somewhere above her head, "Plus, there was the suicide."

"Oh shit!"

Sully squirms in place.

"C'mon Sull…" Rebecca pleads, twisting her watch around. She's running really late now, the inspector will start without her if she doesn't get out of here fast. "Tell me what you know."

Sully slaps his dish towel over his shoulder and leans forward on his freckled arms, his reddened dishpan hands pushing against the counter. "It's a really long story, Rebecca, I don't think you have time. Besides, like I said, it was a long time ago. No one cares about that stuff anymore."

"Cares about *what*?" her voice zings skyward.

Sully sighs, "Look…most of it was just gossip, but I guess you should know that Mr. Deitzhoff's first wife committed suicide there…under… ahh…suspicious circumstances years ago, and…his daughter kind of… disappeared." He whispers "disappeared," breaths it out long and soft.

"Get *out*!"

"Yeah," Sully says sadly, talking to the black and white tiles on the floor.

A few guys from the construction crew who are building a new house on Buttonball Lane walk in with requests for large, black coffees and a dozen mixed donuts. The conversation is over. Rebecca slowly opens the door and turns to see Sully's thin Irish lips pinched into a frown. She can feel the lines between her brows etching deeper and rubs the spot absentmindedly, "I'll talk to you later, Sully." He nods to her silently as she leaves.

6

Sully

Francis X. Sullivan feels jittery, like he's had too many cups of French roast. As he watches Rebecca pull out of the parking lot, he drums his pen on the counter until it vibrates in a nervous fit while the workmen from Don Bastille's framing crew study the donuts as if they've never seen jelly, powdered and chocolate glazed before. They read the menu on the blackboard over his head concentrating like it was the Talmud for cryin' out loud. The men are mostly in their twenties, some have bandanas tied around their heads like hippies, just the way we wore them back in the day, Sully thinks. He wishes they'd hurry the hell up. "Norwegian Wood" flows on from behind him and he whirls around and snaps it off. The guys stop twirling their keys on their thumbs and order.

After they leave, Sully wipes his hands on his apron untying it as he strides to the door, flips over the "Back in Five" sign, slips the latch on the door handle and tells an astonished Birdie to take a break. With his apron balled into his fist, he goes into the storage room out back and sits on a packing box, his hands locked onto his knees. Serena Deitzhoff. He hadn't thought about her in years. Well, that's not quite true. Sometimes her image would come floating out of a radio along with a line from one of the old songs, like the faint scent of a fading perfume. He would shake the image away like a bad chill, just before it took shape, and the memory solidified into something sharp, before he felt the old longing–just before it hurt. Now someone was actually buying that goddamned old house. Wasn't that bastard dead yet for chrissake? What was he, about a thousand years old by now? Godammit!

Sully wants a cigarette. He quit years ago—Moira made him—but just thinking about Serena made him want things he hadn't wanted for a long time. He closes his eyes and imagines the texture in his fingers of the match strike, the hiss of flame; cupping his hands around it protectively, leaning forward with the cigarette pinched between his lips, squinting into the first sweet billow it sent up and inhaling deeply while waving the match dead in the air. Then handing the cigarette to Serena. She didn't smoke, but she always wanted some of his. She would take a few drags and give it back, like she just wanted to have some of what he wanted. Like she couldn't figure out what the wanting was all about and conducted this test each time with the same result, shrugging, and handing it back between two long, narrow fingers. "Nothing," she seemed to conclude each time; she didn't get it.

They were sixteen and not in love. Well, Serena wasn't in love for sure, and Sully, he was in fascination, in awe, and in desire, but was too good a friend to let it show. They were best "buds," had been since Sully moved here when he was twelve. His father got appointed police chief of Havenwood after a decade on the Cape chasing beer parties off the beach and writing tickets to tourists who didn't know the speed traps in a town smaller than this one even. It was a rotten time for Sully. He missed his old pals. They'd biked, swam, shot off cherry bombs in neighborhood garbage cans, shop-lifted Marvel comics, Playboy and tootsie roll pops, and just when things were starting to get interesting with the new Arcade going in, his family up and moved to this snob town. He hated it; hated the preppie boys, and the snotty girls with their phony, hardware smiles.

At first, he mostly drifted over to "the cliffs" to hang out by himself, build campfires, smoke. Then he found his calling. He wasn't a good student, stunk at sports, and band...no way! But, he was a gifted goof ball, and that made up for everything. Occupying the chair outside the principal's office as often as he did, gave him a kind of stature which was way below the jocks' but definitely a cut above the band dorks. And he had no competition for the post whatsoever.

Then he discovered Serena. She occupied a place in school all her own as well. The kids left her alone. The boys didn't make fun of her because she was too pretty. The girls didn't like her because she was too strange, but they didn't pick on her because Serena didn't care. She was unavailable to them, out of reach. They were all afraid of her I guess, thought Sully. Everyone noticed her though. She had those pale blue eyes that were transparent almost, like something behind them was frozen stiff. Sometimes when she lifted her long eyelashes to look at you, it was as if she looked into you and what she saw was a pile of nothing.

Sitting in class, after the pencils Sully had stuck into his nostrils had fallen out onto the floor, she would slowly turn in her chair and look back at him and an icy string would tighten in his chest. What was that, he would think. At twelve years old, he didn't think it weird, he'd think it magical.

Sully sat behind Serena in homeroom watching her platinum hair ripple down her back as she moved. Her eyebrows were a funny, gray-brown color; the color of catkins or Siamese kittens. She sat with her back razor straight always. How does she do that, wondered Sully, sprawled over the entire surface of his desktop, all popping knuckles and pointy elbows, with his chin jammed into both hands? Like she's always at attention, ready for something. Sully lurched through each day bouncing from prank to disaster to reprimand and back to goofing off. Serena seemed to float through time contained in a glossy bubble that kept her away from him and everyone else. He could hardly stand it. He considered bursting that bubble, directing some daring and devastatingly funny prank her way. He longed to get a rise out of her, to see her fuzzy eyebrows come together in consternation, her cool, pale cheeks flush. He spent whole afternoons fantasizing about it, entire algebra classes, a field trip to the Museum of Science, and lessons on the Louisiana Purchase were taken up devising ways to play a joke on her, prick her cover, invade her space, until he realized that what he really wanted was to occupy it with her.

He would trick her, he finally decided, be super nice to her; that would really blow her mind. It was his new mission. He would save her a place in the lunch line, pick up a paper fluttered to the floor, sit with her on the bus, eventually speak to her. A piece of cake, he smirked. What was to follow, Sully wasn't quite sure, but he was certain a really good punch line would come to him.

Serena wasn't exactly hungry for his attention, but she wasn't above thinking he was funny and cute and so she let him into her world, or at least she let him occupy a nearby space while she traveled, temporarily, through that time and place.

Sully came to think of Serena as his special puzzle. Like those little plastic games where you had to get the squares in the right order in the box to win. You keep at it, and keep at it, and your tongue hangs out of your mouth with the effort and when you finally do it you're proud of yourself, but what have you really got? Serena was like that, you tried and tried to make sense of her, but in the end, you still weren't at all sure of who she really was, and what you had won. After all these years, although he tries not to, he is still wondering. And that damned refrain creeps into his head uninvited, unwanted… "All your life, you were always waiting for this moment to arise."

7

Serena

Serena Deitzhoff yanks her duffel out of the overhead compartment above her seat. It's the third time that day she's changed places. She curses herself–and Amtrak–under her breath. Why didn't she just fly, why don't they have designated passenger cars for families with squalling brats, why don't they ban the consumption of cheese like they do smoking in public places.

She hoists her pack over her shoulder and makes her way down the aisle boring through the tunnel of cars one after the other. At each doorway, she pauses to assess its contents and then, disgusted, moves on. Every car seems to have its own dank odor; the smell of dirty snow, of metal and grime, of cooking odors absorbed into clothing– grease, and cabbage. Even in a place like this, where a widely varied mix of people cram together, a place where care is taken not to make eye contact, people stare at Serena. She challenges every glance that comes her way with the cold steel of her own sharp gaze until they cough and look away, pretend to see something else, concentrate on plucking at the lint they spy clinging to their sleeve.

Her hair, white-blonde as lightening, has fallen over one eye and she pushes her lower lip out and blows hard at the stray lock. It flies up in a panic and points at the ceiling. It is remarkable hair, thick, spiked to a frenzy on top, severely tapered down the back of her head and over her ears until it ends in a café au lait buzz at the nape of her neck. Serena loves the way it feels when she rubs her hands over it–the clean scratch of stubble. It makes her teeth click together and smile.

The train lurches a little and she bumps her hip against a seat. She looks accusingly at its occupant as if it's his fault until he turns away in embarrassment as she continues to stride down the aisle with long, confident legs. Serena is tall, moves smoothly, carries her muscles easily, like a man. She comes to the end of the car and pivots, grinding grit under the thick soles of her boots, and takes a quick side step into the last seat, swinging the heavy bag around her shoulder in one smooth defiant motion. The bag thuds down onto the empty seat in front of hers while she flicks her lashes up then down to be sure everyone notices she's claimed both seats before making herself comfortable. She puts her legs up, makes a pillow out of her jacket, and leans against it with her arms crossed over her chest, peering out from the bangs she allows to dip over her eyes like a veil. This is an excellent vantage point, she thinks. Finally, she closes her eyes. The rhythm of the train matches the rhythm of her heart. She relaxes. Her body sways, ever so slightly, rocking, letting the thoughts come.

This is the reason Serena took the train. She needs the time. She needs the distance to shorten slowly, to play out in long miles, so she can get her bearings. She needs an opportunity to shed the protective layers built up over the years, remove them one by one until there is nothing left but sinew and strife. She has to pare down to that old self again and make some kind of peace with it. And she has to figure out what, if anything, she's going to do about that fucking Attorney, Noah Hanes.

So strange that he would find her after all these years. Though, it probably wasn't that difficult to track her down, being in the service and all, even if she had changed her name, twice. Stranger still that he would call at the very time she was planning to go back to confront her father– and the demons that trail her, evade her, kick up dust at her feet.

Hanes called to tell her that her father was failing and incompetent.

The Forgotten Roses

He informed her that he, Hanes, had arranged for power-of-attorney because of Harold's condition, had placed the house on the market and Harold in a nursing home. It was a blow hearing that. Picturing the old man, frail and forgetful, and who knows what else. Not because she felt sorry for him, but because it nearly crushed to dust that hot coal she kept stoked for all these years; the fuel that fired her momentum. She had intended to face her father down, lay it all out. She won't let him avoid her, lie to her, deny her the truth. She let too many years pass, and curses herself for that. Now Serena was left with nothing more than a handful of hazy memories–and the house. She mulls that over–her legacy; a low bubble of laughter forms in her throat and flies out like an escaped bird. She snatches at it, but it's too late.

Why did Hanes call me now? What does he want from me, and how might he screw up my plans, she wonders? These are the things Serena wants to sort out logically, methodically, but when she closes her eyes, she sees her mother.

Julia Deitzhoff, lovely, angelic, immaculately groomed, her hair neatly pinned up, her dress–always a dress–carefully pleated and pressed. She is nyloned, lipsticked, powdered; sitting stiffly in her bentwood chair by the fireplace, eyes closed, her fingers slowly rubbing down the string of crystal rosary beads, her lips moving but silent. Serena tiptoes by this image just as she tiptoed past her mother back then, not wanting to disturb her. In reality, it was not possible for Serena to disturb her mother. Julia was still present, but her eyes, when open, were focused on some distant place; her soul had already fled there and she was waiting to follow. This is how Serena remembers her mother because it is the visage that greeted her for years, all during high school–just before Julia Deitzhoff took her own life. Shot herself dead with her husband's gun. No note. No written apology to Serena, no explanation. Not that I really needed either, Serena thinks.

But, in the buried recess of her heart, the covered up place where the little girl of her resides, there is a want, a whisper barely heard, but insistent. Where were the last words, the final breathed out comforts to linger in my ear? Didn't you love me enough to stay? The question that is always left hanging in the air when the crying stops. The final question. The one that Serena thought she closed the door on when she left for good the day they buried her mother, a month before Serena's high school graduation.

On that day, Serena squeezed every last drop of remorse out of her heart. A heart she believed she had long ago willed to shrink as small and hard as the peach pits her mother saved for planting, laying them out in the sun lined up on the kitchen windowsill. When Serena thought of her own heart, that's the way she imagined it; the scab color of shriveled fruit, pitted, knotted and dry. Sometimes she thinks she made herself that way, other times she thinks she was born like that. Either way, it was a good thing she's the way she is or she never would have survived in that house. Maybe she'd have wound up like Julia.

Noah Hanes had better not get in her way—or anybody else. Okay, she reviews mentally, so now there will be no final confrontation. No questions asked and finally answered. She has to learn to live with that. She may never know for certain if her suspicions are grounded, or, as she occasionally thinks, if it's just what remains of her wild imaginings as a kid, one who was more than a little off base. The rumors maybe were nothing more than the gossip of ignorant, self righteous, maybe even jealous neighbors. Serena has considered that scenario in her head before, and acknowledges its possibility coolly, rationally—but her guts say "no." Her guts clench when she remembers the night sounds. The horrible, high-pitched laughter; big, harsh voices, and small, shrill ones coming from beyond her window where the old cart path leads to the street. She would get up from bed, turn on her light, and look out her window, but it was always too dark, too many trees, too far to see.

Now, there's nothing left to block her view or cloud her vision. All she needs is a little more time to determine how she will put her final plan into action with the complication of Hanes in the mix. The question is how much does he actually know? Chances are, not much. Harold Deitzhoff was the keeper of many secrets. He had fooled everyone, the prison administrators, the townspeople, his wife–at least for a time. He even published papers on his methods, "Respite Therapy" he called it. But, rumors surfaced after a while. Serena began to hear them in junior high. Small town gossip, regurgitated like cud, chewed on twice, embellished, expanded; how much was true?

Over the years, Serena uncovered one immutable fact; there was always an uneasy connection between Havenwood and the prison. Few people know that the prison was part of Havenwood long ago until the town fathers gave that parcel of land to Warington; excised it like something infectious. Disowning it did nothing to rid the community of unease. Havenwood harbored bad feelings–distrust, suspicion, tension, and guilt–that lingered on. Time removed memory of their kinship for some. Possibly some were complicit and tried to forget. Others wouldn't forget and stoked the flames of gossip that ignited over picket fences or down at the Grange Hall; travelling like brushfire across dry hayfields; embers spreading from farm, to barber shop, to cider mill. Tales spread about the women, and the reclusive man who worked at the prison just down the road from his house. "He and his family keep to themselves, won't mix with the townspeople, who does he think he is anyway? Him and his books and theories and articles. Hogwash! Or something worse."

Stories told by fucking hicks, and her own cloudy memories, that's all I've got to work with, Serena concludes grimly. And there's the hidden money. Serena had seen her father hide it one night. He buried it out beyond the garage workshop in what looked like a large metal box; a safe deposit box maybe, she'd thought. At least, Serena believed the box contained money, she knew he distrusted banks, and it was certainly something valuable, otherwise why would he have buried it? Anyway, whatever it was, if was valuable to him, she wants it.

Serena doesn't give a shit about money. Even though she has considered digging up the damn thing herself and taking it with her, money is not the reason she left the Army and stuffed herself into this tin can like so much sausage oozing her way across country. She is going home. It will be like 'The End' in a book whose covers she can close and tuck away; never look at again, she envisions. And if she can't get tangible answers, she will reclaim her past, seal that open wound. Cauterize it.

Serena grinds her teeth until she makes sparks and her jaw sets like alabaster. Her eyes turn inside out, blind white, from the force of looking inward. If the other passengers turned around right now, they would gather up their children, their Burberrys, their cheese sandwiches and run. They would disembark in strange towns, head for home, and lock their doors behind them.

8

Havenwood

Oh *crap*...heart is doing that thing again, that drum roll thing...need to calm down, relax, learn meditation, she thinks. Maybe I'll get Lily to show me how again. *Damn*...a suicide! But that isn't the only reason she's out of breath and agitated. She scowls deeply from the effort of examining her feelings. Maybe it's that strange girl Sully told her about, the one who disappeared; between her, Dana, and that awful story about Rose, Rebecca's anxiety peaks. Panic fills her throat. I'm so frightened for Dana. What am I going to do? It is the question swimming just under the surface of Rebecca's skin all day, every day. When there is no immediate answer for that question, she pushes it back down, along with her fear, and does her best to solve the other problems that come up. She sighs into her cup of coffee and takes a long sip. People are waiting for her. She doesn't have far to go, but she has to hurry or she won't make it there in time.

❧

Rebecca's clients, Gordon and Missy Frakes, are in their late thirties, no kids. He is an engineer, she's a psychologist. Rebecca has shown them twenty-two houses in five towns. They looked at enormous gingerbread laden Victorians in Milton, multilevel Deck houses in Carlisle, and new construction in Sudbury. They have trooped through converted carriage houses and mini-farms, houses with in-ground pools and houses with a view of the Charles. Rebecca thought they'd never buy. She thought, maybe, house hunting was their hobby. Missy told her, "I'll know the right one when I see it. It will speak to me." Gordon agreed, "We're waiting for something special." The Deitzhoff house is special all right, Rebecca sneers.

Finally, it was the land; nine secluded acres, surrounded by heavily wooded town forest and conservation land. Quiet. Solitude. Privacy. The Frakes didn't know that was what they desired most until they realized what a rare and precious commodity it was. They just had to have it. They're nice enough, but Rebecca hasn't connected with them the way she usually does with her clients. Maybe it's Gordon's clipboard, Rebecca considers. Drew always carried one whenever they looked at houses too. Rebecca doesn't know why they're so concerned with listing every shabby detail, since they are probably going to gut it down to the two by fours.

The lot is—like Harold Deitzhoff himself—non-conforming. Nowadays, the town would never let you build on a lot so narrow, so close to wetlands and riddled with ledge. "You won't be allowed to expand the footprint of the house because of septic system constraints, zoning by-laws and such," she had explained, but that actually intrigued them all the more. Now they're percolating with thoughts of treetop aeries and communing with the friggin' birdies, thinks Rebecca snidely. I have got to cut that out, she resolves.

Rebecca doesn't know why she's so hard on them. They are probably perfectly good people. So what if Gordy has a nose so sharp he could cut cheese with it, and hasn't, not once, cracked a smile. Missy makes up for this because she is always smiling, or at least appears to be because all of her teeth show and her lips turn up even when she talks. Like a TV anchorwoman. Her high gloss lips skitter and slide over her relentless teeth trying to gain purchase; finding none, they retreat, self-consciously and wait for another chance.

Before Rebecca opens that can of worms in front of the Frakes–the one marked "suicide"–she should try and get more information. How reliable could one of Sully's stories be? Maybe he has it all wrong. Although…he looked so odd, as if all his freckles itched, when he told her.

One step at a time. Let's just get through the house inspection first. What with maybe termites and, for sure rot, and an old hidden septic tank, there's plenty of stuff that can screw-up this deal before any suicide story has to be brought up, she tells herself as she pulls slowly out of the parking lot. She inches her way out into the morning rush hour traffic stream, waving at the familiar face who nods her a place in line. Timing is everything–one of real estate's tenets–and poor timing due to her conversation with Sully has placed her in line with the moms in toddler packed SUVs on their way to preschool. The kids are barely visible by the tops of their little baseball caps or ponytail ribbons. Sometimes the moms look as if they're talking to themselves, a mile-a-minute with over animated faces. Rebecca cranes her neck out the window to see how far the line extends. It looks like a parade of well-dressed lunatics, chattering and singing to themselves.

Morning traffic flows a little better once you get past the preschool. It's a straight shot all the way through town. The one main road that cuts through what is jokingly referred to as the business district insures an uneventful, uninterrupted, and direct route out. There is no reason for anyone not a resident to stop. One must go elsewhere for dry cleaners, you cannot get a cut-and-blow dry to save your soul or your split ends, and your front end will remain unaligned unless it rolls on out of here. Bread, a stick of butter from an already opened four-pack, and Pot O'Gold scratch tickets are available from Bunny's Convenience Mart; and you can stop the progress of your child's ear infection with a ten day supply of thick, pink amoxicillin from the Apothecary wedged like bologna in a sandwich between the post office and bank. This is Havenwood's version of the strip mall—old brick, white clapboard, and a cupola topped by a copper horse galloping with the wind.

On the outskirts of town there are several small farms where fresh eggs, bales of hay and feed can be purchased. If you know the right people, it's possible to buy—for far too much money—a few slender glass bottles of milk, as wholesome and shapely as young girls. The dairy, owned by a gentleman farmer whose lineage goes back to the pilgrims, and fortune to politics and power, is fittingly bucolic. The milk—unlike Havenwood—is *un*homogonized and the cream floats on top, thickly clotted and yellowy, under blue and white pleated paper caps.

The only time outsiders come to Havenwood to purchase anything is on autumn weekends when the Graingers re-paint their homemade sign and set it out east and west of their farm stand. It is a primitive rendition, childlike, of a Red Delicious, that's all. Nothing else is required to attract long lines of pilgrims waiting to buy any of twenty-two varieties of apples, ice-cold, unfiltered cider, and homemade apple pies at outrageous prices. Yes, the town fathers' planned well.

Although the number of residents is well under four thousand people, there are three churches. Havenwood's gross national product, religion— or sin maybe. Pictures of the Congregational church can be found on postcards depicting small-town New England. Services are at ten thirty a.m. Sunday mornings; always have been, always will be. Congregants dress to the nines and families file neatly out of midnight blue Volvos while the sharp steeple overhead pierces the clouds, points to the sun, as it officially rings out the hour for the whole town.

The Catholics have a mystifying array of times for Mass, from Saturday afternoon through every hour on the hour (except ten o'clock— no one knows why), from six until noon on Sunday, and then once more Sunday evening, except on holidays. Parishioners run in from whatever they are doing and are dressed in what they were wearing at the time.

The Forgotten Roses

They pull up too fast into the enormous parking lot, pile out of minivans and run in ten minutes late.

The UU attendees are a motley group. Their appearance is often determined by the subject of the sermon. One would dress differently perhaps, for example, if the service were an exploration of Goddess ritual than you would for one revolving around Kubler-Ross's views on death and dying. They whiz up in Saabs, twenty minutes early to get a good seat.

The Stop is across the street from St. Mary's, smack in the middle of town. Sully, of course, is there Sunday mornings to provide donuts, coffee, and his views on God and the afterlife to churchgoers of any denomination. The two other churches sit at opposite ends of the center, like guardians or sentries.

The wide main street that offers up each one of the churches as it cuts, dead center, through town carries no secrets. It holds the sunny side of Havenwood to the light for invitation and scrutiny, for all to see. The houses that line the exposed edges of Main Street are unassuming. They are the older village colonials, the homey little capes, or plain-Jane antiques not yet transferred from the hands of townies to those of interlopers.

New buyers will add decks, hot tubs, and dormer third floor attics for conversion to private master suites. They will install new granite topped kitchens and marble baths. They will paint every surface in natural colors like wheat and sage and sand. Safe colors. They will join the Garden Club, The Historical Society, go to town meetings to protest the erection of cell towers—though grumble constantly about the number of dead zones in town—and make complaints about the marauding goats that escape the broken-down fencing at old Frank Eames "Just-a-Mere Farm." The goats resist the resulting ordinance in an act of social disobedience and continue to trample and strip professionally designed perennial beds whenever possible.

Newcomers fall in love with the idea of forest trails, then put up "no trespassing" signs on every public access that nudges their property line. They will zealously mount campaigns to "save the old maple tree" routinely slated for culling because tipsy teens keep hitting it going too fast around the tight curve on Deerfield Road. Every so often, someone chains themselves to the scarred old trunk just as the tree warden revs up his chainsaw, as if it's the last tree in town, as if they are the righteous instrument of Mother Nature herself, as if protecting us all. They will dig their heels in along with mountain laurel and fence posts. They will want to be the very last ones in.

Rebecca takes a left onto Fox Hollow Drive to begin the slalom of winding roads that will bring her to Farpath Lane; roads that look deserted, no houses are visible, no street lights lead the way. A ruse. Concealed behind woodsy acres at the end of long gravel driveways hide old-money estates or new-money McMansions as big as hotels. Tucked unobtrusively behind ancient hemlock barriers, are former farmhouses gutted, "restored" and tripled in size, or telescoping, glass-clad contemporaries sprawled arrogantly on clearings surgically carved out of virgin terrain. Monuments to success, to ego and plenty. Here the residents take their stand against the dense gallop of underbrush and relentless elbowing in of saplings, the press of wild things.

They all do it. Newcomers circle their wagons against the undesirable. Each taking on the colors of the rest, like gang members. They become linked to the old Yankee farmers who put up endless rows of low rubble-stone walls asserting personal boundaries, then got together at night in smoky groups to set the limits of inclusion into the fraternity. Everyone that settles here begins to feel they own membership into a secret society. In thrall with its gifts; endless bridle paths that snake lazily through acres and acres of protected old-growth forest; sheltered vernal pools where fat bull frogs and spotted salamanders leap into the nets of Havenwood children; clear, clean swimming holes that bubble up from hidden springs. Like the Canada Geese on the common who endure the long winters as if there is no spot warmer, no grass greener; as if under a spell cast by the old ones that came before, or by the place itself—the folks who nest here, never, ever want to leave.

9

Invisible

"Rot," Rebecca hears the inspector confiding to the buyers as she follows the path to the front door. The sun is dappling the brick and in the fresh morning light, the house looks almost young again. All the shabbiness seems hidden in shadow pockets, and there is a polite breeze that brings a scent, faint but enough to draw the nostalgia out of them–burning leaves.

Gordy and Missy tip up their noses and smile. But Danny Jalinski is poking around, uncovering secrets. He's squatting by the front doorsteps jamming his screwdriver over and over into the soft sill. It gives like flesh. He continues to sink the sharp metal into the neighboring shingles, the frame, bottom of the door, again, and again until Rebecca winces with each jab. She wants to grab the flannel on his arm and tug at him, shake him like a child so he will stop, as if it is at a living thing he stabs, as if this is a personal violation. The house finally stops him, pushes back firmly at the next parry, "Enough," it signals at last with the thud of solid wood under the relentless blade.

The Frakes' faces begin to pucker like twin prunes. They exchange long fretful glances as if they are communicating through telepathy. Gawd. It's too early for this crap. Too early in the inspection, too early in the day to feel this knot in my chest, Rebecca thinks. She takes a big breath, loosens the knot.

"So sorry I'm late. How are you? What a great day, just smell the pine!" Rebecca gushes, upbeat. She oozes positive. She smiles as if they are all best friends having gobs of fun.

"How's it going Danny?" Rebecca bends down to him, places a friendly hand on his shoulder. She looks into his eyes, tries to ascertain what she may have missed. Was there a disaster before she arrived? Did they stumble upon a sinkhole? Step into a termite nest?

Danny looks at her clear-eyed, straight arrow. "We just started," he reassures her. "We got dry rot."

Danny is a young man of few words. He's good at what he does; thorough but not overzealous, understands the quirks and foibles of old houses. Doesn't panic about uneven floors, the pitch of a roof, the slant of a wall and won't alarm clients unnecessarily about the idiosyncrasies of antiques or minor maintenance issues. Rebecca is always grateful for a common sense guy like Dan to show up, especially with a couple of nit-pickers like Gordon and Missy.

Rebecca likes Danny. He has developed a good word-of-mouth reputation in the area. When he first turned up at one of her other inspections, she thought he must be the inspector's son and just had to ask him how old he was; twenty-eight, he told her a little defensively. He looked like a baby. That's how you can tell you're getting old, when doctors, police officers, teachers begin to look incredibly young, wrongly young.

Danny sands up and brushes off his hands and the seat of his jeans; nicely filled out, Rebecca notices. He's not a bad looking guy, she thinks. Medium height and build, dark brown hair in need of a cut–a little shaggy, it swirls around at the back of his neck appealingly–smooth ruddy cheeks, clean-shaven, a nice boy. She imagines kissing him, her hand stroking that swirl, looks a little too long at his mouth and flushes pink with shame as if he could read her mind, which doesn't keep her from wondering if he's married, has any kids. He stands back from the house and looks up, unhooks a flashlight from his belt and shines it up at the roof still darkened in morning shadow. His hands are large, strong looking with a fine bristle of black hairs dusting the backs. Now Rebecca wonders if he patted his wife on the bottom affectionately before he left home this morning. Stop it, someone should slap me, Rebecca thinks, her mouth twisting into a rueful little smile.

Danny moves along to the side of the house where overgrown yews have choked out access to the foundation. He plows headlong through them, parting them like curtains and shines the light to the right and left along the bottom edge of the house, guides the beam up toward the downspouts at the corners, to the peak of the roof, and the second floor window. He steps back and the yew branches snap shut. Danny goes around back as the three follow in silence: Gordon, clipboard tucked under his arm, Missy, watching her feet as she picks her way through wet leaves and decaying pinecones, and Rebecca bringing up the rear, watching for signs of trouble.

Ivy has attached itself to the foundation and now blankets the cement surface, crawls up the back steps and over the scrollwork of the wrought iron railing. It has latched onto the overhang above the door and green fingers are reaching toward the windows on either side. Rebecca wonders how long it would take ivy to smother this side of the house. Is that what its intention is, to engulf the house and bring it down, swallow it until it is part of the forest carpet, digest it until it is earth?

"Too much moisture trapped around here," Danny says. He is pointing with his flashlight, scratching back the ivy, pulling at it, knocking on the foundation with the butt end of his screwdriver. He comes over to the back stairs where the three are gathered and gets down on one knee, scans the surface of the steps, the surrounding blue-slate flagstones. He looks up at Rebecca and says, "Frass." A bad sign. Rebecca knows that frass is the sawdust termites and other wood-eating insects leave after they have chewed on your house. To the Frakes he explains, "We have evidence of termite infestation. We'll have to get a good look at her beams and joists from the basement, see what we got." He flashes his light up to the roof and illuminates gutters overflowing with pine needles, and blackened leaves.

"Need my ladder," he says and ambles down to his pickup holding down his tool belt against his faded jeans so the hammers don't bang against his leg.

Rebecca tries to engage the Frakes in small talk while they wait. Wanting to distract them from dark thoughts of rotted wood and burrowing bugs, she points out the cardinals in the wild blueberry patch in the distance. They ask about the proximity of Audubon preserves. Their voices bounce off the trees, the tight canopy above, the thick forest carpet below and fall back on their ears with a dull thud. There is no echo. It is as if they are in a padded box; the sounds they make are flat, artificial. Words do not escape from here but keep their muffled company too long, making them uncomfortable and causing them to fall once more into self-conscious silence.

Gordy and Missy take to peering into the forest like explorers, poker faced. The density of the pine grove that surrounds them has choked out the undergrowth and caused the trees to shoot upward like rough arrows. A few saplings, spidery and pale, try to catch a blot of sun below as the wind parts the fabric of branches high over their heads. Missy places a hand like a visor over her eyes and cranes her neck forward. Sacajawea, Rebecca thinks biting her lip to suppress a smirk.

Gordon tips his head way back intently examining the large knot of forest debris caught in the crook of branches in a nearby white pine. A squirrel's nest. Rebecca can't tell if he knows what it is, but she doesn't volunteer the information. Meanwhile, Missy now has her hands spread on her boyish hips surveying the orange-brown bed of needles at her feet, kicking at them a little, as if contemplating a massive cleanup operation. She looks determined. They should have hired her for the Exxon Valdez, thinks Rebecca.

They hear Danny clanking back with an aluminum ladder that he wedges between a couple of evergreens at the back, securing it fastidiously before he begins to climb. The Frakes blink hard in unison each time he bangs the ladder against the house. Empathy blinks, that's a good sign Rebecca notes, the house is already theirs.

Danny negotiates the roof expertly while the others watch. The women grimace with worry for Danny. Old Gordy takes on a vicarious macho stance and looks on, studiously unconcerned, with his balled up fists at his hips atop the wide spread of his short legs.

"Roof's been replaced not too long ago," he calls down from above. Rebecca and Missy release their held breaths as he climbs back down. "Chimney needs re-pointing though," he says almost apologetically.

"What does that mean?" Missy asks Gordon, but he doesn't hear, or just doesn't bother to answer her as he tries to keep up with Danny rounding the corner to the other side of the house. She looks at Rebecca wide-eyed and Rebecca explains with a casual wave of her hand, "Some bricks are loose, that's all. You'll need a mason to cement them back. Your inspector will explain it all to you when he's done." She pats Missy's back reassuringly and they move on.

Danny doesn't spend much time on the other side of the house, and asks to go inside. They walk around to the front of the house and Rebecca puts her key in the lock, but the door gives way immediately. It's open. She had asked Mr. Deitzhoff's attorney if he could see to it that Harold was elsewhere during the inspection. Rebecca didn't want to upset Harold, didn't want the Frakes to pester him with questions, and didn't want Harold offering them strange information and cloudy sodas.

Rebecca walks in first and stops a few steps from the door; the others follow nearly skidding to a halt, like the Three Stooges, and remain balled up at the entry breathing down her neck.

Someone has been here. Someone has cleaned up the place. Things are moved, or gone. The tattered shades and crippled blinds have been removed and the long, heavy burnt-orange damask drapes are closed tight at each of the living room windows. The couch has been pushed back against the wall under the large picture window that has been left open a crack. A gust of wind billows the tops of the drapery fabric outward over the couch; the bottom of the drapes remain pinned. Strengthening sunlight seeps through the dark coverings, bathing the entire room in a bloody glow. It is the color of corpuscles and capillaries, of flush and fever. The wind shifts, and the curtains are sucked inward, then puffed out once again like the slow beat of a heart; they watch, spellbound, as the window pulses and throbs. The rest is stillness. The breeze inflating the damask does not penetrate the room; dust-laden air remains suspended and illuminated. The floating particles twinkle like glitter. The room is warm, close, clotted with expectation.

"Goodness!" says Missy from behind. Her voice is high, involuntary. Rebecca feels she must do something so she takes two steps forward and the rest follow in a clump. Then Danny disentangles himself, steps around and through the room, head down, straight for the fireplace. Gordon follows clearing his throat with purpose. Missy and Rebecca are rooted to the floor that, Rebecca now notices, is bare.

The old Oriental rug is rolled up, pushed against a wall. Who has been here? Perhaps a cleaning company hired by Noah. Although it's hard to imagine Mr. Deitzhoff agreeing to that. Because not only is it clean, it is emptied of much. Rebecca can't quite figure out what things are gone, it was such a clutter before, but a lot is missing for sure. Small things. Big things. The beautiful caved oak mantle, stripped bare. There are no empty plastic medicine bottles, no oil paintings heavy with gilded frames on the floor propped against walls, no stacks of dusty National Geographic and medical journals on the end tables, no matching Tiffany lamps either.

The stale urine smell has not quite departed, the couch remains after all. But it is reduced if not defeated by the odor of furniture polish. It hangs in the air and reaches down the throat, oily and coating—a cover-up. The women have begun wandering like drugged mental patients or lost souls throughout the room trying to identify their surroundings. Rebecca takes a quick inventory: pillows and cushions, gone; ottoman, gone; recliner, gone; almost all the really smelly stuff, gone. Also missing are the photos, the knickknacks, and mementos. She looks around for a box that might contain them, gathered in a pile for poor Harold so he can take them out later, maybe at a nursing home, and place them around his room, perhaps on his new bureau top? Rebecca frets; there is nothing.

Missy has wandered over to the fireplace where her husband and Dan are on their haunches discussing loose bricks and creosote buildup. Rebecca does a double take at Danny. His knees are clean. There is no soot on his hands, no ashes on his knees, his sleeves. The fireplace opening has been scrubbed clean, not just vacuumed out, but washed free of any traces of ash, any evidence of use. "Wow, I've got to get the names of those cleaning ladies," she says to Missy. Missy startles and looks peeved, as if Rebecca has interrupted a train of thought or broken a spell. Maybe I should give her some space, Rebecca thinks. "I'll be in the kitchen," she tells Missy.

Rebecca could see from the living room that the dining room has been tidied as well, but as she steps through the arched opening, she realizes how far the cleaners went. The doors of the massive mahogany breakfront were left wide open and someone has emptied the shelves. There are piles of dinnerware on the swept-clean wood floor arranged like pyramids: dinner plates, desert plates, salad plates, and saucers, with teacups arranged in a circle at the bottom. A stack of creamy china—Limoges, Rebecca confirms—with a platinum ring around the edges.

This floor is also missing its Oriental rug, nowhere to be seen. On top of the dusted buffet, lead crystal decanters with round tops as large as doorknobs stand murky with caramelized remains. There is a tarnished, mottled-black candelabra with five tall arms. It's richly ornate patterns, pressed into the wide base, look like lotus blossoms and urn-bearing Greek goddesses. Rebecca picks it up with two hands, feels its weight, probably solid sterling. An array of mismatched crystal candlesticks gather at one end, some with candle stubs still in them, scribbles of wax hardened over the lips and puddled at the bottoms. Many candlesticks have tall candles in them, used but with no melted drips—new candles. They look out of place, Rebecca thinks and she touches a candlewick; the charcoal comes off between her fingertips, powdery soft.

Someone took the time, and trouble to place the leaf into the oval dining table. An odd thing for cleaners to do, Rebecca notes. Silverware was carefully arranged—as if to admire it—sorted by pattern. And a small silver teapot has been singled out, polished to glowing. Rebecca lifts it, holds it up, and turns it around admiring the way it shines even in dim light. Someone loved this once, she thinks, maybe someone still does.

In the corner, the drawer of the built-in china cabinet was left open; papers dropped messily on the floor. Rebecca stoops to pick them up and turns to see what the Frakes are doing. Missy catches her eye and Rebecca smiles at her. "I guess these cleaning ladies are not so hot after all," she kids with Missy as the three enter the dining room. Rebecca gathers the papers together and drops them back in the drawer, slides it shut and wonders why they were pulled out and thrown down, and by whom.

Rebecca expects to see the kitchen cleaned-up as well, but it is not. It remains as Mr. Deitzhoff left it, soiled, and littered like a beach after a shipwreck. Awash in the detritus of life, the broken evidence of what was once whole and useful, now broken and decayed.

The cleaner must have started in the living room and became exhausted, couldn't face this mess. Probably a woman, Rebecca thinks. A man would not have arranged the silverware so carefully. He would have gathered each grouping in one hand and deposited them on the table like a bundle of sticks. Only a woman would have fanned the knives out like spokes on a wheel or separated the chipped cups from smooth.

Danny takes a big breath as he stands in the doorway. "Whew," he says nicking his red Jalinski Inspections baseball cap back off his forehead with the knuckle of his finger. He walks to the center of the kitchen, takes off his hat as he looks around, swiveling on his hips, running his hand over the top of his dark curly hair and securing the hat back on. He whips the flashlight off his belt and shines it on the sack of sunflower seeds, walks over to it, tips it away from the corner and looks behind it. "Mice," he declares; though the evidence is fairly obvious.

Missy gives a little shudder, "Don't they carry deer ticks?"

Danny and Rebecca look at each other but no one answers her. This isn't the first time she's asked about ticks. Missy is obsessed with deer ticks, and mosquitoes, or more precisely, Lyme disease and equine encephalitis.

She and Gordon are from a different kind of suburb. The kind that hugs Boston and is considered still to be "the city" by its more far-flung neighbors. The houses there are mostly turn-of-the-century and sit stiffly on eight thousand square feet of chemi-lawn surrounded by chain link. Car exhaust helps keep mosquito numbers down. Although Missy adores the idea of country acreage, she is fearful to the point of hives about the unsavory element it harbors. She wants to know how many deer per capita. Where and when was the last outbreak of triple E? Will the town allow spraying? Can she put fencing up to discourage deer? What about raccoons? And now mice; next she'll be asking about hanta virus, Rebecca thinks.

"Poor little things. They're trying to store foot for the winter," Rebecca says. She would drag out one of the girls' old Beatrix Potter books to illustrate the point if she'd thought to bring it along. Mrs. Tittlemouse sitting on a mushroom nibbling Harold's sunflower seeds from a button plate. How adorable.

The Forgotten Roses

They continue on to Mr. Deitzhoff's bedroom. When Rebecca first showed the house to clients, after they visited the other disaster areas, everyone visibly braced for the disgusting sight that surely awaited them in his bedroom. But it was always bunker straight, bed made, corners tucked tight, drawers closed. The room previously was a guest room. The real master bedroom, children's bedroom, as well as two more baths were upstairs on the second floor. But Mr. Deitzhoff could no longer reach them.

The upstairs bedrooms and baths are a tacky portrait of times gone by, museum quality circa 1950's. There was the ubiquitous maple four-poster the color of Kraft caramels, his and her nightstands with natted doilies gone ecru with age, under twin milky-white hobnail glass lamps. An oval braided rug under the bed, olive green chenille bedspread over it. On the tiny window, organdy curtains droop, a mockery of themselves, over a thick hunter-green oil-cloth shade; room-darkening shades. A concept so foreign to Rebecca she winces. Why the Deitzhoffs felt the need for them is incomprehensible since the bedroom windows are so small, tucked into eave space at either end of the house, and shaded by evergreens.

Rebecca leads the way into the smallest bedroom. The daughter's room, the one who disappeared, Rebecca remembers. "Disappeared," listen to me for godsake, what does that really mean anyway? Honestly, Sully is such a drama queen. The girl probably got sick of this place and took a powder, joined a commune, eloped.

There is nothing of her in this room; no flavor, no trace. Only shadow. It's as if this room exists in the narrow space between night and day, forever dusk. The walls are paneled knotty pine; the knots, big dark random fists. The furniture is the same maple set as in the master bedroom, scaled down to child-size: a twin bed, minus the tall posts, wedged under the sloped ceiling and covered with the same bumpy chenille bedspread, a yellow one. A small student desk is topped with the only lamp in the room; a rearing horse of cast-iron similar to one Dana had when she was little. Rebecca pulls the chain but the bulb is dead so she steps over to the little window and yanks at the bottom of the shade. It springs up and she gasps, reeling in shock at the hooded eyes, the hooked nose and cold stare pressing against the outside of the window.

She spreads her arms wide, like wings, and stumbles backwards shielding the others. A short and guttural shriek escapes from Missy. Danny forces Rebecca's arm down so he can see. He maneuvers around her brandishing his flashlight like a club saying "What the hell?" as he steps toward the window but Rebecca pulls on his arm to hold him back. His muscles are flexed and tense under his shirt, his bicep warm and hard. She wants him to stay with her and the others, safely backed against the closet doors. Danny obeys Rebecca's insistent gesture and stops in his tracks. He lowers his flashlight and illuminates a huge owl. They all jump in unison, a foot off the floor, as if the thing might fly through the glass panes and carry them off, or rip out their eyes. They realize by the time they land that it is not a living thing because it does not move, nor ruffle a feather, or swivel its big head; it does not even blink. Danny rushes up all at once, unhooks the latch, shoves the window up with the heels of both hands, leans forward and raps it with the flashlight. "Copper I think. Hollow," he says. Rebecca lowers her arms slowly, like a railroad signal, and allows the Frakes to pass by so they can take a look.

It is merely an owl replica, cast in metal, mounted on a bracket just outside the window. "It's quite beautiful really," Gordon proclaims. Its feathers have weathered to a soft, mossy green edged in mottled brown shadings like tortoiseshell. They are awed by the hungry curve of the beak, the rough scaly texture of the talons; their deathly grip. It is remarkable; they nod in agreement, trying to blow the last fumes of fright away with reasonable words spoken casually. The owl scowls at them behind empty eyes until they look away.

The Forgotten Roses

"I've seen something like this before. It's like a scarecrow, to keep away woodpeckers," Danny says.

"Well, why is it facing the window then?" Missy asks.

Another of Missy's questions goes unanswered. They stand and regard each other dumbly. Rebecca sits down on the bed hard, looks over at the window, and wonders about the girl that lay there at night with only the owl for company. She looks to the big, angry bird for answers, but it is fiercely mute. Her wings shrugging and silent, her talons clenched in frustration. Perhaps it has seen too much. Rebecca has.

She is tired of these people, this house. She tries to obliterate thoughts of the girl on whose bed she is resting. She needs to close her eyes to blot out the sight of that damned owl staring at them, at her. In the blank metallic eyes, Rebecca can see the reflection of their intrusion into the still life of this room. But as her lids drop, she sees fragments of the day, like shattered glass flying by. They swirl together, a spinning constellation, trying to come together into something whole. Rebecca tries not to see the piece that is the missing girl, tries to avoid the piece that contains questions about Rose, about Dana. And prisons; the kind with barbed wire and locks, and the other kind, internal, with familiar diaphanous walls that hold us back and not always against our will. Rebecca opens her eyes because she doesn't want to see.

This room is too damn dark for a child. Rebecca gets up wordlessly and walks out. She leans heavily against the curved oak banister, all the way down the stairs and into the room that is the color of heartbreak. It is like being trapped inside a person. She feels it pulse around her. Just as she considers escaping to the outside, the others clomp down the stairs looking sheepish, as if they had shared something too intimate, illicit, and embarrassing. Avoiding her eyes, Danny asks Rebecca where the door to the basement is.

There are three rooms down there; two are finished, the third contains utilities and the door to the bulkhead. Danny fairly licks his chops entering the utility room, in his element. "Meat and potatoes," he says happily as he charges ahead. Gordy and Missy seem rejuvenated under his enthusiasm and gaze upon the old boiler as if it was the Holy Grail.

Rebecca disengages from them. Ever since she was a little girl, she has been able to slip in and out of a room totally unnoticed. She learned very early to be so quiet, so inconspicuous that she was virtually invisible to those around her. When her father was in a rage, when he was in a mood, when he was tired, just home from his daytime job, eating dinner, leaving for his nighttime job, remodeling for Eva; those were the times that Rebecca practiced invisibility. She is the oldest; her sister, Joanie, the baby, had no need for the talent. The boys stunk at it and suffered the consequences.

Even when she got older, it was a useful skill. Until it became an inclination. Sometimes, she was invisible when she didn't want to be. It happened a lot in high school. But by the time she went to college, she thought she'd shaken both the need and the tendency. Then she met Drew.

It was early spring at UMass, students were feeling overconfident, certain the warmth would stay. They cut off their jeans and wore their Bass Weejuns without socks. Rebecca was a freshman looking for a physics tutor. She pulled a card off a bulletin board in the student union and trotted over to Orchard Hill, one of the senior dorms. By the time she got there she was hot and out of breath. A sheen of sweat glazed the tops of her breasts under the blouse that she had knotted above her waist and left half unbuttoned at the top. She was breathing heavily when she knocked on the door. Drew opened it. He wasn't the tutor, he was a senior at Amherst, just waiting for his friend to come back. He looked down at her, leaning against the door jam with his hands in his pockets, smiling his perfect even smile while she stammered out her story. He wore a pale blue denim shirt with rolled up cuffs and madras shorts over

The Forgotten Roses

long, tanned legs; his calves bulged from track. His hair was sandy brown, streaked, as if he had it done, with blonde highlights. And the most expensive looking watch, nestled into the thick dark-blonde hair on his arms. She was shocked when he offered to help.

"I almost passed out," she told her roommate, bowled over, "he is so cool!" she gushed. In truth, Rebecca felt over her head in every way. She was way too short for that lanky guy, her stringy cut-offs no match for his creased madras, her braided friendship bracelet couldn't compare with his beautiful gold watch. Drew's parents belonged to a country club and golfed wearing matching pink and green shirts with crests over the pocket. Rebecca's parents belonged to St. Patrick's parish and renovated in their underwear.

Drew was so easy to fall in love with. Nothing ruffled him. His grey eyes were serene; his lips on hers were like butterflies. Once they became a couple, she felt tranquil, secure, and very adult. He talked about writers like Kazantzakis, and Carl Jung's theories of the collective unconscious. He gave her gifts of books that she read and stacked up forming a tower next to her bed. When she was alone and felt unsure of him, she picked up each volume—like plucking daisies; loves me, loves me not—setting them down neatly in another location, moving the tower back and forth, here and there, as it grew.

Rebecca was satisfied that he was nothing like her father; moody and volatile. She vowed never to wind up with a man like that. Drew was even-tempered, and unchanged from day to day; clearly not someone for whom a stubbed toe would set off an angry outburst that would sour an entire afternoon. She found Drew's predictability admirable, his calmness reassuring. But what filled her with joy—the thing she believed with all her heart—was that he possessed all the qualities that would make a great father. Their children would never have to run for cover when he came home. Their lives would be peaceful, quiet discussions would replace hot-tempered yelling. And he would be proud of them all.

Rebecca worshipped him.

Rebecca was different from most of the girls Drew knew–high maintenance types, entitled, opinionated. Drew was drawn to Rebecca's warm smile, her unassuming good-nature and earnest sweetness. But mostly what cinched his interest was her trim little figure, tiny waist and those delicious boobs; big and round, sweet as apples. She had long dark hair, that she sometimes pulled back and up all in one smooth graceful motion and quickly knotted, ballerina style–she looked like a Modigliani painting. And those full, willing lips; Rebecca was an amazing kisser. Drew never realized how great just kissing could be, which was a good thing because she wasn't easy. Rebecca was a good girl–a virgin.

A while after Drew and Rebecca started dating, she had begun to feel a bit lightweight. After Drew graduated and earned his Master's at Brown, she dropped out of school to move in with him and worked while he went for his Ph.D.; by the time they left Providence, she was winking in and out like a traffic light.

After they married and the children were born, the tendency to disappear went dormant like herpes; maybe she was too busy, too needed. Then, years later, at a faculty dinner party, she had a relapse. Rebecca was sitting between Drew and Susan Langley, a Ph.D. in psychology with tenure, long blond hair and perky little tits that shimmied, braless, inside her black silk evening suit. Rebecca was trying to dip into her lobster bisque without disturbing the flow of conversation they were having around her when she realized that it didn't matter how carefully she timed her spooning for their convenience, they were totally oblivious to her. She wasn't even an annoyance, she just wasn't there.

Of course, this recurrence was disturbing at first, but then Rebecca remembered she could actually turn it on. She could skirt the perimeters of a cocktail party, and observe, with mean glee, the painful forced conversations in which she would have to engage, had she been visible. It's surprising what buyers and sellers will reveal, and truly awe-inspiring how quickly and thoroughly invisibility can occur when in a room full of pompous intellectuals or egotistical real estate attorneys; oh the places they'll go! After a lifetime of observation from edges and shadows, Rebecca had learned, better than most, to read people, detect nuances, predict outcomes—a gift.

Rebecca does it now. She sinks back into the recesses of the cellar, backing up slowly until her heel scrapes against the cement wall. Makeshift shelves wobble next to her. She looks over at canned goods bulging and dangerous and cloudy glass preserve jars with thick globs of unidentifiable substances seething greenly inside. Rebecca can just see the headlines in this week's Havenwood Press: "Broker decapitated by shrapnel from antique beans."

Here in the cellar, the smell of mildew clings like cobwebs. The dampness is of the seeping variety; very soon they will become uncomfortable all the way through to the marrow. Rebecca watches the trio of busy explorers. They don't notice her, but she sees them clearly, as if looking directly over their shoulders. She observes the self-important way Gordon folds his arms across his chest as Missy strains forward to hear what is being said. Missy swings her head back and forth, back and forth, as if she is at a tennis match, listening to the conversations between the two men. Rebecca can see that Gordon doesn't understand any better than Missy about well-pump maintenance and filter variations. It is crystal clear to Rebecca, that Missy feeds Gordon's ego with her deference, his omnivorous black hole of an ego.

Missy's behavior grates on Rebecca, it has from the moment she met them, she now realizes. Rebecca would prefer that they did not buy this house. She would like never to come here again. Perhaps Danny will find structural beams with long, bubbling channels of termite inroads, eaten through like blocks of Swiss cheese. Perhaps this house is decrepit, ready to fall in under the weight of itself, like Mr. Deitzhoff. Perhaps it is infected. Or haunted.

Missy is calling for her, as if from a great distance. "Rebecca...?"

"I'm right here," Rebecca says as she steps forward, present once again.

"Well..." Danny sighs, taking off his cap and scratching his head. "The good news is that all her systems have been maintained on schedule, the roof is sound, and the rot won't be hard to fix. The bad news is that there is definitely termite infestation."

Gordon writes furiously on his clipboard. It is on the tip of Rebecca's tongue to say, "You do know, Gordy, that it is totally unnecessary and annoying of you to be scribbling away on that damn notepad since Mr. Jalinski, who is actually in the inspection business and unlike you, knows what he is doing, will be furnishing you with a detailed written report." But that would be pointless because it is not the information that he scratches down that is important to good old Gordon, but the exacting portrayal of himself as the master of all things.

"What else is down here?" Danny asks Rebecca.

"Just the workshop," Rebecca answers leading the way. She turns on the fluorescent bulbs and they nervously flicker to a steady bluish hum. The room is paneled in what looks like black-speckled Styrofoam.

"Sound proofing," Danny explains before anyone asks.

There is a rough wood workbench, empty of tools, against one wall. The floor is concrete painted barn red. There is nothing here for Danny. He stands in the center of the room and hooks his thumbs into his tool belt. "Huh." It is a statement. Danny is looking upward; they follow his gaze to a huge metal hook, fat and curled like a worm, hanging from the center of the ceiling. Rebecca never noticed it before.

"That's where they hung the bodies," Danny says. It is a joke. The Frakes titter appreciatively, though a bit nervously.

But Rebecca feels something close down tight in her head. It clangs like great metal doors slamming shut. She is trapped. The hair stands up from the back of her neck all the way down to the base of her spine. Her hands and feet prickle with hot needles. She begins to pant as if she's in labor. The walls feel too close. She raises her hand, touches her cheek where it burns. Can they see this? I don't want them to see me, she thinks.

The constellation descends once again, fogs her brain, clouds her senses. It spirals into a whirlpool, tightening into a continuous reel of unending pictures, then slims out to a string like DNA. Rebecca cannot read the information. She knows it's all there, everything she needs to know is contained in that pattern, but she cannot yet crack the code. Something interferes, like static disrupting a signal. She hears her mother repeat "twisted" over, and over and sees Eva's knuckles, bloodless, whitened like a string of big pearls as she demonstrates. And in her hands, Rebecca sees those shoes. Bad girl shoes—hard and beaten, black as licorice. "Twisted."

Rebecca thinks she is turning now to go upstairs. She cannot feel her legs, but seems to be moving. Perhaps now I am invisible even to myself, she thinks. The others fall in behind her like ducks in a row. I must look okay. I must not appear to be stricken, thank God, otherwise they would not be following so willingly.

Rebecca wills her hand to unlatch the front door, her feet to cross the threshold. I am crossing the threshold, she tells herself. I am outside. The sun is high overhead, Rebecca looks up and it is thankfully blinding. Her eyes water and there is a white spot in the center of her vision which prevents her from seeing any further into the core of Gordon or Missy. Rebecca is grateful.

She wants to quit while ahead. "Look at the time! I'm sorry, I have another appointment." God, I am so clever; actually talking like a real person. "I'll call you later today. Will you be home? Good. I think it went pretty well, don't you, Gordon?" She believes herself to be smiling; she can feel her lips curl, the air against her teeth. She wants to thank Danny but is out of breath. Her brain commands, "smile encouragingly" and she thinks she does. Under the blind spot, the eclipse that is her vision, she can see a spray of sparkling stars. Hyperventilating. That's what I'm doing. Go to the car. What are you supposed to do for that? I have no paper bags, what's wrong with me, I should have paper bags. Deep slow breaths, you've seen Lily do it. Deep slow breaths. The stars are spreading into an iridescent field. Not a good sign, Rebecca thinks. She leans her head against the steering wheel. Someone knocks on the window. It's Danny. Rebecca can't actually see his features, but can tell by the color of his red shirt.

"You okay?"

She talks through the glass, waving merrily. "Sure!" she tells him brightly, turning the key in the ignition. Get out of here, Rebecca. She waves again at Danny, turns back to wave at Gordon and Missy. Look how well I'm doing this. Danny's mouth is slightly agape, but she swears the Frakes do not notice a thing. Rebecca's hands are slick with perspiration. It's just the stress of this sale, she tells herself. Then she thinks of Rose. Could she have been one of the "hung bodies?" Don't be ridiculous, Rebecca. Snap out of it. Rebecca tries to resist, with all her might, the urge to goddamn peel out of here. She should wait until she calms down.

The tires spin for a moment, spitting crushed pine needles and dirt while Rebecca waits. Suddenly the car lurches forward, squealing. Rebecca relaxes the crushing grip she had on the steering wheel and lifts off the break, relishing how good it feels to be moving forward, and in the right direction.

10

Bitch

Tandy Michaels is a bitch. That is why Rebecca likes her; she does it so well. One could imagine "Tandy Michaels is a bitch," scrawled on various bathroom stalls, men's and women's from junior and senior highs all over the South where she was raised as an army brat, to Northeastern University where she briefly studied business administration. Sometimes Rebecca wonders if that is the reason Tandy found her way out here, to escape the cursive scrapings of her past. Rebecca imagines Havenwood is a good place to escape into, swallowed whole.

Rebecca is lying face up, stretched out like a corpse on the newly upholstered couch in the conference room of Country Lane Properties. The sofa is deep and soft with wide rolled arms, the back lined with plump welcoming down-filled pillows. In this incarnation, it is covered in flame-stitching of soothing colors. When people sit, they sink so deeply they have trouble getting up. It is a couch for clients. The brokers hardly ever use it, lying here Rebecca feels like a malingerer even though she is blind with a migraine.

The owner of the company, Sophia Lane, has just had the office completely redecorated and the brokers are awash in Santa Fe shades of adobe, turquoise, and maize. The chemical smell of new carpet, and fresh paint fumes, are sharpening Rebecca's headache to a fine point. Tandy stands over her with her hands on her hips.

"What is wrong with *you*," she asks with concern doused with annoyance.

Rebecca keeps her eyes closed while holding down a damp paper towel folded over her forehead. She has no illusions about attempting to enlist Tandy's sympathy or understanding over the events of this morning. She wouldn't even know where to begin. How far back would she go? She does a quick peddle backwards in her mind, back to Sully's revelation, back to Dana, to Drew, to the taste of warm ginger ale drunk out of a greasy glass, to her mother's eyes narrowed in warning. No, it's all too murky, too untidy, and in no way concrete, or more importantly for Tandy, not directly enough related to the sale. She wouldn't get it. But, if Tandy smells drama in the air, she'll throw herself onto the stage with relish.

Rebecca forces her eyelids to part; through the slits, she slides her eyes toward Tandy. It feels as if they are rolling over broken glass. "Have you heard anything bizarre about the Deitzhoff house?"

"Bizarre? Like what?" Tandy's ears practically prick forward like a cat's. She's picked up the scent.

In fact, Tandy has always reminded Rebecca of a cat, or kitten to be more precise; a ginger kitten—one full of piss-and-vinegar. Tandy is tiny and curvy, kind of plush. She has feathery eyelashes that fan down over her eyes rather than curl upwards. A faint downy fuzz of fine blond hairs brushes along her cheeks and stops at her perfectly lined lips. Her nose turns up and is more than a little pugnacious. Her bushy strawberry blonde hair is cut boyishly short to curb its unruly tendencies but on Tandy it is as feminine as ringlets. Tandy was born with a manicure. She inherited long, red nails along with amber eyes and size five feet.

Tandy hasn't much of an accent left. She has been trying to bury it, along with her past for the last ten years. But a touch of a drawl lingers although she hates to admit it and Rebecca teases her about it unmercifully when she "furgits."

Last year she married Max Weinstock, an optometrist, which as far as

The Forgotten Roses

Tandy is concerned "is as good as being a doctor." Since then, her wardrobe has taken on an obsessively upscale bent. She only shops at Barney's now, or Saks, and is partial to heavy lined silks that are chalky to the touch. Today she is in "aubergine"–last year it would have been plain old purple–with shell pink mother-of-pearl earrings, ringed in solid gold, the size of quahogs.

Tandy recently lived in a condo in neighboring Reedsville, but soon after she snagged Max, she "hauled ass" over to Havenwood to stay. Now she sits on the planning board, giving the stink eye to every newcomer with blueprints.

Rebecca feels Tandy's eyes running up and down her prostrate frame, assessing her outfit, the mud on her boots. Tandy wouldn't dream of wearing jeans for anything less than a round-up and doesn't even own a pair of sneakers. She wears her expensive designer heels even to house inspections. She says it conveys a high level of professionalism. Rebecca thinks it's a pretty obvious way to avoid getting your feet dirty, as in, "Oh y'all go on ahead to the paddock. I'll stay here in the solarium and wait for you."

I bet she'd like to slap my boots off the sofa. Screw her, I'm not moving, Rebecca thinks. Tandy's position as office manager gives her an outlet for her bossy nature and permission to lambaste the other brokers over such matters, which of course, they pretty much ignore.

The brokers at Country Lane are all women. Sophia assiduously avoids hiring a man. Calls male brokers "used car salesmen. I won't have them peeing all over the toilet seat and farting around in my office." And so it remains an office of women only. Farters need not apply. The atmosphere is womanish, that is to say it is low key, competitive but homey and there is no hierarchy. Except for Tandy, who is better suited to charming disgruntled clients and putting down uppity attorneys than managing co-workers. Disputes among the brokers are handled in matriarchal fashion by Sophia. She dispenses motherly wisdom and

Solomon-like decrees accompanied by large doses of bribery; much like the mother of any large, contentious family.

Practically the whole town knows that Sophia Lane started this business a couple of decades ago after her husband took off with the babysitter, leaving her with five children and little else. The scandal was delicious fodder for gossip in little Havenwood back then; people still talk about it, wondering if there was something about Sophia that drove him off.

She nursed the company from a one-woman kitchen-based operation to the most successful real estate company in the county. Within five years, she moved out of two cramped rooms above the bank after purchasing and renovating Jersey Johnson's garage on the edge of the business district. It was nothing more than a long low cement block box until she transformed it into the sleek contemporary building it is now. Three big rooms in a row with enormous windows overlooking a wide lawn with a gathering of honeysuckle along the stone wall and a patch of black-eyed Susan near the walkway which the brokers take turns watering during the summer months, adding flats of Pansies and Petunias, planting mums in the fall. The grassed area covers the enormous–large enough to accommodate a hotel–state-of-the-art septic system that the town required Sophia install. "Board of health bullshit! The *bastahds!*" Sophia always adds in her thick Boston accent when telling the story. Before the lawn came in, the enormous mound looked for all the world like an old Indian burial ground.

When she started out, committee members regarded Sophia as abrasive and pushy; a woman who wouldn't take no for an answer. Now, she is considered one of the town's most beloved and colorful characters; back then they complained bitterly of what a big pain in the ass she was and gave her a hard time.

Rebecca has heard how Sophia bulldozed through those years smiling through gritted teeth, armed with cardboard shirt boxes filled with homemade fudge brownies or Toll House cookies. She would go before planning boards, to selectmen's meetings and board of health hearings laden with baked goods, and reams of meticulously prepared paperwork. She was one of the first people to see the dollar potential of Havenwood, one of the first local developers to stake out a couple of parcels on abandoned cornfield along a bumpy road and call it a cul-de-sac. She fashioned a couple of small neighborhoods out of overgrown pasture and attracted the first few executives who didn't mind the hour commute to the financial district. She was selling tranquility and pastoral country life. She was selling a dream. And she was charging dearly for it.

The town has come to forgive her. After all, she was one of them—sort of. Sophia raised her children here, stayed on through thick and thin, but never really felt wholly a part of the community; she didn't have time for it.

She hit the ground running when Jake left and knew enough not to take back her maiden name after the divorced. Sophia Fanelli, entrepreneur, would not have gotten as far as Jake Lane's wronged wife trying to keep body and soul together. Although, she has told Rebecca she was nothing less than thankful when the asshole skipped town, Rebecca isn't sure she believes it. She asked no one for help and got none. And while she swears she didn't want their charity, she nevertheless sourly resents them, the townspeople, more than she ever resented Jake, for the way she had to struggle so hard for every inch.

A few years ago, Sophia talked Tandy into becoming the office manager. Tandy, to her credit, was doubtful about her leadership abilities, but overcome with the prospect of "a lot less troopin' around with every jackass wanting heaven on earth convenient to the Mass Pike, and a top notch golf course." Tandy's high heels are mud free today and she is eternally grateful and as loyal as a terrier to Sophia for that.

Nowadays, Sophia mostly travels. She breezes through the office between trips–and affairs–like Auntie Mame, calling them all "Dee-ah" in a sing-songy voice while bestowing generous gifts of hand painted Chinese silk scarves or Venetian glass bead necklaces. She billows through, all six feet of her, in flowing silk-screened pantsuits and low comfortable heels with her hair–gone totally white–pulled back into a low pony tail. She hugs each of them, circling their shoulders in overpowering arms until the women wince under their smiles, bones crackling like kindling from the force of her.

When back home, Sophia attends weekly office meetings and gives loud advice that is out of date and slightly off kilter, then grabs her Yves St. Laurent sunglasses, her enormous pocketbook, the size of a trash can, and tears out all in a rush leaving them waving after her fondly and more than a little relieved. The broker ladies at Country Lane Properties love her, but they love her best when she is in Luxembourg or Lisbon.

Rebecca's migraine pills have kicked in. She sits up and tugs at the bottom of her jacket, fluffs up her hair where it's mashed in the back. Tandy is impatient but aroused; if she had a tail, she'd be flicking it.

"Have you heard that it might be…I don't know…haunted or something?" Rebecca asks

"No! Why? What have you heard? You were there this morning weren't you? Did you see somethin'?" Tandy's into it now; she's bristling.

Rebecca examines the paper towel, turning it over and over in her hands. "Well, Sully mentioned something about Mr. Deitzhoff's first wife committing suicide there. And other rumors. She shakes her head and shrugs. "I should ask him more about it I guess." She glances up at Tandy, "I might have a disclosure issue on my hands," Rebecca tells her, on more solid ground now.

"Because of the death," Tandy nods in agreement. "Maybe I'll call Greg Boynton and make him get off his lard ass and actually work for his retainer. But what about it being haunted? *Did* you see something?"

"No…I felt something."

The Forgotten Roses

"You *felt* something?" Tandy says "felt" like it had a bad taste. "Like what? Did the thing touch you, or was it a cold blast of air…anything like that?"

"No, no. I mean I had a feeling. Something wasn't right." It is on the tip of Rebecca's tongue to tell Tandy about the owl, the hook, but as soon as the thought enters her mind, it sounds foolish even to her. Tandy is waiting for a good story. But the one that waits behind Rebecca's lips is as substantial as smoke. As if she woke from a dream, attempting to describe it. What seemed plausible while dreaming–with detail so rich and vivid–sounds like muddled nonsense in the harsh light of day.

"It must be pms," Rebecca jokes instead. She can see Tandy hesitate, suspicious. Rebecca gets up and walks over to her desk. "I just need to have a talk with Sully about the first Mrs. Deitzhoff." She doesn't mention the girl. "You're sure you've never heard anything?"

"I'm sure. When did she die?"

"I don't know." It's true, I don't know anything, nothing at all. Except that there was a suicide, and a disappearance… And Rose. Maybe I could ask Mr. Deitzhoff if he remembers her. Oh my God, I can't do that, Rebecca thinks. She plunks her elbows on the desk and holds her head in her hands. I must be losing it, she tells herself.

She needs to keep her priorities straight, keep events in perspective. She needs to put it all in logical order, like an equation. "Let's see…what do I know…" Rebecca mulls out loud, head in hand, foggy and slow from the after-effects of the migraine and medication.

"You sure you're alright? You look peculiar." Tandy actually looks alarmed.

"Oh thanks, Tan, now I feel much better. Just let me think… I know that the suicide must have happened quite a long while ago; probably thirty years or more."

"I bet Sophia would know," Tandy offers. "But she's in London till

Thanksgiving. When she checks in, I'll ask her about it. What was the woman's name?" she asks.

"I don't know," Rebecca replies wearily. "*Mrs.* Deitzhoff," she says snidely.

Tandy lets out an exasperated sigh, "Well, talk to Sully then, but don't nose around too much. We don't want to be the source of rumor ourselves. That'd be a *disastah!*" She pretends a little shiver, but smiles mischievously and Rebecca has to laugh because they both know how much Tandy enjoys mayhem. She's famous for following the fire engines that scream past, flying behind at break-neck speed, then reporting back, flushed and breathless with gory details. Tandy's another one who's missed her calling–fire dog. Or arsonist.

"And don't mention anything to your clients just yet. Not until we can get a handle on the situation with our attorney, confirm it and all.

So…you had a feeling huh?" Tandy regards Rebecca from under eyelashes heavy with mascara, eyelids at half-mast. Rebecca looks into the fringed cat eyes, nearly concealed. She looks straight into them, unwavering, and holds her gaze but doesn't answer. Tandy's eyebrows rise a bit over the glowing amber of her eyes; the centers widen and contract–a fleeting acknowledgement. Tandy despises weakness, but like most women, respects intuition. "Alright then," she says before walking over to her desk.

"By the way," she turns back to Rebecca, "your one o'clock called to confirm. The Greens? How's it going with them?"

"Great!" she tells Tandy enthusiastically just the way Tandy wants to hear it.

Thank God for the Greens; a refreshing antidote to the Frakes. Clients like the Greens are the reason Rebecca loves this business; all the nice young couples with high hopes and a scraped-together down payment. They sit around Rebecca's desk and put their heads together while she helps them make life plans around the handful of facts they offer up. Rebecca examines them like a fortuneteller reading tealeaves: salary, savings, credit history, assets. They talk of interest rates, p.i.t, and mortgage insurance.

Rebecca gets to know them, grows fond of them, listens to their problems, and offers recipes and advice on toilet training. Sometimes the women wax poetic about their dream home and Rebecca gently lassos them down from the clouds back to the reality of split-levels and fixer-uppers. She brings coloring books and puzzles to keep the kids busy, lugs diaper bags through house tours, sympathizes with wives over husbands missing in action on extended business trips, and scrapes melted crayons off her car seats.

Rebecca is very protective of "her people." She will not take them to houses within zapping distance of a power line, eliminates developments built over landfill and discourages building lots that overlook picturesque apple orchards where undetectable clouds of insecticide may float on the breeze and land on a sandbox. She gives them guided tours of any town that strikes their fancy, at any time, on any day. She does it for the sale, the commission, yes, but she also does it for them.

Herb and Maggie Green are looking for a good school system and a friendly neighborhood for their three kids, seven, five and one. They want a yard big enough for a garden shed, a play set and a happy slobbering dog. A little privacy, not isolation. He wants a garage, she a screened porch, they both want a private master bath. These are the things they tell Rebecca, but Rebecca knows even more. That's what makes her a good broker, an exceptional broker. Because she has read their tea leaves and has seen the pattern of their future.

Herb doesn't yet realize that he wants to be in the Fourth of July parade with the other Cub Scout dads in the precision lawnmower drill-team. And Maggie wants to wheel baby T.J. alongside Joshua and Jillian who will be riding bikes decorated with red, white, and blue streamers. Herb will coach soccer and head up a fundraising committee to improve the playing fields at the middle school. Maggie will join the Newcomers Club, the Friends of the Library, volunteer at Elder Affairs and run for school committee, but not until the kids are older. They don't care much about easy commutes, proximity to malls, or diversity.

They are not so different from the immigrants who came all the way across the ocean only to gravitate to pockets inhabited by people from the old country. They want to be able to identify the cooking odors that float out of their neighbor's windows. They want to feel secure, bolstered by familiar faces of those with similar backgrounds, comforted by sameness. And they want to sink deep roots in a community of others who want exactly the same things.

Rebecca becomes their surrogate mother, their confidant, their best friend for a while. Sometimes she does battle for them; often they are not even aware that she had to. She finds them their dream, not necessarily their "dream home," and sees them off to a good start. They come to her adrift and leave settled.

"They're getting anxious; they want to move before Christmas. Of course, they love Havenwood, but can't afford anything on the market right now. I'm keeping my fingers crossed about Mrs. Parker's little house coming on the market in time."

Tandy nods approvingly, "Good, good," she says marching away–her sharp heels digging pockmarks in the virgin carpeting–and then stops, turning around to say, "Dana called looking for you."

11

Bruised

Dana rubs the spot where her boyfriend, Corey, grabbed her last night. There are three oblong bruises on her upper arm. She pokes at them angrily, presses hard where each mark hides under her shirt. It smarts and she's glad because it's better than the achy, empty feeling swimming around at the pit of her stomach.

"That asshole!" she tells her friend Amy. Amy concentrates on looking concerned. She feels concerned, but she wants to make sure that her face shows it. She frowns and juts her chin out, nodding enthusiastically so that her flat-ironed hair stabs at her shoulders.

Dana and Amy are sitting cross-legged outside behind the high school cafeteria, on a tired patch of crabgrass under a scrub oak that doesn't even attempt to shade. It has a scabby trunk made permanently smooth on one side from propping up the backs of generations of lolling teenagers trying to catch a few rays between classes. It is lunchtime, but Dana and Amy aren't eating; they're sneaking a joint.

"Look out, here comes Bennett," Amy says. They turn their backs, wave the air in front of their faces hiding the joint inside Amy's cupped hand under her backpack. "Hi Mr. Bennett," they chirp and wave to him. "Aren't you girls having lunch?" he calls to them. They shake their heads and tell him, "Diets!" As soon as he gets out of sight, Amy bends over, hangs her tongue all the way out of her mouth as if she's gagging and rolls her eyes until only the whites show. "I can't stand him…stupid turd flunked me. Course, I never did one page of homework," she says laughing and gagging aggressively again.

Dana knows it's funny, but she just can't laugh. She's still thinking about last night.

"So, what happened?" Amy asks finally.

Dana sighs, "So, I told my mother I was going over to Stacey's house and I met Corey there. Then we went to Todd's because his parents are away and he had a thirty rack."

"Why didn't you call me?" Amy asks indignantly.

"I didn't know 'til we got there. Anyway, we're drinking and Corey starts hanging on me, you know how he does when he gets drunk. I was buzzed, but not out of it, you know. Corey must've been drinking way before we got there because he's shitfaced at this point. So he's acting like Chester the molester and I tell him to get *off* me. He gets really, really nasty and starts pushing me around. I get so pissed, I whack him and he takes a fit! He throws his beer can at me and grabs me and shoves me against the wall. My head banged so hard I saw fucking stars!"

"Jeez!"

"That wasn't the worst part. The worst thing was when my head hit the wall, my jaw kind of snapped shut. Like my teeth smashed together or something and now my front teeth are loose a little bit."

"No shit! What are you going to do?"

"Well, I might tell my mother that someone hit me by accident in gym and I need to go to the dentist."

"No, I mean about Corey."

Dana shrugs, "I don't know... Todd and the other guys got mad at him and stuff, kicked him out. I don't know how he got home. I kinda feel sorry for him. You know he only acts like that when he's hammered."

Amy takes a quick drag and holds it in as best she can while still talking. "I know, most of the time he's really, really sweet," she says in a high squeaky voice.

"He'll probably be all like, 'Oh I'm so sorry. I didn't mean it,' and all that, when I see him. Have *you* seen him?"

"No," Amy exhales apologetically.

"I've been looking for him all morning. Maybe he's at home hung over. I tried to sleep in, but my Mom got on my case. She's such a fucking pain in the ass."

"What did she do?"

"Oh, you know, the usual crap," Dana straightens and stiffens to mimic her mother. She tightens her lips, makes her voice shrill and screechy. "Dana, you have to get up blah, blah." Dana gags just like Amy did and they both laugh though Dana doesn't do it nearly as well as Amy. "Why can't she just leave me alone," Dana sulks and pulls up fistfuls of grass. "Can I have some?" she asks Amy.

Dana sucks in the smoke through her teeth, squeezes it down, pulls it into her throat. The dope tickles by her tonsils. It sears the cilia, seeps into the bronchia and flows into her bloodstream like warm milk. At least, this is how she imagines it. Dana closes her eyes and waits to feel better. She wants to feel cottony and removed. She wants her headache to go away, the one she has had since last night when she cracked her skull against the wall. She doesn't know why she didn't tell Amy that part. Like she's almost embarrassed about it or something.

"I called my mother," Dana says with her eyes closed. She wonders if you can get a brain tumor from hitting your head. Probably not.

"You did? What for?"

"Well, I was just going to tell her about my teeth 'cause I think maybe I should really go to the dentist today. Maybe I can get dismissed." Dana feels close to tears for some reason and that makes her mad again. "She's probably out with one of her fucking clients. God, I hate her so much. She's either like in my face, or totally not there."

"I know. Do you want some more of this cause I'm going to put it out before we get caught." The bell rings, lunch is over. Amy daintily pinches the end of the roach before she tucks it into the pencil compartment in her backpack. "Are you coming?" she asks Dana as she gets up to go to class.

"Yeah, but I'm going to the office first to try her again."

Dana waited too long, and now she is forced use the school's phone to call her mother with the office trolls listening in on her conversation. "Fuck!" she says under her breath. Some little freshman twerp beat her to it and is telling her nanny what time to pick her up from band practice. What an idiot. Dana moves in closer until she's breathing on the girl. She can smell the kid's shampoo. It's probably Johnson's baby shampoo, Dana sneers. The girl speeds up like she's on fast forward, "OkaythanksI'llseeyoulater g'bye."

I am so mean, Dana exults as she calls her mother. She turns her back on the woman working behind the desk and whispers into the phone, "Mom? It's me. Um, something happened in gym today and I think my teeth…I mean someone hit me by accident and kind of made my front teeth a little loose so I think I better get to a dentist. Like now!

"No, I didn't tell the gym teacher. No, it can't wait until after school, and I don't give a shit about your appointment, my fucking teeth are about to fall out of my head!

"How can I calm down when you don't even care! All you care about is your fucking clients!

"Okay, okay, so call the dentist and call me right back. Okay! Bye!" Dana leaves the front office and leans against the wall in the corridor hugging her books to her chest. She sees Amy walking toward her. Dana thinks Amy looks stupid with that dark purple lipstick she bought at Urban Outfitters—what did she call it? Poison? Decay?—but she's afraid to tell her because she might get all bent out of shape and there's no way Dana's going to hurt Amy's feelings again.

When Amy had shown her that ugly, black yin-yang tattoo on her hip,

The Forgotten Roses

Dana almost puked and she told Amy right away how stupid it was and how it costs like a zillion dollars to get it removed by laser. Why, Dana asked, didn't she get one of the roses or butterflies on her ankle like they'd always talked about instead of that big black thing sitting under her waist that looks like mating worms on a white dish? Amy didn't speak to her for two weeks, and really Dana was the one who should have been pissed because Amy went and got it done without her, when they had planned all along to get tattooed together.

Dana really missed her. And she worried about her too; Ames can be kind of a flake. Even though Dana has lots of other friends, mostly kids she's known since kindergarten, and Amy isn't the brightest bulb and—even though she tries hard to be—she's not the coolest either. Still, she's the one Dana usually confides in. But, right now, Dana doesn't feel like talking anymore. Her head is throbbing and she feels like shit.

"What are you doing?" Amy asks.

"My mom's calling me back. I'm going to wait here. You better go to class."

"No, I'll wait with you."

"You're gonna be late."

"What's one more detention?" Amy shrugs. "How else would I get my homework done?"

The office troll waves Dana back into the room to talk to her mother; Amy trails behind. "Yeah? Okay. Bye." she says into the phone and sighs heavily as she hangs up, as if she's been holding her breath for a long, long time. "My mom is picking me up in fifteen minutes," Dana tells the secretary who directs Dana to go to the vice principal's office.

As Dana walks down the corridor to Mrs. Pinchon's office, Amy asks, "What do you want me to tell Corey if I see him?" Dana mulls over this vital question, chewing on the inside of her lip. A little while ago, she might have said, "Tell him to go to hell." But she doesn't feel mad anymore. Or, she could just say, "Ask him to call me." But right now she doesn't feel like talking to him, doesn't want to hear the sound of his stupid voice and his stupid excuses. Dana doesn't know exactly how she feels about Corey. She wants to pick out the right feeling. It's like picking apples from a tree; this one's not quite right, that one isn't either. Most are too remote to grasp and she's too tired to try.

Dana just wants to get home. She wants her mother to bring her a cup of hot, milky, tea with sugar and feel her forehead with her lips. She wants to sleep until dinner and come down to eat in her bathrobe and socks. She wants to zone out in front of the tv wrapped in her comforter. Maybe her mom will make buttered popcorn and hot chocolate with marshmallow tonight.

"I don't care what you tell him. I'll talk to you later, okay Ames?"

Dana rounds the corner and into the office to speak to the vice principal. Mrs. Pinchon peers at Dana over her glasses. They are on pearl strings that droop under her double chin like reins. She reeks of disapproval, her mouth puckers in displeasure. "Your mother called, Dana, but I told her that due to your record of absences and tardys you will be required to get a note from the dentist. And your guidance counselor will want to see you about making up lost class time. Is that clear?"

Why doesn't she just take the fucking glasses off, let them flop onto that shelf she calls breasts, Dana thinks. It's a wonder she doesn't get a stiff neck from holding her head that way all day long so she can see over them. She must think it makes her look important. What an asshole. Dana tries to picture Mrs. Pinchon having sex because she thinks the image would be hilarious. She envisions the old bitch flat on her back with her legs straight up in the air, but it only makes Dana queasy. "Yes, Mrs. Pinchon," she replies politely so the old hag won't throw a fucking fit and choke on her dentures.

Dana sees her mother through the windows of the office. She is trying to find a parking space close enough to the front door, but there is none, so she swings around the driveway again. "My mother's here," Dana tells Mrs. Pinchon.

Mrs. Pinchon sighs, as if it is a personal defeat that Dana is getting to leave. She dismisses her with a wave of her hand, pretending to be too busy to say anything further.

Dana pushes open the heavy doors and watches her mother pull up right in front where the handicapped parking is, so Dana won't have too far to walk. Dana is aware of her mother's considerate gesture. She takes note, with satisfaction of her mother's worried assessment of her as she slides into the front seat. Dana is filled with relief, but feels sheepish over it, which turns to irritation as soon as Rebecca opens her mouth.

"Are you all right? Let me see your teeth."

Dana lets out an exasperated groan. Like I'm going to open my mouth right here in front of the school and let her look in, she thinks. What an idiot! "Not here mom! Let's just go!" Dana slinks down into the seat so that only the top of her head is visible from outside as her mother pulls away.

"Are you okay, honey?" Rebecca asks.

The sound of her mother's voice grates on Dana's last nerve. She feels like crying again. She closes her eyes, clamps them shut. If her mother says another word she'll burst. She'll scream. She'll start bawling like an idiot. Why doesn't the woman just shut the fuck up?

Rebecca looks over at the top of Dana's head. So familiar...just like when she was little, when her hair was in pigtails and she used to hold my hand while we drove. Dana's hair shines on in wild disarray, pushed up in back like a golden waterfall, by the motion of her slide down the seat. Underneath, her face looks pinched and pale. Her eyes look like they are rimmed in dark blue eyeshadow. She is as limp as her old stuffed dog, ragged around the edges and colorless. Rebecca's throat constricts as if she is being strangled, until it hurts too much to swallow and the only relief, the only remedy for it is to reach her hand out, take Dana's and squeeze. To Rebecca's surprise, Dana squeezes back. A good sign, she thinks the second before Dana snatches her hand away.

12

Dreams

Three thirteen glows from Rebecca's clock radio. She tries to slow her breathing as she casts her mind back to the nightmare. Babies spread-eagled, pinned like moths to a circular wheel, someone spins it, the babies cry, their mouths great, gaping black holes. Empty. Starving. Hopeless. In the dream, she pulled back on a wooden lever. The implements were medieval; the lever heavy, oaken, rough-hewn. She leaned her shoulder into it; it wouldn't budge. She pushed and pushed, panting, grunting, and it finally gave way. But the wheel didn't slow, instead it sped up and the babies were flung off, propelled into the dark air landing in broken heaps, their arms and legs sticking out stiffly at odd angles like plastic dolls. What have I done, what have I done, she wailed. Then Rebecca woke, breathing hard, heart pounding, hair tangled and sweaty at the back of her neck.

She tries to calm herself, to shake the overpowering dread. She sits up, turns on the light, changes the subject in her mind. *"Think-a sweet tings, and you'll have-a sweet dreams,"* that's what Nana used to say at bedtime. Rebecca turns out the light and closes her eyes again thinking about her sweet Nana.

Rebecca's fondest memories are of weeding through tight garden rows with Nana, surrounded by the fragrance of spicy leaves warm in the sun, and Nana's round back bent over as she gathered ripened tomatoes into her apron. Weekend sleepovers in the summer meant days spent in the garden: watering, pinching off long green beans from tall curling vines, picking only the young, tender cucumbers, the smell of bee balm and marigolds, gathering squash blossoms, the taste of a begonia petal popped into her mouth; it crunched and was tangy.

And, whatever the season, early Sunday mornings, waking up to the fragrance of onions and garlic simmering in olive oil, the first step of many for spaghetti sauce–*sugo*–and the low murmur of Italian spoken between grandparents, Gina and Vincent. From her bed, Rebecca listened, lulled and comforted by the constant flow of hushed conversation; like a pot of continually, gently percolating coffee. She marveled at how much they had to say to each other.

In winter, before Christmas Rebecca and Nana would go shopping: Grover Cronin's, in Waltham, Barron's, Filene's Basement in Boston, when it really was the basement–the dingy underbelly–Grants and Woolworths's–the fabulous "five and tens."

When Rebecca and her Nana walked the two miles from Nana's two-family to Grant's in West Newton Square, she held Rebecca's hand tight down by her side as if Rebecca was a balloon that might fly off. Nana wore her good wool coat, a stiff square pocketbook over her arm that she kept compressed protectively against her ribs, and a mink pillbox hat. And nylons of course, always wore them, even at home when she would roll them down to her ankles before putting on her slippers. Before they set out, she pulled on thin rubber galoshes over her heels. Rebecca's boots had a lining of fake fur and were big enough to accommodate two layers of thick socks. Nana's feet must have frozen.

At Grant's Rebecca chose between marshmallows covered with toasted coconut, or big cellophane bags of hard honeycomb cubes that, after you ate a handful, left the inside of your mouth raw and shredded: fireballs, squirrels, Mary Jane's that only the grownups liked, and tiny wax bottles with sticky sweet liquid in them. Rebecca would suck out the contents until the bottles stuck to her tongue and she showed Nana the trick. Nana would cover her eyes in mock horror and Rebecca would be delighted down to her toes. Grant's always smelled, deliciously, like popcorn.

With her savings, Rebecca bought big white handkerchiefs in packages of three for fifty cents for the men, and delicate hankies that sales girls would produce from narrow drawers, sliding them out from behind the counter like they were slices of gold. Some had monogrammed letters or days of the week in every color of the rainbow. Rebecca chose, ever so seriously, between filmy, blue scalloped-edged ones, or the snow-white ones with clusters of embroidered roses and tiny red French knots dotting the edges. These were bestowed upon special people: Nana of course, Rebecca's mother, a special teacher, and cost dollars.

Grant's offered fascinating riches: pink crackled-glass candy dishes, ceramic ashtrays the size of dinner plates, Evening in Paris perfume in little dark blue bottles with glass stoppers, glamorous rhinestone clip-on earrings, nurse kits containing plastic vials filled with tiny round candy pills. What Rebecca wished for the most for herself, were the metal cowboy cap guns that looked just like Roy Rogers', but settled for a box of red cap rolls that she took home and banged with rocks on the sidewalk, exploding the tiny black gunpowder centers with a vengeance. The smoke was acrid, dangerous, satisfying.

Nana bought corsets there. Sometimes she bought Rebecca Barbie accessories. Nana couldn't get over Barbie's figure, her bathing suits and lingerie, Ken. Barbie treasures were displayed on glass counters in grid-like sections; one compartment contained little red high-heels, another dresses, fur stoles, pocketbooks, packets of jewelry. Once, Nana purchased a teeny string of pearls and miniature nylons for Rebecca's Barbie.

Rebecca could not get those nylons on Barbie no matter how hard she tried; she thought there was some trick to getting them on that she was too stupid to know. Other girls must know, but the secret was kept from her like when mean girls whispered behind their hands while they stared right at you. Rebecca's cheeks flamed in frustration. She still remembers how hot and tired her eyes felt in their sockets from the tears and the trying.

Nana and Rebecca sat in the kitchen with their heads bent together over Barbie's smooth inflexible, pink plastic legs spread in a V between them, her pointy toes poking into their faces. Rebecca remembers the glare of the overhead kitchen light, the look of concentration on Nana's face as she tried and tried to get the stockings on Barbie. Nana had square hands, strong hands, rough and calloused from pushing a thick sewing needle in and out of course woolen coats all day long. She carefully tried to thumb the narrow nylon casings past Barbie's too shapely, unforgiving thighs. Beads of sweat formed and glistened like jewels on her upper lip that made Rebecca feel sadder than anything. Rebecca's sweet old Nana muttered to Barbie in Italian, *"Piglia in culo,"* she said. When Rebecca was much older, she realized Nana had told Barbie to, "stick it up your ass."

Rebecca smiles at the thought, but it doesn't help, she still can't settle down. Why did I dream about babies? Such a disturbing, sickening nightmare! She turns on the light once more and gets up to check on Lily and Dana. An old habit, besides she's worried about Dana. All evening Dana was sullen, which is normal, but oddly subdued, as if the stuffing had been knocked out of her. She didn't hole up in her room with her music blaring as usual. Dana stayed downstairs with Lily and Rebecca in the living room watching Lily's favorite shows. She brought her comforter with her and lay down on the couch wrapping herself into a cocoon. Rebecca made the girls milky sweetened tea and buttered cinnamon toast sprinkled with a little bit of sugar. When it was brought to Dana on a tray, she sat bolt upright and sighed a long tremulous sigh as she settled the tray on her lap. She even said, "Thanks Mom" in a pleasant voice that caused Lily to look over at her in wonderment.

The Forgotten Roses

Drew came home late and Rebecca got up from bed to tell him about it. He said, "Well, maybe she's finally turning around. Don't look a gift horse in the mouth." He sounded just like his father. Then he wanted to know what the dentist said, what exactly was the course of treatment and the expected outcome, how much would it cost, how much would insurance pay. Rebecca didn't have all the answers.

"Damn it, Rebecca, don't you ask? Don't you listen?" He looked tired, the flesh around his eyes puckered.

"Where were you tonight?" Rebecca asked.

"Faculty meeting," he responded too quickly and then said belligerently, "Why?"

Rebecca shrugged with forced nonchalance, "I really don't care what you do with your evenings Drew," she said with her chin tipped up defiantly. She argues like the Griffins now. She becomes haughty, contemptuous, her lips purse. Sometimes she merely waves her hand dismissively. Rebecca has learned that the dull arrows hurt the most. Besides, it was quieter that way; she never wanted her children to feel the need to run and hide, as if an air raid warning had sounded–duck and cover–the way she did when the yelling started.

She believes he is seeing someone and watches him for signs. She probably should just confront him, but he might actually tell her. I am not ready for this, she told herself, and, recognizing a good exit point, turned sharply, marching off as dignified as possible in shuffling slippers.

Rebecca finds Lily in bed with Willow who is curled on top of her head like a fur hat. Lily sleeps flung out in every direction, her covers kicked off, her mouth open as if she's about to speak, her hair electrified. She is totally abandoned to her dreams. Free. Her window is open too wide. I should lower it, Rebecca thinks. The night air has chilled and is filled with mischief. There is a bright moon that drops blots of light onto the trees; when the wind blows, the lights scatter like sprites. Maybe Lily is one of them; maybe at night her spirit escapes to play in the moonbeams like Peter Pan. Maybe Willow guards her, watches her nocturnal foray enviously, waits for her return. Rebecca doesn't disturb them.

Dana's knees are drawn up to her waist; she is lying on her side, her hands tucked under her face as if clasped in prayer. Moonlight has turned her hair to liquid silver; it flows out behind her spilling onto her pillow in long gentle currents. Dana does not look angelic though; she looks like a porcelain mask of the real Dana.

She sleeps neatly under her blanket, composed as if for a portrait. Even Dog is careful on the pillow next to her, all four legs straight by his side, his good eye watchful as ever. Dana sleeps perfectly; she does not drool or snore. She could model sheets or mattresses. But her brow is slightly furrowed, as if she is angry or worried even in her dreams.

She is so still. Rebecca tiptoes over to her and watches for signs of breathing. She did this a couple of times each night when they were babies. Almost hourly when they were newborns, holding her own breath until she could see the rise and fall of their tiny chests. She gently places her hand on Dana's back to feel the rhythm, just as she did back then, and keeps it there until she is convinced. While she's bent over her, she cannot resist; she takes the tips of Dana's hair, where the ends bend in half-remembered curl, and rubs them between her fingers.

When Dana was small, her hair would curl on whim: when it was humid, when the sky was pink, when she ate lollipops. It would spiral down in tendrils around her face and glow like a halo. Rebecca would rub the silky ends between her fingertips as if she could make wishes on them.

Something grips Rebecca's shoulder and she whirls around startled to find Drew behind her. "What are you doing?" he hisses at her.

"I…I'm just checking on Dana. To see if she's okay." she whispers back, feeling defensive, embarrassed. He motions her to follow him and she does. He closes the door carefully behind them and Rebecca can see a lecture starting to form like a cloud over his head. Soon it will be raining here in the hall. She will be drowning in condescension, soaked to the skin in Drew's opinion of her over-protectiveness, dripping in blame for Dana's bad behavior. I should turn on my heels and run, she thinks, but plants her slippers stubbornly and grits her teeth in defiance instead.

She puts her hand up like a traffic cop, "Don't even start with me, Drew."

He shakes his head, "Do you see what you're doing? You're smothering her."

Incensed, Rebecca takes two steps forward until her face is directly in front of his chest to make sure he can hear her; it causes him to lean back some. "Are you talking about Dana or yourself? I feel sorry for you if you think love and concern are suffocating. But Dana is not like you, thank God. What do you know anyway? Spinning in your own little world!"

"What were you doing in there pawing at her?" Drew says between tight lips. He is all the way over the mean line now. I pushed him there, she thinks. Walk away now, Rebecca, she tells herself.

"Pawing? *Paw*-ing? Jesus! You can't even recognize affection when you see it," she says viciously through gritted teeth. "Cold goddamn fish goddamn selfish prick!" her voice inadvertently rising steeply with each word.

Drew just stands there clenching his jaw until Rebecca feels the chill of his resentment through the thin cotton of her pajamas. "Cold fish?" he leers. "There's someone who doesn't think I'm cold at all."

Oh shit, here it comes. Rebecca swallows, wishing her legs didn't feel like mush, as if there were no bones under the skin. How can you walk away with no bones, she asks herself.

"Believe me, there is someone…"

Rebecca feels the sting of his face against her hand and realizes she's slapped him. Hard. He looks stunned. His head is turned sideways from the force of the blow. She didn't mean to hit him, she just didn't want him to go any further.

"I'm...sorry," she says though she's not sure it's true. Rebecca looks at her open hand in surprise, like she's never seen it before, closes it into a fist, and hides it behind her back. She backs away from him slowly, and finds the sight of him receding before her fascinating. He clearly finds the sight of Rebecca infuriating, which is mildly satisfying if not downright funny to her. "I'm sorry," she says again but it's not at all convincing.

She backs up to her bedroom door, turns the knob, slides in, locks it, and stands with her back pressed up against it waiting. What am I waiting for? she asks herself. Drew is not the type to batter down the door; he doesn't have the fire for that. I bet he's still standing there in his blue and white pinstripe boxers looking hateful.

She expects that any moment now the daggers he is surely throwing out his eyeballs will penetrate the door and stab her in the back. She waits for their sting, for their penetration and the slicing of flesh. But nothing happens and remorse covers her like a wet blanket. Rebecca slumps to bed and sits on the edge feeling let down. Her shoulders ache, she is unable to square them, she feels as if they are round and small and weak. It seems like she's been waiting forever—for things to change, for things to happen, for signs.

At first, eons ago, she waited for an intimacy that never came. She thought that with time, things would get better between them. Rebecca was sure that she could make it better. She cooked overly complicated meals from *The Joy of Cooking*, tried to learn about wines to impress his parents, audited courses to keep up with Drew, stretched her secretary's salary as far as it could go so Drew wouldn't have to worry about bills while he was studying. Rebecca showered him with affection, and waited for him to respond in kind. Each sweet kiss, hug, tender stroke of an arm, soft touch on a stubbled cheek, every gentle reach; lessons taught, but never learned.

She waited for Drew to get through grad school hoping he would be less distracted, recognizing even then that Drew was somehow disconnected from her, like a phone with faulty reception. That was around the time he started telling her he needed some "space." So Rebecca gave him that too. When he drifted around the apartment looking as if he was on a different planet, she resisted the urge to throw her arms around him to bring him back. She used the time at dinner when he would be silently reading a book at the table, to plan her next most memorable meal. She would have served him her heart on a stick, roasted with garlic and oregano if she thought it would make a difference.

Rebecca waited for Drew to agree to start a family believing that it would solve everything. And, having the girls did make a difference; she was right about that at least. He finally came out of himself. He relished the orderly running of a household. Family rules were important to him: making sure they were all home for dinner hour, seeing that the girls kept their rooms neat, planning family vacations and signing the girls up for swimming, skating, tennis, basketball, volleyball, ballet. He went to every event, performance, and game. He bragged about them constantly.

His favorite thing to do with Dana and Lily was to sit down on the sofa in the evenings, with one little girl on each side, and read from *Old Mother West Wind*, or *The Little Prince*. Later, when they caught his love of books like a fever and could read on their own, he would still gather them together and encourage them to read a page from *Jane Eyre* or *Robinson Crusoe* to him. The girls adored him. Especially Dana.

As soon as she could talk, precociously and in full sentences, Drew's eyes shined most brightly around her. She was so smart, Drew taught her to read while she was still a toddler and by the time she reached kindergarten Dana could read the newspaper, the cover of Time, and the contents on cereal boxes. She was so thoroughly his. Until Dana reached puberty and grew thorns along with her budding breasts. Rebecca often wonders which Drew feels more betrayed by: Dana's nasty behavior, or the fact that he is no longer the sun in her universe.

I shouldn't have implied that he was a shitty father, Rebecca thinks. She wanted to cut him, but he refused to bleed alone. No, maybe Drew is not cold, even though Rebecca has told herself that for years; used it as an excuse for him, as if he suffered from a birth defect and couldn't help himself–waited for him to heal. It's something much worse, something she has just begun to suspect. All this time, Drew has withheld his heart from her–like an underserved prize.

The certainty of it suddenly feels as solid as stone. There is something good about having that piece of the puzzle in her hands to examine. But the weight of it makes her unbearably sad–and undeniably angry.

Anyway, it doesn't alter where they are at this moment in time; still bound together as a family, making a home, raising children, Rebecca thinks digging her heels in. Now she's moved them down the slope to another level. I have no one to blame but myself, Rebecca admits.

Rebecca's mother would agree. It's up to the woman to keep the marriage going. Men are weak. Women are in charge of the home. If it goes to hell, it's her fault. Her shame. Eva would tell Rebecca that–has told her that and more. There is only a narrow criteria for divorce: beatings, child abuse, laziness. The rest is up to the wife–cheating, drinking, gambling–these are merely weaknesses in men that require patience and management. But this is written in stone, in blood; good wives find a way to work it out, good women stay for the children, for the family. It is all that matters.

13

Secrets

Someone else waits on this night filled with mischief and dreams. She, too, has spent a lifetime waiting, waiting to leave, waiting to come back. Serena Deitzhoff sits in a tiny log cabin located deep in the woods near the home where she grew up. She hugs her knees to her chest listening for noises in the dark. Buried memories ambush her every so often, and she feels like a child again, as if she's been sucked back in time instantaneously and against her will. She shivers, but it is not from cold.

She looks over at the doorway and conjures up the figure she saw when she was a little girl. It was illuminated by the backdrop of sunlight filtered through saplings, and shimmered there a pale sparkling green, like a woodland fairy. At five years old, Serena thought it really was one of the fairies that she and her mother built tiny, earth-bound huts for. Julia and Serena would find thin willow branches and bend them over, poking each end into the dirt until it formed a short, curved tunnel, a miniature home. Then they covered it with the biggest, most perfect maple leaves, decorated it with blossoms and lined the bottom with a bed of moss as soft as kitten paws, or fragrant mint leaves from her mother's herb garden. In return, the fairies left tiny gifts like a red-capped mushroom, or a perfect rose. Other times Serena would find a smooth white stone, a foreign coin, a blue barrette, and once, a chocolate covered cherry in a pleated, brown paper cup.

On that day long ago she had wandered from her play yard, followed the direction that the tall grass blew and the bend of the lowest oak branches pointing the way. She eluded the blockade of pine. Serena tucked her head under an arch of vines and found a pussy willow path, saw a gathering of pink Lady Slippers, so wild and rare that she knew not to pick any, and tried to locate the thin call of a hawk looking for a mouse lunch. She scooted under a crook in a hedge and only got her hair caught once, passed a rabbit lodge at the base of an old stump and when she stopped to find a stick to poke into the hole, she saw the little house up ahead. Serena rubbed her eyes with balled up fists, she was that amazed. She never once realized she was lost.

Serena heard her mother calling her name, but it seemed far, far away and unimportant; Serena wasn't ready to go back yet. Inside the cabin smelled like cedar chips, wood-smoke and the moist, brown-dirt scent of the forest. There was a cot with a worn quilt tucked tight around a thin mattress. The striped pillow was too flat to be comfortable. A messy pile of split logs leaned against a woodstove in one corner, and one lone chair, looking punished, stood in another. There was an oil lamp on a shelf, and thick canvas squares nailed to the tops of the windows, parted like pigtails and held aside–not with colored ribbons–by string ties.

The sunlight shone through the windows in perfect straight lines just the way she draws them with her colored pencils. She watched as a million tiny stars danced inside the rays. She felt warm and drowsy, sat on the floor, and leaned her head against the edge of the cot. Her eyelids felt heavy. She could hear her mother still calling but would not, could not shout out loud herself. Hush, hush Serena wanted to whisper, she wanted her mother to be as quiet as she, as quiet as the spider waiting in her web along the windowsill, as quiet as a secret.

Serena could tell this was a secret place, and maybe the secret was for her alone; it could be a playhouse or a gift from the fairies. Maybe it is the giant queen of the fairies now at the door and this is her home, she had thought. Serena lifted her arms up high toward the vision, the luminous glow of light at the doorway. But, when the figure moved forward Serena saw that it was only her mother in a faded housedress and not even the Blessed Virgin which would have been her second guess because bolts of light appeared to be rising off her head, just like the pictures she had seen of Mary floating to heaven.

Julia Deitzhoff's yellow hair stood out in zigzag wisps that had escaped her French twist on her fight through the woods to find Serena. Her nylons had runs that looked like puffy fat scars running up her legs. There was a circle of pink high on each of her cheeks that was so round and perfect and fever bright that it looked as though it might have been painted there by a doll-maker, the lipstick had been chewed off her lips that were as parched and white as tissue paper, and her eyes looked too wide. A spark bounced off the gold cross hanging around her neck as she bent towards Serena.

But it was not a fairy encounter, or visions of the Virgin Mary, or being alone in the woods that alarmed Serena; it was the expression on her mother's face that made her freeze in place. The look in her eyes was so foreign to Serena that it caused her to stare in confusion until her mother reached down and yanked her up by the arm and squeezed her too tight, then pulled her all the way home while Serena screamed in outrage. Her mother spanked her hard for the first and only time that day and told her never to wander from the yard again. And to never, never dare go back to the little house again. She told Serena that bats and snakes lived in the house. Julia told Serena that a bad man might steal her. She told her that witches went there at night. She made Serena get down on her knees at bedtime and pray for God to protect her from all the bad things. Serena's mother knelt down beside her, closed her eyes, and moved her mouth, but the prayers were swallowed by the dark. Then she tucked Serena into bed, and leaned down close to her. Serena felt her mother's warm, moist words puff into her ear, "Don't tell father." They echoed there all night, like the tapping of mice feet in the attic; little whispered warnings.

Serena didn't believe any of her mother's stories, not really, but she didn't like getting hit, and she hated the way her mother looked at her when she found her at the little house. Serena disliked the way spit gathered in the corners of her mother's mouth and the way she trembled when she scolded about the cabin that day. So she stayed away–until she was older. She tucked the cabin aside in her mind, didn't think about it at all until a few years later when she began to wake in the night. People were in the woods way past everyone's bedtime and Serena knew in her bones exactly where they were headed. On those nights, something nagged her to consciousness, to turning on her pony lamp, and to her window.

Her father must have noticed her light from his post down on the cart path, perhaps even saw her at the little window. He must have considered his options, weighed them meticulously and clever man that he was, came up with the owl to block the view.

When her father showed them the owl, he told Serena and Julia it was to scare the squirrels from the attic, to keep woodpeckers from making holes in the wooden gutters. Julia worked her hands like she was trying to stretch them, until they were blotched and dry as autumn leaves, until father put his big hand on her shoulder, looked into her fretful eyes and said, "I don't want you giving it another thought, mother. This will take care of everything nicely." To Serena he said, "This is Big Bertha, she will protect the house. She is beautiful, don't you think?" as he stroked the decoy's cold head.

Serena thought the owl's eyes resembled her father's somehow. Even though the owl's round stare was different from her father's piercing blue eyes. His eyes were sharp enough to penetrate tender, hidden places but opaque as a closed door; the owl's were still and deep as a pond, connected all the way through to the center of her. It was the peaks that framed their eyes that made them appear similar–the owl's pointed, ruffled feathers and the silent, watchful scowl that hooded her eyes; and her father's bushy brows, overgrown as a forest, dark as menace–as if their intentions were bunched up on their faces for all to see.

Serena was a wakeful child. From that night on, whenever she heard the noises in the dark, instead of getting up she looked over at the big owl standing guard on the other side of the window. Serena believed the bird was as detailed inside as she was out, with no empty spots, or hollow spaces where uncertainty could blow through. She thought the brain might consist of gears and winding things like a clock, that her stomach was solid full all the way through, and her heart was a fearless rock the size and shape of Serena's small fist. Her father was right oddly enough, his idea worked but not in the way he had calculated. Bertha protected her all those years.

The decoy was fierce and hard, an impenetrable barrier. Bertha never let the voices get near, she, not God, kept the bad things out. Serena talked to Bertha until the outside voices faded and Serena's eyes grew tired. After a while, she slept through the night. When she got old enough to piece things together, she wondered what it was that her mother needed to get through the nights.

Now, the little house doesn't frighten her, it never really did. She is quite comfortable staying here. She feels calm and in control, even peaceful, and that strikes her as ironic. She cocks her head. There is only the hum of wind through bare branches, the shush of pine, and the dry rustling of grasses. The sun stole every last drop of warmth on its way down; the night quieted as it hunkered down against the frost. She reaches into her backpack for her down jacket and slides her arms through but leaves it unzipped even though her shirt is open at the neck. This is easy, she thinks, not like bivouac. Serena couldn't take the freezing cold, the kind that was permanent, night and day relentless, and left your fingers and toes aching, your lips cracked, too numb to speak. She hated the forced marches of her youth, the damp and discomfort.

Other than that, she found Army life had suited her. The routine, the structure, the boundaries and restrictions: others felt stifled by them; Serena felt comforted, secure.

She reaches into her pocket, feels a package of lifesavers, and pops one into her mouth. Wintegreen. She should lie down and try to sleep for a bit, but she is too excited. Like a teenager, she thinks and the tension in her face gives up to a wide smile. What she feels is not the heart pounding, hand trembling kind of excitement that leaves you breathless that others describe, this is more of a spreading warmth, an expectation of pleasure. Serena is infinitely relaxed, she gets up, yawns widely and stretches, stamps her hiking boots on the floor, puts her hands on her hips and twists from left to right getting the kinks out.

She looks out the window and can just barely make out, through the filter of brush and tall grass, the dark outline of the house down the hill. Or maybe she can't really see it, just knows it's there and so imagines the black outline of a building. She places her hands against the rough log frame of the window and leans forward with her nose nearly pressed against the glass pane trying to get the house into view. "Hocus pocus, now you see it, now you don't," she says to herself as the clouds part and she catches a brief glimpse of the front door until it disappears back into shadow. She gazes up at the sky, the clouds that are balled up sliding by the moon are few, but there is a choppy breeze that pushes at the tallest tree branches so that the shadows shift. She looks back at the house and sees only emptiness.

During the day, with her binoculars, she can see clearly the goings on there. She watched the real estate lady and the others this morning and, later in the afternoon, she watched Hanes as he went into the house, stayed for a few minutes and left. Hardly anyone knows about this place, she thinks. Serena is not surprised that her father did not mention to anyone that there is a small one-room log cabin further up the hill. It was built for seclusion, camouflaged. A wall of dense brush and brambles at the back protects it, so that if you were to walk the property line along the old cart path on one side and then down the bridle path on the other, you would never see it. It's low—Serena can barely stand up in it—set into a small hollow and, like Sleeping Beauty's castle, flanked by thorny briars. The roughness and color of the logs and weathered cedar shingle roof conceal it from every angle. And all around, a conspiracy of pine.

It does not exist on any plot plan, map, or deed. There are probably only a handful of people left who know about it and they would likely try not to remember. Maybe they have dreamed, as Serena has, that it has crumbled into dust, or blown away in a storm, or ignited setting ablaze everything standing for miles and miles. Maybe, in fact, there are only two remaining who remember and dream. Or one.

The iron bed frame is still here, rusted raw, and the narrow woodstove in the corner with the crooked pipe, the small wooden table with a pitcher and bowl in the center, frozen in time like a primitive still life. They are covered with cobwebs, leaves and dried insect hulls. Serena swept out the floor before she set out her things, but tried to ignore the rest. Now she looks around and in the dark, they seem to stare back in reproach.

Serena hears the crunch of movement outside and holds her breath. She stands still, but flexed for a quick flight if necessary. The door slowly swings open and when Serena sees who it is she takes two quick strides and holds out her arms in welcome. She shuts the door and their lips find each other in the murk, a long soft kiss. Velvet. Sweet and melting. Serena moves her mouth along the chin with baby kisses and licks playfully at the cheek. Their eyes meet, in the dark they are the same color, the deep formless blue of newborns. They are almost the same height, well matched, tall, slender, lanky.

"You came! I missed you so much," Serena whispers.

They strip off their clothes quickly and slide into the sleeping bag pressed up against each other, arms and legs entwined. "Lord! We shouldn't be doing this here."

"Don't worry," Serena murmurs and nuzzles. "No one will ever know. Ghosts can't talk."

They make love slowly, as if a long familiar song plays in their heads. The steady heat of their languid lovemaking builds until they are incandescent, until the sleeping bag smells of ironed sheets and the metal zipper burns to the touch. And still they continue until the sky over their heads blushes red, and the crows set to gossiping.

14

Running

Drew's car pulls out of the driveway slowly, silently, lights out–like a ghost. Morning gray is seeping through the blinds. Rebecca turns the wand so that the slats part slowly, revealing a sky as flat and dull as her heart. The tree branches look like they have been etched onto the surface, scratched there by angry hands. She needs to think. The girls won't be up for school for over an hour; she has time for a run. Running helps Rebecca think.

Before getting dressed, she walks into Drew's room, the cold under her feet echoing the cold inside of her. It's the neatest goddamn room she's ever seen; even in his haste to leave, he hasn't left a sheet corner flipped up or a bookmark fluttered to the floor. She walks over to his dresser and looks for clues, to what she's not certain. As she pulls open each drawer, she notices a blank space in each one: socks with their immediate neighbors gone, only one row of rolled up boxers left, a couple of sweaters absent here, a few polo shirts there. Rebecca knows exactly which ones because she purchased them all. Drew abhors shopping, "the new opiate of the common," he's fond of saying.

Someone who doesn't know him as well might think that this partial leaving is a sign of ambivalence, or a merely temporary flight. But Rebecca, who knows a decision of Drew's when she sees it, whispers to herself, "It's his way of holding out." Rebecca almost feels sorry for her, whoever *she* is. Even if *she* goes to Brooks Brothers and buys him all new outfits–neatly placing them inside the perfect English Country armoire Rebecca imagines the *she* as owning–he'll find other things to withhold. Things he will hoard, and be as unable to share as the starving man his last crust of bread. Rebecca sighs, but something releases along with that knotted breath, and she feels a little lighter.

Rebecca pictures Drew leaving in tiny increments, just enough to cause both of them, Rebecca and *she,* wanting more. Rebecca slides each of Drew's dresser drawers all the way out and dumps the contents onto his freshly made bed, pulling out each of the tucked tight corners of his sheets and tying each end to end, forming a giant bundle that she will roll down the stairs, through the dining room, out the French doors, and into the garage. She will do the same with other sheets, filling them with books and bow ties and neatly pressed pants still on hangers. The thought of his immaculate things in a rumpled ball next to the weed killer and trash barrels gives Rebecca a start. She glances at herself in his full-length mirror and sees herself there surprised, dark, and smiling.

Rebecca hurries now to get outside; she pulls on an extra t-shirt over her sports bra, and quickly throws on her sweats and thickest crew socks. She finds some mittens. She hates to run in the cold, but dislikes the boring treadmill at the fitness center almost as much. She makes the switch to inside when her nose starts running and her face begins to sting after the first slap of Canadian air, usually just around this time of year. Rebecca really needs this run, she needs to push herself all the way to the limit and feel her lungs struggle to fill, she longs for that ache.

When Rebecca first started running, she could only get to the end of Partridge Path–about a quarter of a mile down the road–before she had to stop, gasping and wincing from a cramp in her side. For the first year, the blood pounding in her ears drowned out the rustle of leaves as chipmunks scampered for cover at her feet and prevented her from hearing the chickadee calling–Lily says he calls for his mate, Phoebe...*fee-bee* –the fragrance of crabapple blossoms, and fresh cut grass couldn't get past the dry taste in her mouth.

Now, as she has grown stronger, she notices everything. Her route takes her by cornfields, green and gold and dense as a forest in the summer, bleached now, pale as bones, rustling stiffly in the breeze. Hay bales randomly dot open fields as if giants have tossed them there from above. Cardinals, crows, and sparrows, delayed robins and early titmice flit through the providence of berry bushes by the roadside like the ones at the end of her own driveway—Rebecca has no idea what they are—that her Portuguese cleaning lady tells her makes good wine. "Strong, very strong!"

Today she soaks it all in with her head up, eyes wide open, and can run a pretty steady three miles in a little over half an hour. She feels good about that, about setting that goal for herself and achieving it. Maybe what I need is a new goal, she thinks.

She has always wanted to learn to shoot; not just learn, but to be a crack shot. That would be fun. Nobody knows this about her of course. Rebecca thinks it unseemly, but the idea electrifies her anyway. Privately she would love to shout, "Pull!" and take down a half a dozen clay pigeons in a couple of seconds until the shards fall like confetti onto the grass. Or, even better, to fire down a long tunnel hitting a target figure square in the chest so that the paper explodes into a big, ragged hole right about where the heart would be.

Growing up, Rebecca had yearned for only a very few things. She wanted to fall in love, marry, and have children, a home of her own, a dog and a cat. When she was a child, she used to say five Hail Mary's each night requesting those blessings. They were the only things her parents wished for her as well; nothing more, nothing less. Not too much to hope for—or pray for. I am forty two and I have everything I've always wanted, except the dog—and the ability to blow away a target at fifty paces. What is wrong with this picture?

When Rebecca turned forty, she cut her hair and took up running.

Other women her age have face-lifts, or go back to college to get law degrees. Lately, she's been thinking about pumping free weights, about quitting real estate, about having an affair.

The truth is no one has ever asked. Of course, casual flirtations are commonplace in a town as small as this one. Tandy gets propositioned all the time, in the supermarket by lonely shoppers, at Barneys by bankers on lunch breaks, even at the Brimfield Antique show she and Rebecca went to recently, the guy selling the sterling silver trophy cups practically asked her to step into his RV.

"How do you do that?" Rebecca asked Tandy.

"Either you have it or you don't."

"So I don't?"

"I don't mean it like that. Listen, you just don't send out the signals. The 'I'm available' signals"

"Well, I'm really not…and neither are you, I might add."

"See that's your main problem. You've got a 'goody two-shoes' problem."

"Oh shut up! That's not true."

"Your other problem is when a guy actually notices you, you don't know what to do with yourself."

"Don't be ridiculous."

"Honestly! You avoid eye contact."

"*What!*" Rebecca says, indignantly. Tandy might have hit a nerve after all.

"I'm totally serious! I've seen you do it–many times." Tandy covers her eyes with her hands, as if she's playing peek-a-boo. She needles Rebecca, "Who are you hiding from? Ought

to get Sophia to pick up one of them burkas for you. What's the matter, don't you want to get laid ever?"

Tandy's right. Rebecca thinks maybe she should go to a bar and pick someone up and have some of that anonymous sex that you hear about.

The Forgotten Roses

Hot, ferocious sex. In a car, or against a brick wall in an alley like in paperback novels from the grocery store. Although, as Tandy says, she doesn't exactly know how to pick someone up and it may be possible to do it wrong and get laughed at or turned down.

Probably what she needs instead is a real relationship with someone she likes a lot, but casual, with no angst; friends but with sex, good sex. It's been way too long without sex, longer than Rebecca cares to remember without good sex. It was good at first with Drew, she recalls. But eventually novelty has to be replaced by something else, and they never got to that next level. Something was always missing, and it always seemed to be her fault.

What she really wants is to meet someone new and have her heart catch in her throat at the sight of him. She would like to fall in love all over again. Who *doesn't?* Don't be an ass Rebecca, she hisses under her breath.

Anyway, all those possibilities are fraught with either danger or aggravation. First of all, there are STDs. There is murder by a sociopath, there is stalking. Then there are the logistics of an affair that seem exhausting. Like finding the time, the place, providing appropriate alibis. Whose car would we use, she wonders. What would I wear? I'd have to get rid of all my cotton panties and buy silk ones. Thongs. Would I be the 'other woman?' "Jesus, Mary and Joseph," she blurts out loud. "I do not want someone else's husband!" And if he's single, why would he want a married woman, what the heck is wrong with him anyway? Probably I'd have to get a bikini wax at the very least; maybe a tummy tuck or a boob lift. Rebecca reviews all possible complications and consequences; works them like worry beads.

How do you find these men, these affair prospects? She has looked around a bit. Either they have suspect mustaches–Dana calls them molest-aches–or comb-overs. Dr. Harwich, her dentist, was pretty appealing until she saw him at the apothecary in tight sweatpants with the front sticking straight out in a sickening little tent. Rebecca wonders why it is that most men that she meets lately are as pale as insurance salesmen, or they stare at her chest while talking, are full of themselves, or dull as dirt.

Then if you do find someone who has potential and make it to the hotel room or whatever, there is the possible ick factor. What if he didn't smell right? Feet can be a problem, toenails a critical area. Even things like linty socks, or tighty-whities could make her gag. What if his legs were like sticks? What if he couldn't get it up?

And there is the very real possibility of winding up with someone exactly like Drew. This is the most disturbing scenario of all because it is the most likely, and because it implies she is doomed to repeating the same mistakes over and over, like a sci-fi movie involving time warps.

Running this morning was a mistake, she thinks. It's too cold. It's too dark, which is just as well, Rebecca supposes, because her nose is running uncontrollably and she wouldn't want the neighbors to see the snot shining on her upper lip. Where is the sun for godssake? All she sees is a bleaching at the horizon, as if the thick coating of night has rubbed off around the edges. Her ears are frozen. She figures she could snap them off and they would crumble in her hand like tortilla chips.

Infrequent headlights glow yellow and syrupy pushing thickly through the gloom in front of them. Everything else is the same color as Rebecca's sweats: the pavement, the sky, all gray. She should be wearing reflectors; she could get hit and no one would know. Rebecca thinks she could easily slip on wet leaves, slide into the path of an oncoming car, and lay for hours, bleeding out, her legs stuck straight into the air, like a dead skunk–road kill. Isn't dawn the most dangerous time, the time you're most likely to be picked off? Dusk and dawn; the in between times when substance fades to vapor, neither here nor there. This must be what depression is like: this heavy, murky haze, without warmth, without color or form. I'll never run in the dark again, she vows.

The Forgotten Roses

Someone honks and Rebecca nearly jumps out of her skin. It's no one she knows, just a man driving, seeing a woman running, alone. He feels the need to startle her, he wants her to notice him perhaps, and know that he can make her jump. His eyes follow her as he drives past, a sharp look, dog-like. Does he expect her to look friendly? Pleased? Does he believe his honk to be an invitation? She wonders if his headlights reflected the glistening mucous under her nose. Maybe that will be reason enough for him not to pursue her, not to stop a ways down the road, turn around, and pull up alongside her with fetid suggestions. She knows better. It doesn't matter if there are fluorescent green boogers dripping down to her shoulders. It does not matter what she looks like, or how old, or what condition she is in. It is just being female and alone that is the compelling thing.

Rebecca's mind goes back to her childhood when she and her best friend, Linda, walked everywhere. They were not quite teenagers, still skinny little girls with knobby knees and arms as big around as pencils. They hiked miles to get to the best blueberry bushes and blackberry patches. They would disappear for hours trekking to the florist where perfectly good flowers were thrown out in back that their mothers would go ga-ga for in which case they might get extra money to buy Archie and Veronica comics when they were sent to the corner store to buy bread and milk later. It took only thirty minutes to get downtown on foot where they spent hours at the library giggling in whispers between the stacks, or at the drugstore leafing through Beatle magazines. The beach, the tennis courts, the drugstore for vanilla cokes and a bag of chips, wherever they went, up and back, men would honk. Men in trucks, in station wagons, in Nash Ramblers and Chevys. Old men, young men. The girls would wave back at the ones that seemed friendly, the ones that looked like grandfathers or brothers, even though they knew they really shouldn't. Nice girls didn't wave at strange boys, they knew that much, although they didn't know why not and, since they didn't it pleased them to be that bad.

Sometimes a car packed full with boys, wriggling and roiling like caterpillars in a nest, would race by. The boys would hang their heads out the windows like puppies and make yelping noises and sloppy kissing sounds. They would seem so happy and pleased with themselves. Occasionally someone, some lone man, would give them the finger. She and Linda always had the same reaction to both events: they would scream to each other in a mixture of shock and fascination, their eyes comic strip wide and bulgy, then break out in gales of laughter after the car drove by, at the absurdity, the stupidity of it. They would crack up, double over, hold onto each other's arms for support, and stumble towards home drunk with the fun of being them.

We never sensed danger, Rebecca recalls. We knew nothing of rage and sex and violence. We were as free and light as sparrows, grown-up enough to walk all the way down town, and young enough to race each other there in our new Keds–invincible. When we turned into teenagers, we slowed down and clutched our library books in front of our chests. Our shoes were stiff, our steps were smaller; we knew to be careful.

Suddenly, Rose pops into Rebecca's mind. She wasn't careful. What did that get you, Rose, Rebecca thinks even though she realizes it's her mother's kind of thought. It feels sad and mean in her head. She asks it out loud as if expecting an answer and because she really wants to know, "What did that get you?" As soon as the words fall from her mouth, Rebecca trips as if a stone landed at her feet and she nearly takes a spill. She recovers and quickens her pace, panting loudly, willing herself to go harder. She sees the turn to Fawn Road up ahead as she steps onto the wooden bridge that crosses the narrow part of Buckle Brook. The soles of her sneakers tear into the worn lumber, scattering splinters and sending the frogs at the water's edge diving into the mud. Her eyes tear because she smells something burning, like cigarette smoke and thinks of her father. She wonders if he would be proud of her if he could see her run like this? Her ears flame as if someone is talking about her, as if someone with a fever is whispering in her ear, a hot breath carrying searing words straight into her head.

"Don't bother your father. Be a good girl."

Part of an equation begins to take shape in Rebecca's head. She sees the fragments once again, just as they appeared at the Deitzhoff house. But this time the pieces begin to crystallize. Rebecca's father was a hard worker, a faithful husband devoted to his wife. But he took little pleasure in his children beyond babyhood, as if they were a troublesome, difficult project of Eva's that never ended. We wore on him, Rebecca thinks, like sandpaper. He tried to ignore us, and if we made that impossible for him, he got angry. He was always angry, mean mugging throughout the house, barking orders. Rebecca thought if she were really good her father would take notice. But being noticed hardly ever turned out to be a good idea—not in the way she hoped—usually involving commands and chores. Eventually she recognized it was best to just disappear when he was around.

Rebecca kept her eye out for someone who was the complete opposite of Joe. Then she found Drew, the antithesis of her father in every way; or so she thought. And when that aloof young man said he loved her, she fell for it; this must be right, this must be heaven. That is what we say to ourselves as we unwittingly fashion our futures from the patterns of our past.

Having this nugget in her pocket does not slow Rebecca down. She sets her jaw and lengthens her stride as if answers to other questions lie along the next stretch of ground. Does knowing the root of the problem make it solvable? Should she try, once more, to hold it together? What is better for the girls? How much does this strained and stunted relationship between her and Drew cost Dana and Lily? What would the cost be if she led them off this path, and onto another? And the cost to me? Rebecca finally allows herself to consider.

Rebecca pushes her lungs to bursting and pounds her feet along the pavement until tiny bits of mica work their way permanently into the rubber soles making sparks as she goes, but the answers don't come. The sky is brightening; there are stretches of pink that look positively hopeful. Her heart is beating so hard she can practically see it through her sweatshirt, and with a final burst she gets herself to a place that is above the pain. She knows she has gotten somewhere that she hasn't ever gotten to before and it feels good. Though unfamiliar, it feels like pride.

❧

Rebecca is surprised to see Lily at the door, she's up early. Her little face is full of worry. "Why didn't you tell me you were going out to run?"

Rebecca stumbles in and can only pat Lily's shoulder in comfort, until she finishes a half a glass of water and catches her breath.

"I'm sorry, honey. I didn't think you'd mind. I didn't want to wake you," she pants.

"Well I don't mind, Mom, it's just that you weren't home and neither was Dad and I didn't know what was going on."

Dana walks in the kitchen saying, "The little creep woke me up! I told her you'd probably be right back. What a baby." She sounds disgusted.

"Shut up," Lily shouts.

"Dana, just be quiet," Rebecca warns.

"Whatever," Dana replies as surly as ever.

Rebecca doesn't know whether to be relieved or depressed that Dana's back to normal. "I'm sorry Lil. You're right, I should have told you." Rebecca can see out of the corner of her eye, Dana's eyes rolling in her head. "I wasn't thinking," Rebecca tells Lily and hugs her. Lily relaxes and turns on cartoons on her way to the kitchen table. "What would you like for breakfast?" Rebecca asks.

"I'm not eating," Dana declares.

The Forgotten Roses

"How about French toast?" Rebecca asks cheerily.

"I told you I'm not eating. I can't eat with this thing on my teeth," Dana raises her voice.

Rebecca closes her eyes a second to shift into reasoning mode, turns to her, leaning on the counter for support. "Dana you have to wear the retainer for weeks, maybe even months. You'll just have to get used to eating with it. I understand…"

"You don't fucking understand anything! I told you I'm not eating. Are you deaf?"

"Dana!"

"Just leave me *alone*," Dana whirls on her heels and stomps out the door.

From the window, Rebecca follows Dana's flight and sees Corey waiting in his car at the bottom of the driveway to take Dana to school.

Lily watches with wide, liquid eyes. She sits motionless. After Dana leaves, their eyes meet and they are silent together for a moment. "What would you like, honey?" Rebecca says quietly.

"I don't care," Lily says and dejectedly leans her head on her hands at the table.

"I'll make French toast."

"Okay."

Rebecca beats the eggs, melts the butter, dips the bread, all the while watching Lily who stares blankly at the tv. It's clear to Rebecca that Lily is not registering *Rug Rats*, she's a million miles away. "Lily? What's the matter?"

"Nothing."

"I know Dana is a big pain, but…"

Lily jerks up in her seat. "What's her problem anyway? I just asked her a few simple questions and she acted like I was a freak or something!" Lily is close to tears.

Rebecca's stomach knots in anger, in disappointment. She can't stand the thought that in the absence of both she and Drew, Dana would not help Lily. This sickens her, makes her feel almost panicky. Maybe this is not a phase, she thinks. It begins to dawn on her that Dana's behavior may not be a temporary rebellion but something more insidious, the reflection of a serious character flaw. Maybe Dana is just turning out bad.

"Oh don't pay any attention to her. You're right, Lil, she was way out of line. I promise I'm not going to let her get away with being mean to you like that," feeble words that droop in the air like limp balloons. Rebecca brings Lily her plate of French toast, the bottle of maple syrup and kisses the top of her head. "Just eat your breakfast now and don't think about her." Lily glances up at her mother looking for confirmation that her mother really understands what happened, how much Dana hurt her.

"*Mangia, mangia, bello giovane*" Rebecca tells Lily, because those words were a comfort to Rebecca long ago, and cups Lily's chin in her hand, just like her Nana did back then. "I know," she says to Lily finally.

❧

Rebecca watches Lily walk up the driveway to catch the school bus. An odd gust agitates the treetops; a vibrating arrow cuts across the murky sky –Canada geese making a determined getaway exchanging loud warnings. The back of Rebecca's neck tingles; she shudders and clutches her robe tighter around her throat protectively. There is a change in the air, as if the barometer has dropped. New Englanders are sensitive to variations in the atmosphere. This region is known for sharp, untimely turns in the weather. Nor' Easters, Alberta Clippers, ocean effects, and low-pressure troughs breed hyper-vigilance and practiced readiness for approaching squalls. Something is brewing. Rebecca braces and makes plans.

She begins to mentally put the day in order: check in with the Frakes, get Sully to open up about what he knows, talk to Noah Hanes, and there's the Greens; Rebecca needs to find them a home. All the while, Rebecca will be arming herself for a confrontation with Dana. Teasing out the points she needs to make, reaching for the right words, the correct tactics–demanding or concerned, soft or hard, tough love or unconditional.   Weighing, balancing, devising, revising–a churning undercurrent running beneath the placid surface Rebecca maintains.

Maybe I'll call Drew, Rebecca thinks, reeling herself in, taking a step or two backwards. And maybe I'll tell him I'm sorry about last night, that it was my fault. I overreacted, I'll say. We were both tired. I'll tell him that it's important for us to present a united front for the girls' sakes, particularly at this difficult stage with Dana. And I'll remind him that we need to stick together as a family; that's the main thing–our family. That sounds good, I should write that down, Rebecca says to herself and goes upstairs to her desk to find a pen and paper.

When she gets there, she looks across the hall at Drew's closed bedroom door, thinks of the pile of clothes tied up like an enormous dumpling and forms the image of cooking it, wonders if it would fit on the gas grill and imagines that it would actually smell sweet–satisfying and delicious. When she gets to her own room, instead of reaching for the pen on her nightstand, she twists off her wedding band and drops it into the little clay pot Dana made in kindergarten that holds loose change and safety pins. As she gets ready for the day, Rebecca's nostrils twitch with the scent of barbecue.

15

Diner

Rebecca relaxes into the order of desks in a row, the glow of her computer screen, paperclips exactly where she left them. She's the first one in the office so she makes the coffee, watching as it percolates into the glass pot. The process calms her, the fragrance soothes. She settles into her desk and takes control of her day, or at least this little corner of it. The Greens need a home and she happens to know exactly where to find it.

"Mrs. Parker? It's Rebecca Griffin from Country Lane Properties. How are you?

"The reason I'm calling, Hannah, is that I understand from June Warren that you're thinking about putting your house on the market soon. I wanted to tell you about some clients of mine, a really sweet young couple, Debbie and Herb Green. They have three children.

"Josh is seven, Jillian is five, and the baby, they call him T.J., he's absolutely adorable! They really want to raise their family here in Havenwood and your house would be perfect for them, they're coming out to look at another property tomorrow and... Oh, that's perfect. They'll be thrilled! We'll see you then. Take care, Hannah. Bye-bye."

Tandy is lurking by the door. "I don't know if June's gonna appreciate that. I think she'd like to be the first one in the door with clients seein' as it's her listing and all."

"Does she have adorable clients that are dying to get in?"

The Forgotten Roses

"I don't know."

"Well, if she does, she should have told Mrs. Parker about them. I can't worry about June's clients, I have to worry about my own," Rebecca replies testily.

Tandy keeps looking at Rebecca, as if she's expecting something more. Rebecca shuffles her client cards industriously trying to ignore her. Rebecca thinks Tandy looks really pretty today, glowing; marriage is agreeing with her this time. She's wearing a deep raspberry suit with a short jacked nipped in tight at the waist, from the back her bottom looks as round and lush as a Georgia peach. The color is just beautiful on her even though you might think it would clash with her redhead's coloring, but it lights her up and softens her at the same time. Rebecca thinks she should tell her so, but the words won't leave her mouth because there is too much going on in her head. Besides it might open her to comparison. Rebecca's wearing a long skirt, leather boots and a white blouse with a wide leather belt that has a beautifully hand-wrought silver and turquoise buckle. Drew brought it back from New Mexico a few years ago. She always liked the way it showed off her small waist—Drew did too—and when she saw it hanging in her closet this morning, she pulled it out and wrapped it around, cinching it in tight. She can't think why, but it made her feel secure, as if it had the ability to keep her pulled together today.

Tandy knows better than to say it to her this morning—Tandy can tell something's brewing besides the coffee—but Rebecca knows what she would just love to ask: "Is the rodeo in town?" Normally Rebecca would think it funny.

"I'll call June," Rebecca promises Tandy, mainly to get rid of her.

Tandy dips her head a bit in satisfaction, tucks her little sweetheart chin into her silky chest. She's so smug; Rebecca wishes she'd take a friggin' hike.

"What's new at Deitzhoff's?" Tandy asks.

Oh shit. I don't want to talk about that place right now. "I'm working on it," she says shortly.

"Is that all you have to say?"

"It's holding together, Tandy," Rebecca tells her irritably. "Everything is okay. I'm going to meet with Sully in a few minutes, see what he knows. Septic inspection is first thing in the morning. I'm on top of it," her voice rises a little.

"Didn't say you weren't. Why are you so touchy?" Tandy scowls at Rebecca in puzzlement.

"It's just that…I have a lot of calls to make, and I'm running late…as usual," Rebecca replies and dives into her address book. She doesn't bother to smile. She doesn't even bother to make herself sound sorry.

Tandy backs off. She tsks prissily as she walks out as if she's offended when Rebecca knows she's not, it's just show. It's really such a relief that Tandy, underneath her cotton candy exterior, is as cut and dry as crackers inside. Others would carry Rebecca's prickly remarks around with them like cockleburs stuck to their skin, rubbing them raw and leaving lasting sores. Then they would require either retaliation, tit-for-tat, or mea culpas before they could heal over. Such a tiresome, time-consuming process. Tandy's skin is a mile thick, and it takes a lot to wound her. Rebecca knows she hasn't even come close; she would never want to. Maybe later I'll go into her office and tell her how lovely she looks in pink, Rebecca thinks.

Rebecca will close the door to Tandy's office and Tandy will turn off the police scanner she listens to all day as if it played music. They'll kick off their shoes and sit with legs folded, tucked under their bottoms. Rebecca will talk about Drew, just a little, enough to be entertaining and not bellyaching. Tandy will rant, just a little, about how "men are dogs" and tell her about some obnoxious thing Max did as she cracks a window open, and has a surreptitious smoke leaving raspberry stains around the cigarette she will stub out after only a few puffs. They'll have weak office coffee and laugh over Sophia's latest love conquest–"Remember the one-legged ferry captain from Nantucket? He sure could Polka," Tandy will snort; she loves that story. Tandy can always make Rebecca laugh.

Rebecca just has to make a few calls first. "Sully? Hi, it's Rebecca. Are we still on for this morning? Meet you in Westville? At Frank and Crystal's Diner? Okay, see you in a bit."

"Hello. Yes, this is Mrs. Griffin. What do you mean she's on the absent list? She left for school this morning, her friend Corey picked her up. He's absent too?" Shit! She says to herself. "Thank you for calling, Mrs. Pinchon. I understand. I will take care of it." Jesus! Now what!

❧

Rebecca can see the back of Sully's head in one of the end booths; she recognizes the thinning cowlicks. Frank and Crystal's is much bigger than The Stop. They have real seating instead of stools and counters; laminated menus and waitresses working the mother's shift instead of an illegibly scribbled blackboard. There is no Francis X. Sullivan serenading you with "Twist and Shout" while you're eating your tuna melt banging elbows with the guy teetering on a stool next to you dropping sauerkraut onto your shoes. Rebecca notices that Frank and Crystal's has been freshly swathed in nick-resistant antiqued heather-blue paneling and smooth new pleather covers the seating. God, I hate this place, she thinks.

She's still out of breath–as if she's been running–since that last phone call, the news that Dana has skipped school. Lucky Dana, Rebecca thinks ruefully. If only Rebecca could skip a day, or a week. Where in God's name did she go?

"Hi Sull, how's it going? You look like hell," she tells him sliding into the booth across from him. He looks as if he hasn't slept. His skin looks thin and blue, like skim milk; it curdles around his mouth. His shirt is a mass of wrinkles.

Sully curls his lip towards his nose in personal disgust and says, "Man, I feel like hell." He hangs onto his cup of black coffee with both hands like an alcoholic trying to sober up. "Moira's away," he tells her, as if that explains everything. He leans against the back of his seat and stares up at the ceiling.

"Oh? Where to?" Rebecca asks making small talk, not really giving a hoot where Moira's gone. She's itching to find out about the Deitzhoffs, about the house. She feels like she should be out trying to locate Dana, not that she could actually find her...and Corey...the two of them... having a great time somewhere no doubt.

"Her sister had the baby," he says listlessly.

"Congratulations, Uncle Sully. What'd she have?"

"Boy, I think."

"You think?" Rebecca shakes her head and has to give up a little laugh; he looks so forlorn, so pathetic. She pats his hand, "How long will she be gone?"

"A few days...her mother's there too, and her sisters–the Irish Mafia on estrogen. Jesus, you couldn't pay me to be within ten miles of that house! I pity the husband, poor bastard."

Rebecca thinks it's himself he pities. He plops his head into his hands, pushing his fingers through his hair so that he looks like a hedgehog–the sharp pink nose and narrow face framed in peppery spines.

Sully is talking like Sully, but he looks off balance–more than usual that is. Rebecca expects him to start eating cheeseballs with toothpicks. He keeps adjusting his collar, as if a pin is sticking into his neck, and looking at the clock. A waitress comes over to take Rebecca's order and he jumps a mile.

"I'll just have a cup of tea, and some crackers if you have them." Rebecca has been queasy since Dana left. "I won't keep you, Sull," she tells him. Now he seems sheepish, embarrassed that he's so twitchy, maybe. He's beginning to make her nervous, let's just get this over with, Rebecca thinks and continues, "I just really need to know about the Deitzhoff house, you know, because I have a deal going and I need to disclose to the buyers anything that may affect its resale value. You mentioned a suicide?"

Sully puts his coffee down, stares into the cup as if it contains the information he is about to give her. "Okay, so here goes," he says sighing in resignation. "Serena... I mean... Well, there was the women's prison..."

He looks longingly at the door then back at Rebecca and she leans forward towards him, rounding her shoulders over her teacup, raising her eyebrows in encouragement. His eyes lock onto hers and he begins again.

"Serena Deitzhoff was a good friend of mine. We were kids together, I guess you could say we were best friends. She had this screwy upbringing. Her father worked at the women's prison in Warington, a psychiatrist or something, and her mother, she was some kind of religious nut. Anyway, between the two of them—they were like a couple of hermits—they never let Serena play with any other kids, so she grew up pretty isolated up there on that hill. Didn't have any friends that I know of, until I moved here in Junior High. She was...different; really beautiful though. Had very long, light colored hair?" He demonstrates with his hand, sawing at the small of his back. "Platinum. Like a space age material, silvery and shiny. Not of this world," he says dramatically and drifts off into space himself.

Rebecca glances at her watch. "Go ahead Sull."

He talks into his cup, "I was never actually in the house; Serena couldn't bring anyone home...or wouldn't. But I was on the property a few times." He shifts in his seat, moves his head around as if his collar's choking him. "Never met the old man, or the old lady for that matter. Serena used to tell me things sometimes. She was kind of close-mouthed, but every once in a while she would come out with something, something that would knock your socks off."

"Like what?" Rebecca's palms itch. She notices the cloying smell of deep frying hanging in the background.

"Well for one thing, it seems old man Deitzhoff had a pretty rich night life. According to Serena, all kinds of things went on there at night. She would hear voices from outside, from out in the woods. And sometimes he would come into Serena's room while she was asleep and stand by her bed and just stare at her. Of course, she wasn't really sleeping, she would pretend."

"What did he do that for? Oh my God, did he molest her?" Why are they frying fish at this hour?

"No," Sully says slowly, "To be honest though, I've always wondered about that. She never had boyfriends, just me; 'course, I wasn't really her boyfriend, just a friend. She didn't seem to have any interest in, you know, romance or anything..." Sully drifts of, clears his throat and continues. "But she never told me he bothered her, and with Serena, if anything like that had happened, I don't think she would have held that in." His voice drops and he says to himself, "No way, she wouldn't have kept that from me." He picks his eyes up and says to Rebecca, "I think he was just watching her–weird son-of-a-bitch."

"I found out this morning that he went into a nursing home. His attorney told me. God, I felt so sorry for him, but now..."

"Now, he's the prisoner," Sully says.

"What about the noises? And what about the suicide?" she asks, feeling nauseated.

"I'm getting to that. So anyway, Serena would tell me these things sometimes, and I would just accept it, the way kids do. Parents are always doing strange things, and hers were a little stranger than normal... okay, a lot stranger but," he shrugs, "that was it. Until we got into high school. Then we heard the rumors."

The Forgotten Roses

Can't they open a goddamn window in here?

"The story was, Deitzhoff was somehow bringing girls out of the prison and doing things with them."

"Jesus!" Rebecca feels a prickling that is starting at the base of her skull and running down her spine—tiny hairs all along the path are coming alive; she feels each one. She gulps down self-control like a fat pill. "What things?" she asks calmly behind the safety of her teeth.

"Well, there were a couple of different stories. Some kids thought he was performing experiments on them like a mad scientist or something," Sully says waving his dishpan hands as if he's batting at flies. "Or that he had his own private harem going. But the one that stuck, the one that got the most play, was that he was selling the girl's favors." He looks her in the eye, steady finally. "Prostitution," he says.

Rebecca hears a sound in her head, like a whip cracking. The tension in her neck tightens like cold plastic. She puts her fingertips to her temples, gathers her thoughts, ferrets out a reasonable question. "Did anyone ever find out for sure?" she asks.

"Uh,uh." He shakes his head. "Remember, Havenwood was the sticks back then. Hardly built up, houses were few and far between. He had a lot of privacy going for him. People thought he was some kind of eccentric genius—maybe he was," Sully shrugs. "For sure, he could do pretty much anything he wanted to up on that property and who would'a known?"

Rebecca stops listening because she remembers what her mother said about Rose. "She knew something." Could this really be it? She can imagine someone like Rose going along willingly at first, then realizing she had traded one trap for another. She pictures Rose, led through the dense, dark forest as alien and inescapable as any prison, her heart pounding from fear and anger, muttering vows through clenched teeth. Plotting revenge.

Rebecca lines up her crackers in order of the questions she should be asking Sully. She picks one out, "I guess Serena might know—and her mother. What about the mother?"

"That's where the suicide comes in." Sully's face twists in pain. "She took herself down into the basement, got a hold of one of the old bastard's guns, and shot herself square in the heart."

"In the basement?" The obvious ramifications to the sale jump to the front of the line and Rebecca immediately feels mercenary and ashamed, petty in the face of the troubling issues Sully is unraveling.

"In the basement," Sully repeats. "Serena found her. Took off for good a few days later."

Rebecca picks out another question and pushes it from her mouth. Others tumble out behind, tired of waiting. "But, but…you mean she never told you anything about the girls, the prisoners? You said she started hearing rumors in high school; what did she *think* was going on?"

Sully squirms in his seat. "She told me about voices in the dark, lots of times, but," he looks at her, his eyes pleading, "we were kids, we were so stupid, naïve, what'd we know? She could never make out conversations or anything, she just heard…noise.

"Serena had a wild imagination, that's for sure…me too! But the stuff we'd come up with between us was about witches and evil spirits. Sometimes when we talked about it, we'd laugh, like it was all a big, fat joke."

"As we got older, we just stopped talking about it. She once told me that she had been following her father at night; he had hidden something and she was trying to find out what it was. I remember, she was really excited about it, like it was gonna be the answer to everything. But she never brought that up again either. You gotta understand, if Serena didn't want to talk about something, she'd cut you off at the knees. You didn't screw around with her. After a while, the subject was dropped, period."

Rebecca tries to picture Serena as a young woman, the way she may have looked the day she left home. She wants to care about her. Rebecca recalls the young girl she saw in the photo. Her shoulders looked so small under her father's big hands holding her in place. Try as she might though, Rebecca cannot remember Serena's face, whether she was pretty, or sad, or frightened, only that her wrists dangled from the ends of her sleeves, the bottom of her coat too high above her knees, as if she'd outgrown it unexpectedly. The girl looked out directly, challenging the camera's eye. But Serena's image remains incomplete, like a photo before it's fully developed.

Rebecca does care about a girl with a father like that, a mother who couldn't help her; a girl who needed a fortress around her feelings to survive. A lonely girl. Rebecca wonders about the woman that she became–but she doesn't really care about her.

"I feel...guilty," Sully reveals suddenly, bringing Rebecca to attention. His face looks pinched under his freckles. Rebecca cares about Sully, a lot. He has the kind of undernourished look that switches on maternal instincts. She has the urge to reach over and smooth down his hair.

"Why? You couldn't have done anything," she says soothingly. "Besides, who knows if the rumors have any truth to them? Serena never actually confirmed any of it...did she?"

"No, no, it isn't just that. Even if none of it was true, still, her father was a creep and her mother was gonzo. She was so alone in that nuthouse. It had to be pretty damn bad up there to drive the mother to blast a hole through her chest. And then Serena had to go and find her. Man, that must've been freakin' gruesome.

"I think I could've been a better friend. I think I should've..." Sully shoots Rebecca a quick, edgy glance, "wanted her less, and cared about her more." He clears his throat as if there's something lodged in it. "And then she was gone," he mutters so she can barely hear him.

Wow, the way he said wanted. Was that longing in his voice? Sully looks depressed and Rebecca's afraid he's going to cry. Why is it such a horrifying prospect. She's never seen Drew shed a tear in all the time she's known him. This realization suddenly fills her with panic. Rebecca reaches her hand out and holds onto Sully's. "You can't blame yourself for her disappearance."

"Serena used to talk about leaving Havenwood all the time, we both did. We used to make these plans, y'know, kid type plans. I was going to be a vet and she was going to have a stable of horses. We would own a farm together and take in stray animals, grow our own food, milk our own cows. We wouldn't need anybody else; it was going to be just us."

Sully is swimming in his past—drowning in it. Between missing Moira, regrets and old memories, he is the picture of remorse. His narrow shoulders have drooped so, the only thing holding up his neck are the wrinkles on his collar. Rebecca considers moving over to his side of the table, putting her arm around his shoulder, patting his back.

Suddenly, he straightens, pushes his empty cup aside, and folds his hands on the tabletop. "So tell me, are these people really going to buy the place?"

"It looks that way." She straightens up too, and pushes aside the clutter of thoughts in her mind.

"When?" he asks.

She clears the unspoken questions from her throat and tells him, "The closing is scheduled about a month from now. Providing the septic inspection goes well."

"Do you think there will be any problems with that?" he clips out.

"Who knows? No one's quite sure where it is. I have someone coming out tomorrow with a metal detector and a back hoe to try and locate it." Sully nods, taking in the information like he's cataloguing it. "Why do you ask?"

"Just curious," he shrugs. Sully begins to fidget in his seat again, looking around for a way out. He waves madly at the waitress and asks for the check when she rushes over. Rebecca reaches to pay it and he stops her.

"But I asked you for this date," she kids him. "Lets at least go Dutch."

"Go Dutch? Reba, no one says that anymore. What are ya, old or something?" He pokes her in the side as they get up. Next, he'll be giving her a noogie.

"Thanks Sully. And thanks for talking with me. I can see it was hard for you, I'm sorry I made you dredge it all up."

"No pro-blem-o," he smiles goofily. "Besides, I needed to test the competition." He bends down to her and stage whispers, "punk coffee."

"You drank two cups!"

"I was being polite."

"You wish," she smiles back at him, glad to see he's his old self again—at least there is one thing in place at the moment. Rebecca hangs on to this normalcy, this everyday joking back-and-forth as if they had not been discussing suicide, abuse, and perversion. As if two friends had merely been weighing the pros and cons of adding breakfast sandwiches to his menu; sausage vs. ham, bagels vs. croissants. The little fleshy commas that form at the corners of Sully's mouth when he smiles make her sigh in relief.

She feels the overwhelming need to order things; locate Dana, straighten a few things out with Drew, do something special for Lily—set everything right.

When they are outside, before Rebecca goes to her car, she stops Sully, taking hold of his arm and asks, "Do you think he actually prostituted the inmates for money?

"Maybe he did," Sully says tightening his lips. "But I doubt it was for money," he says jamming his hands in his pockets, then turning quickly, he walks away like he's in a big hurry.

She wants to ask him more, but he's almost to his car. Besides, she is taken aback from what she saw in his face before he turned to go.

Rebecca had never seen Sully angry before.

If not for the money, then for what? She tries to picture poor, bent-over Harold Deitzhoff running a prostitution ring. Ludicrous! It's an image that won't form. She remembers the last time she saw him, sitting in his stained and sagging armchair, his shriveled body, his wasted arms outstretched. Then she remembers his eyes. Compelling, dark at the centers, glittery–like tacks.

16

The Cliffs

Dana and Corey have been parked on the access road by the railroad tracks in Havenwood deciding what to do with their stolen freedom. Skipping sounded like a great idea earlier this morning, but Corey is beginning to piss Dana off. He doesn't want to hang out in Harvard Square and he doesn't want to drive all the way to Mt. Watchusett like he first suggested, he just wants to sit around in his fucking car and talk. What's there to say anymore? First, he was hanging all over her with apologies, now he wants her to admit that she deliberately does things to get on his nerves when she knows he has a bad temper. "Bad temper," that's what he calls it.

"Look, Corey, let's just forget about it for now. Why don't we just go into school late, say we had a flat or something."

Corey is getting agitated, he starts to say something a couple of times then stops, he slams back hard against the back of the seat and his face clouds over. This unnerves Dana. "I just want to fucking get out of this car," she says. She means it to sound like a command, but it comes out pathetic, like a whine.

Corey looks at her for a long time, as if he's considering her request. "Let's go to the cliffs," he says getting out of the car and slamming the door.

"All *right!*" Dana answers in exasperation. At least it's *movement*, she thinks. She gets out of the car and they start the two-mile walk down the railroad tracks. It's a freight line, hardly ever used now, that bisects a tiny corner of Havenwood. The land juts up in steep jagged slopes and is treacherous with loose rock which makes it unsuitable for horse trails, but a perfect stomping ground for teenagers; it's secluded, it's trouble, and it's all theirs.

Years ago, kids forged their own sloppy trails through this scrawny neck of the woods. Knowledge of the place passes through them like radiation the moment they enter junior high. They go there at night to smoke, to drink, and to hang out. The directions are simply passed on by word of mouth. "You go down the tracks a couple of miles until you see the two birches on your left that lean together and look like the letter A. Walk under the blue spruce trees and you'll see the trail in front of you." Dana sometimes wonders what would happen if the birches straightened or someone cut the spruce for Christmas trees. Would generations of teenagers wander forever, bored and lost, like the tribes of Israel, through Havenwood's forest?

Dana and Corey climb the trail silently. It's hard going and you better watch where you put your feet or you might twist an ankle or skin a knee or worse. Dana thinks about that phrase, "watch where you put your feet," and has to smile. She remembers Nana Eva pointing a wooden spoon in her direction and looking into her eyes. "Watch where you put your feet, young lady. Boys only want one thing! Why buy the cow when you can get the milk for free? Huh?" Then Nana nods slowly at her like she's just uncovered the most profound truth since the Dead Sea Scrolls. Dana thinks Nana Eva is hilarious.

Dana curses to herself because she has to pee and she's frying in this sudden heat, otherwise, she has to admit it's a beautiful day to be walking in the woods. She pulls her sleeves all the way up and tucks the bottom of her shirt under her bra leaving her waist free to the air and exposing her pierced belly button over the low, hip hugging waistband of her jeans. Corey is up ahead. Dana watches him climb up the hill, jumping over exposed roots and boulders effortlessly. She watches as his ass tightens and flexes as he climbs. She herself is a little out of breath, out of shape. She'd quit field hockey last year because it just took too much time from other things, Corey mostly.

She loves him, but she vowed to herself last night to tell him that he ran out of second chances about a hundred chances ago. She just can't stay mad at him though. Even now, having to wear this stupid retainer, and knowing she's going to be in major trouble for skipping today, just the sight of him up ahead leading the way makes her feel shivery. She still loves the way his dark hair falls over his forehead and the way he shoves it back all at once with his hand. His brown eyes can look so sad, and his kisses... She feels a little thrill at the back of her throat. Dana loves kissing Corey. His kisses send her to another dimension, she actually feels as if she's floating, though she wouldn't say that to anybody because it sounds so dorky. And the sex is great too. Corey's not the first boy she had sex with, but he's the first one she actually enjoyed doing it with. He's great. So hungry for it, for her. It makes her hot just thinking about how desperate he is to do it sometimes. When they finally get the chance, he lasts forever, wants her all the time, can't get enough. Unless he's drunk, and then everything just sucks, which, come to think of it, has been most of the time lately, she realizes.

"Jeez, it's really gorgeous up here in the daytime," Dana says as she comes into the clearing. The "cliffs" are actually ledge outcroppings at the top of a hill that overlook miles of meadow and forest below. The rock face leads straight down to the Charles River, but when it gets there there's nowhere to go but in the drink so no one makes the trip down even though you can see that it wouldn't be that hard. Dana stands with her hands on her hips feeling exhilarated, like a conqueror, surveying the view. Corey's preoccupied; he's poking a stick at the black ash of old campfires in a depression at the base of the first tier of ledge. Dana squats down beside him. He looks like a little kid, she thinks. She wants badly to kiss him to make him feel better, but he won't look at her.

"Dana, I'm really sorry about the other night…"

"I know you are," Dana says.

"Wait a minute, let me finish," Corey says sharply. Then he inhales loudly and continues while jabbing at the ashes. "I don't know what happens to me when I start drinking. I mean it's only when I've had too much, I guess. I need you to help me, help me not to drink so much. I don't want to hurt you Dana, I really don't. It's just that you get me so mad sometimes. But that's not a reason for hurting you and I know that, I know that…" he trails off. "I wouldn't blame you if you wanted to dump me, but if you give me another chance, I promise I'll never go off on you like that again." Corey looks at Dana with his big puppy eyes and she wants to hug him, but she's not stupid, she resists the urge because she's heard this speech before.

"You've said that to me before. *Now* look at me! I have to wear this stupid thing for who knows how long!" She takes the retainer out of her mouth and shoves it in her pocket because it makes her lisp and she feels stupid trying to argue with him sounding like Sylvester the cat. "I can't forgive you this time, Core. I just can't!"

Corey spreads his hands. "Just tell me what to do and I'll do it. Don't give up on me!' He sounds desperate. "You know I love you. I knew you were going to say this to me," he groans and holds his head in his hands. "Don't do this to me, Dana."

"I didn't do anything to you, you did this to me, remember! I just can't take that shit anymore. I won't!" By this time Dana knows she's not going to dump Corey. She knows that he loves her, and she knows he's hurting. He's all stressed out about grades and applying to college, his parents always on his case. And on top of that Corey has this major problem, this drinking problem, and she probably is the only one who can help him. She should have kept a closer watch on how much he drank, tried to steer him away. She knows how he gets when he's wasted.

The Forgotten Roses

She should have known better than to give him shit when he's like that. He definitely needs her right now. But first she wants to see him squirm a little. After the way he's been acting, it serves him right if he's all bummed out now because he thinks she's going to dump him.

Dana sits back on her haunches and hugs her knees, turns from Corey and stares, sulkily, towards the horizon. She drops her chin onto her knees and her lips poke out into a hard little pout.

Cory takes a look at Dana and goes silent and broody. He moves off to another boulder to sit by himself. Good, let him stew, Dana thinks. I hope he falls off the rocks and lands in the river.

The sound of a motor distracts Dana. She squints into the sky and sees a model airplane doing noisy loop-de-loops in the air. There is no one visible in the meadow, just the miniature plane above, the flicker of sunlight on its wings as they twist doing silvery, show-off nosedives, figure eights and spirals. High over the little daredevil is a line of tender white fluff. The buzz of the motor, the scribble of metal in the sky as the plane flies straight up into the clouds, impossibly high, reckless, makes Dana hold her breath. Suddenly it sputters hanging in the air like a star. For that one sparkly moment it has no ties to earth. No one can control what comes next, it's just holding its own, Dana thinks and roots for its bravery, its freedom. Just before beginning a fatal plunge, it noses up and turns parallel to the ground, zooming by, buzzing the river and tipping its wings right and left impertinently. It flies off skimming the meadow at top speed, the noisy rev of the engine growing fainter, and disappearing.

Dana sighs and rests her head on her knees. The sky is bluer from up here. Looking down on the treetops, there's more color left on the branches than you notice when flat on the ground. A raggedy blanket of rusty oranges, yellows, and browns spread out below, overlooking the river that snakes through the valley and under the train bridge. The Charles River is just a narrow spit at this juncture—the slimy green-brown color of frogs—barely reflecting the patchwork quilt above. The train bridge is only a short wooden link to shore held up by an enormous cement pillar. Guys often jump off the bridge onto the pillar the kids long ago named "the pickle." They jump down so they can reach the sides of the bridge to attach license plates they have liberated. They do it because it's hard to do and more than a little dangerous, they do it because they're guys. The girls back at the cliffs watch the boys shove each other, wave, and hoot like wild baboons. The girls think the boys are simultaneously idiotic and brave; they admire them and they laugh at them. The girls know they could do the same thing if they wanted to, but none of them wants to.

"I'm going back," Dana tells Corey. She's getting tired of his moodiness, and she still has to pee. Let him deal with it; she'll take him back when she's good and ready.

Corey stands up and brushes off his hands. "Wait a minute," he says to Dana belligerently. "How come your friend, Todd, got so bullshit at me? How come he kicked me out of the house? I should'a beat the crap out of him!"

"What are you talking about? They kicked you out because you were making an ass out of yourself, that's why. It wasn't just Todd. Nobody wanted you there spilling beer everywhere and throwing a fit!"

"Are you fucking Todd? I just wanna know, are you fucking Todd?" he yells at Dana.

"What? I don't *believe* you!"

"Just answer me," Corey walks across the rocks to her and stands close enough for her to see how hard he's breathing. He's only a little taller than Dana and she prides herself on being strong; she figures she could take on anyone her size in a fair fight and she doesn't like to feel cornered. Corey's face is beet red and his fists are balled. I guess he wasn't just stewing while he was sitting there, Dana thinks, I guess he was boiling. It strikes her as kind of funny until he closes in on her.

Dana hates that Corey has made her feel this way again, fearful and angry and having to cast about frantically for a strategy to get herself out of this. She needs to calm him down, so she reins in her anger and says with all the sincerity and coolness she can pack into it, "No, I am not fucking Todd, or anyone else. Just you." She'd shove him, but he might fall off the ledge, or shove her back, there's no telling. "Get away from me!" she shouts at his face.

Corey grabs her arm. Her first instinct is to twist away from him but she's afraid to struggle too much. She looks behind her at the ragged layers of ledge below; the water looks cold at the bottom, and deep. She's trapped. Corey is pressing his fingers into the flesh of her arm, deepening the bruises that are already there. Dana looks back again and watches as gravel kicked back from her shoe skitters down the slope and plops into the water forming gently spreading circles. She backs up just enough to let fly another scattering of stones and watches these with interest as well. Corey's grip changes. She sees fury turn to irritation then puzzlement in his eyes. She moves back, just a little, once again and Corey hollers, "Man!" and "What the fuck!" His confusion has turned to fear which gives Dana some satisfaction, but she turns away from him once again to the ridge and the river, watching the way it eddies pooling under an overhanging limb directly below. She buckles her knees some, putting resistance against Corey's grip and feels her shoes begin to slide over the granite and her heart beat faster. Life is full of options, she thinks and throws her head back to feel the sun on her face. Dana opens her mouth to say something to Corey but what comes out sounds like laughter. She suddenly wonders who will give in first, will he release her if he thinks she will pull him over the edge with her? How far can she go? Will she crash on the rocks, or splash in the river? She savors the prospects in splits of seconds, rolling them over her tongue like candy.

"Dana, please," Corey chokes out. He eases his grip and tugs her towards him. Dana lets him. His arms drop to his sides and watches, deflated and astonished, as she turns her back on him and walks away calmly. He mumbles, "I can't help if I'm jealous." And then calls after her, "I wouldn't be jealous if I didn't love you so much."

Dana won't even look at him, she marches down the hill as fast as she can. "Dana wait. What the hell are you doing? I had to *know*," he pleads. Dana keeps plunging down the hillside while Corey trots and stumbles after her. "Jeez, Dana," he says then, "Fuck!" twisting his ankle.

Dana can't stand another second of Corey's blabbing on about how much he loves her; bullshit! Dana thinks the whole day is a stinking bust, she might as well go home and figure out some story to tell her mother. Maybe she'll make cinnamon toast again tonight.

"Be careful," Corey comes up alongside her and tries to guide her down the rest of the way. She wrenches her arm away, "Get off me, what do you think, I'm crippled?"

"Course not, I'm just trying to help."

"Help yourself, Corey. You need it," she tells him. Her mouth is dry, she's sweating like a pig, and she's had it.

They arrive at the bottom of the hill under the spiky boughs of the spruce. Corey turns Dana around and holds her by the shoulders. His eyes are testing her; they are repentant and soft. She feels the hunk of hot rage at the center of her dissipating like vapor. He puts his arms around her and kisses her, he smells damp and clean like clothes from the washer. Moisture rises from their bodies, steam heat, forming droplets on the spruce needles around them. The baby-blue bower sparkles like diamonds, like magic. Corey puts his hands around her waist and runs his thumbs up and down her bare stomach. His kisses are questions that become demands, his tongue reaches for hers as he presses his hips against her and murmurs into her neck, "Dana?" He's as hard as a rock Dana notes, and toys with the idea of dropping down with him under the sheltering branches. She tastes the craving of it. If he slips his hand down inside her panties it'll be all over.

She slides her hands from the back of his head, down his arms and pushes him away. "Not now, Corey. I want to go home." He licks his lips and nods as if he's in a stupor. "Okay, okay. But, can I see you tonight?"

"I don't know… I might be able to get around my mother, she feels sorry for me lately." The truth is, Dana isn't sure she wants to go out with him tonight; her mother is just a convenient excuse. When Dana really wants to do something, she just does it, and deals with the consequences later.

Between the pressure on her bladder and the heat between her legs she feels as if she'll burst if she doesn't get away from him, and get home. She thinks he's wavering and he might start to kiss her again and she doesn't want to get him mad. Dana feels nervous all of a sudden, overloaded with ambivalence. She gets another mental image of her legs wrapped around him under the branches and feels her resolve crumbling. She pushes Corey hard, but says playfully, "I'll race you," and takes off down the tracks.

17

Heartbeat

The sun spreads through the sky, pushing every smudge of cloud out of the way, refusing to give in to the shortened day, insistent. Bees fall to the ground in confusion and the forsythia loses track of time, forcing a few hopeful blooms. They shine, like waxy yellow stars, under the dark shadow of leaves the color of dried blood; tiny blurts of optimism amidst the ruin. The bald trees are unable to buffer the hard slant of light as it comes slicing through bare branches, so the heat is unforgiving and unnatural. Even the birds are fretful and call out in stunted worrisome chirps.

Every autumn day in New England is a crapshoot. The heat presses against Rebecca's shoulders like fat thumbs, her armpits are sticky. I've got to get out of these long sleeves and boots before I lug in the rest of the groceries, she thinks; maybe Dana will actually help me. Dana called Rebecca to say she was home just as Rebecca was about to drive over to the school to canvass Dana's friends about where she and Corey might be; right when Rebecca started thinking about calling Drew. Now, Rebecca hopes she may not have to tell him at all providing Dana has a reasonable explanation, or even a minimally plausible one. Rebecca's glad they're the only ones home, they need to talk.

Dana is in the living room sprawled in Drew's club chair casually reading a book. She changed to shorts and a tank top and her long bare legs drape over one side, her hair, pulled into a ponytail, dangles over the other. Dana ignores Rebecca as she comes in with a heavy grocery bag in each arm. Rebecca kicks the door shut behind her and places the bags on the kitchen counter, pushing aside Dana's dirty dishes. Willow winds around Rebecca's legs, yowling so piercingly–as only Siamese can–even the squirrels fly off the feeder and flee for their lives; her bowl is empty. Rebecca worries that Dana's disregard may have driven Willow to snack on the baby chipmunks that live under the stone wall–a grisly addiction.

Rebecca looks over at Dana again. There's a bag of chips leaning against the base of the chair, a half full glass of soda and ice on the floor next to it. Her foot taps the air in time to private rhythms piped in through headphones.

"Dana, please help with the groceries," Rebecca yells over to her loud enough for the neighbors to hear.

"I don't have any shoes on," Dana answers without taking off the headphones, without so much as looking up or skipping a beat.

Rebecca walks to the chair and stands over Dana with her hands on her hips, "Get some on then. Please."

Dana raises her eyes to face Rebecca for a second, then lowers them, unplugs the headphones, bends back a corner of the page and flings it on the chair as she gets up. The paperback bounces and lands with its pages crumpled in the middle.

Dana screws up her face, but doesn't look Rebecca in the eyes as she sidles off to look for shoes.

"I'm going to change. I'll be right down. Please put the frozens away," Rebecca says marching off thinking, please this, please that. I am so polite to Dana. *"Please please me, oh yeah, like I please you."*

Dana knows she's in trouble, so Rebecca has some leverage. She whips off her belt, unbuttons her blouse, yanks off her boots and grabs a t-shirt and a comfortable pair of cropped jeans. She slides her feet into a pair of new shoes; leopard print flats with a bow at the toe and an elastic strap, like a ballet slipper. Rebecca looks at herself in the mirror and murmurs, "I think they look cute," a little defensively. Dana will surely tell her different.

It's a wonder mothers of teenage girls ever leave the house at all for the brutal honesty their daughters employ when critiquing their mother's appearance. Teenagers complain that mothers are overly critical too, except the girls don't really care about what their mothers think.

Rebecca hangs up her things and looks in the mirror once more before she goes downstairs, trying to see herself through Dana's eyes. A bad move. Now she feels matronly and squat, as if she's looking in one of those wavy carnival mirrors. Good grief, my legs are so short, she mutters to herself walking down stairs. I should never wear flats at all, not ever.

Rebecca begins putting the groceries away and Dana comes in carrying three bags, one in each arm and one gripped by hand. She sweeps by Rebecca and plops them too hard on the counter. "Thank you," Rebecca says.

"Nice shoes," Dana smirks. Her voice is clean, but her intentions are muddy.

Rebecca looks down at her feet as if she's just noticed them and says bravely, "I like them." Dana laughs as she walks by, a short shot expelled over the tongue. Currents of air that seem to belong to Dana only eddy around her and whoosh past Rebecca as Dana goes by. It's as if Dana is a separate planet, contained in her own charged atmosphere. Rebecca is barely a blip on Dana's radar screen.

Rebecca sits on the couch across from Dana and watches her for a while before speaking, trying to get a handle on Dana's state of mind. Dana has struck a pose of extreme nonchalance, frowning into her book as if she is concentrating too hard to notice Rebecca. Dana reaches casually down to her glass, her nostrils pinch together ever so slightly in response to Rebecca's presence. Her nose not only looks like Drew's, it behaves like his, Rebecca thinks.

The Forgotten Roses

"Dana." No answer. "*Dana!*"

"What!"

"I want to talk with you."

"So go ahead and talk," she says still reading, still keeping time.

"Dana, put down that book, take off the headphones, and look at me."

At first, Dana doesn't respond. I suppose she's weighing the consequences of ignoring me completely against giving in to avoid a hassle, Rebecca thinks. Dana sets her mouth into a hard frown as she complies, then folds her arms across her chest pressing back against the chair, daring Rebecca.

"This is not a lecture, Dana. This is Mom trying to figure out what's wrong." Even Rebecca knows what a cornball she sounds like, but plows on while Dana's eyes roll to the ceiling. "Listen to me please. I know we've had some rough times, and we haven't been getting along very well lately, but I just want what's best for you, and I want us to stick together. Dana, you've done some things that have upset me, some things that made me really angry and things that are not good for you. But this morning... This morning, you let me down, you let Lily down, you let us all down as a family."

"What are you talking about?" Dana scowls at Rebecca furiously; her green eyes are stormy waters. She expected her mother to light into her about skipping; but she's so self-absorbed that she doesn't count the hurts she inflicts on others as important.

"This morning you were in charge. When I'm not here and it's only you and Lily, you know that you are responsible for her. That's what it means to be the oldest, that's what it means to be part of a family."

"*Whatever!*" Dana is beginning to get the drift, and slumps deeper into the chair. The fabric of her tee shirt knots up behind her back and that is when Rebecca notices them. The marks. Three purple, pear-shaped bruises in a row, each with its own sickly yellow corona. Unmistakable.

Fingerprints. They sidetrack Rebecca. She stares at them comprehending and uncomprehending. They are the marks of being grabbed, terribly hard. Angry marks, sore and shameful. Rebecca's thoughts clear to form the word as if it is being written slowly letter by letter in her mind–Corey. She swallows hard; this she isn't prepared for. She's prepared to talk about family unity and responsibility, she's prepared to talk about school and screwing up and compromising the future. Rebecca's face begins to flush; it starts at the collarbone and spreads upward infusing her face, causing the hair at her temples to prickle and her forehead to itch with sweat. Rebecca turns away from the bruises, blinking to wash the image away. Maybe it's not what it looks like. She clears her throat and forces out the rest of her speech.

"You did something really stupid today, and I want to hear what you have to say about skipping school, but first I want you to realize that the way you treated Lily this morning is the most disappointing thing you have ever done as far as I'm concerned."

"Big deal. She's such a little twerp. Running around, practically looking in the closets for you. 'Where's Mom, where's Mom?' What a baby."

I'd like to reach over and slap her face. She'd probably slap me back, Rebecca considers and her teeth grind, chewing on Dana's callousness. Try to keep a lid on it, Rebecca. "Lily looks up to you, she depends on you when I'm not there."

"Oh give me a break. Poor Lily. All you think about is Lily. 'Give me a kiss Lily. Here honey. Sweetie pie.'" Sarcasm dripping out of her mouth.

"I'll put it this way then," Rebecca tells her menacingly, tightening her lips over her teeth, fury seeping out. "Next time you are alone with Lily, you *better* treat her with respect and consideration," she says squeezing her hands together until her finger tips turn white, leaning her upper body all the way forward, as if she might spring at Dana at any second.

The Forgotten Roses

Dana recoils in shock continuing to scowl, but looks wounded and forms a pout feeling sorry for herself.

Rebecca takes a deep flushing breath, the kind you learn in Lamaze. Then another, which snags a little on its way out, catches in her throat like a fish bone until she releases the grip she's had on herself and settles back in her seat. She waits before speaking again, until she readjusts the muscles in her shoulders, evens out her breathing, checks in on her real intent.

"Now, what about skipping?"

"I know you're not going to believe me, but after Corey picked me up I just started, like, feeling sick." Dana twists her ponytail around and around her finger. "So I made him pull over so I could lie down in the car for a while because I was feeling dizzy and sick to my stomach–probably because of my teeth and everything–but I thought it would go away. Then I got a headache too, a migraine, so I came home to take some medicine." She stops and thinks, like she's reviewing, making sure she isn't leaving anything out. Satisfied, she says, "And then I called you." She looks as if she doesn't care if Rebecca believes her or not. And Rebecca does not.

"You seem fine now."

"I guess the pills worked."

"I guess. You do know that you'll have work to make up; your grades are slipping again. I intend to go to school today and pick up your homework."

"Fine," Dana says sulky, resigned. Bored really.

"Where's your retainer?" Rebecca asks. Dana pulls it out of her pocked and places it in her mouth dutifully. Even though Rebecca's been thinking this talk has gone badly, she can see now that Dana maybe looks remorseful. She is no longer as closed off, she's just sitting there calmly looking out the window, lost in thought. She almost looks open. Do I dare? Do I dare mention the bruises? I have to, I absolutely have to,

Rebecca decides.

Outside there is the distant whine of a chain saw, the low rumble of a truck probably headed for the construction site on Buttonball Lane, a dog barks, then all goes quiet. The silence drops like a curtain between them, thick and weighted; Rebecca knows she must lift it, now.

"What are those marks on your arm?" Rebecca asks softly and watches carefully for Dana's reaction.

Dana darts her eyes at Rebecca with a quick surprised look and then recovers. "What marks? Oh these? Nothing."

"They look like fingerprints to me. Did Corey do that to you?"

"Corey? Of course not."

"Who then?"

"I don't know. Nobody, I mean. I don't know how they got there." The flush has spread from Rebecca's cheeks to Dana's.

Rebecca doesn't know what to say next. She considers the fact that Dana is still in the chair and not flying out of the room screaming, "Leave me alone!" Dana looks nervous, then picks up her book and pretends to be instantly engrossed.

Rebecca wants to go over to Dana, hug her, push the wisps off her forehead and tell her "mummy loves you." But she knows from past experience that would be Dana's signal to bolt, escape to her room and lock the door. Why is she covering up? I can't believe my Dana–strong, willful Dana–would allow this to happen.

"Dana, please, if he's hurting you, you need to tell me."

She slaps her book down and says, "Look, it was an accident, all right? I can handle Corey."

"You can *handle* Corey? What is that supposed to mean? What is there to handle?"

Dana pauses, takes aim at Rebecca and tightens her mouth into a mean little grin. "You know, Mom, the way you handle Dad."

Rebecca's stomach clenches, as if it has been punched. "Excuse me?"

she says indignantly. "Your father has never laid a hand on me. I would never put up with that!"

"Oh come off it. He treats you like shit, and you put up with *that*. We're always tiptoeing around here trying not to *distuuurrb* him…," Dana draws out the word leering snottily, "like everything he does is *sooo* important, like he's King Tut! And you're all over him to get his attention, or get a reaction, get *something* that he doesn't want to give. Don't you get it Mom…he just wants you to *leave him alone!*"

Dana makes her voice whiney and fawning, "'Drew what do you think about this, what do you think about that? Is this all right with you Drew?'"

"I do not!" Rebecca argues. "I don't do that, not anymore."

"Maybe you don't say it anymore but you're still acting like he rules your life. It's sickening. So he moved out of your bedroom, so what. You still look at him like you want him to *like* you. And he's still looking right through you. Why don't you get a life? You're such a fucking wimp!"

Rebecca springs off the couch, straight up like a rocket. "I'm trying to work things out. For *all* of us!"

"Don't do it on my account," Dana says coolly. "If I have to watch you apologize to him one more time, I'll puke."

"Apologize? I *never* do that! You're just talking nonsense."

"Oh yeah? Not with words maybe, but you're always fucking acting like you can make everything just peachy. Like everything is just fine around here, when it's *not*," she says with bitter contempt. She bats her eyelashes, pushes her lips into a phony smile and continues in a sugary falsetto mimicking Rebecca, killing her. "'We're just one big happy family.' What bullshit!" Dana stretches her neck forward, her eyes black with hate. "You make me sick!"

"Stop that! What is *wrong* with you? How can you be so mean?" Don't say it, Rebecca. Don't tell her she's just like her father, she thinks under her pain, her rising anger, struggling to keep herself in check.

"At least I'm not like *you!* The only thing wrong with me is that I have to fucking live *here*," Dana screeches into Rebecca's face.

Rebecca finally can't keep it pushed down, the fury leaks out like liquid nitrogen, fogging the air around them so that they don't know where they stand. "No, you don't *have* to," she says harshly. "*Don't* live here anymore. Get. *Out!*" She takes a step forward and Dana backs up, bumps her heel against the chair and sidesteps out of the way.

"*Gladly. Fuck you*," Dana screams as she flies out the door.

Rebecca watches the scene as if from above it and not a participant. From that far off place, she reassures herself that Dana will probably go to Amy's. She'll call over there in a while, talk to Amy's mother. Rebecca tells herself that they will survive this. And Dana will be back in a heartbeat. She tells herself the things that will keep her own heart beating, preventing her from falling to the floor.

18

Eva

Premonitions are commonplace in Rebecca's family: fateful dreams, visions, signs. There is an old family story, told often, about Rebecca's grandfather, Vincent. As a young man, already betrothed, he had a strange dream–so real–of a beautiful young woman waiting for him in the next village. It took hold of him like an enchantment; he just had to find her. The next day he rode a donkey there and saw her sitting by a window watching him pass; he knew at once that she was the one in his dream, his one true love, his Gina. The women in Rebecca's family put great faith in such dreams.

Ever since her father died, pictures of her mother, in perfect detail, pop into her head like bubbles of pure loneliness–sad little daydreams. Rebecca wouldn't be surprised if the thoughts were visible, like circled words hovering over the heads of cartoon strip characters. The images that float into Rebecca's consciousness are in slow motion: Eva doing ordinary things, bathing in her pure white tub, reaching for the soap as if it contained comfort itself, the shy shush of water against porcelain echoing through the house; so quiet now. Eva standing at the foot of the bed she had shared with Joe for so long, lifting the top sheet into a billow, spreading it out until it falls evenly, parachuting softly into place. She tucks under first her side then the side no longer in need of tucking, smoothing the comforter, running her hand down his side of the bed like a caress.

Guilt follows. "Why don't you come and stay here?" Rebecca asks Eva.

"I don't want to leave my home," Eva replies pacing hollow rooms, hearing too clearly the sound of singular footsteps on oak flooring Joe installed.

"Are you okay tonight? Want me to come over?"

"I'm alright. I just have to get used to being alone. Don't leave your family."

Eva put in an alarm system that she has no confidence in. At night everything appears altered, foreign, threatening. Joe always made her feel safe; she had faith in him. Even when he grew weaker by the day, even when he was on oxygen and confined to bed, Eva slept securely. Now, she times arrivals and departures by the slant of the sun, not wanting to leave or enter her home in the dark–the dark is her enemy now.

Rebecca's father had the power to make them all feel safe from outside threats, the bad things that might happen to them. Though they feared him, they knew he was hard and brave and would protect them to death if it came to that. Maybe because his children knew he was in the Army during the war, and they grew up with John Wayne heroes and Hollywood versions of strong, silent men. He was that all right. When Rebecca was little and woke in the night it was the smell of burning tobacco drifting up to her bedroom that soothed her back to sleep.

"Let's go out somewhere, there's a new bakery in Reedsville, *North End II* I think it's called. I hear they sell *pizza dolce* and *porchetta*."

"No. Don't leave your family. Last night the kitchen light blinked on and off; the one your father put in. He was sending me a message."

"How about a trip, Mom? You always wanted to go to Italy."

"I heard that Gypsies throw babies at you, and when you try to catch them, they steal your pocketbook."

"That's silly, Ma!"

"I hear they watch your house and when you go on vacation, they break in." Eva is afraid of "they" and "them" now. Eva will never feel safe again. Or whole.

So when Eva asks Rebecca to take her to East Boston this afternoon, how can she say no? How could she possibly explain that she told Dana to get out of her own home. That Dana left yesterday and is now staying with someone else's family. Rebecca called Amy's mother, Meg, last night. Meg was understanding, sympathetic, told Rebecca not to worry. She said, reassuringly, that Dana was welcome to stay there and, "probably just needs some time to cool down." Rebecca told her she was probably right–wishing it could be that easy– and thanked her profusely.

These *girls*," Meg exclaimed. Rebecca can only imagine what Meg Connor has been through with that hare-brained Amy and says a silent Hail Mary for both of them. Now all Rebecca can do is wait to get Dana back. She jumps when the phone rings: waiting for Dana to return her calls, waiting for temperature changes in Dana–cool and cloudy, or hazy, hot and hateful.

The phone rings endlessly like a taunt–the Greens, June, the backhoe guy, Noah. Rebecca writes their needs in her datebook, portioning the hours for the next day in inch high blocks. Tomorrow she will be at Harold Deitzhoff's house while Bud, one of the Grainger boys, maneuvers his backhoe around the grounds digging in likely places hoping to uncover a tank, a pipe, a metal cover. It could take a while; that's what she told Noah when he said he should be there too. They talked about Noah's condo, he's newly divorced and wants a market analysis, he told Rebecca. He's thinking of moving out of Newton. Maybe away from New England altogether, perhaps a warmer climate, he confided.

"I know it's a little out of your territory, but I wonder if you could help me."

"Of course," Rebecca replied, "I'd love to." She was flattered; her face grew hot which made her feel foolish. He is meeting them at

Harold's house at ten. Rebecca is embarrassingly pleased at the prospect of seeing him again, even if it is over a septic tank.

Then Eva called. "We have to go today," Eva is frantic. Rebecca's sister, Joanie, can't drive until tonight and Eva doesn't want to travel in the dark. "Aunt Josephine's sister-in-law is stopping by with the jewelry she brought from Italy. She's invited the old crowd, I'm bringing the cannelloni. I hate to ask you Rebecca, I really do. I know you're busy with your real estate."

Rebecca doesn't want to leave home right now. She can't bear the thought of crossing Havenwood's borders and it has nothing to do with real estate and everything about a child loose in the wind nearby. But Eva and the aunts have been talking about the 18-karat-gold-jewelry-from -Italy-lady all summer long. It is the most long-awaited arrival since the Pope's. If Rebecca lets Eva down she will surely melt into a puddle of brown sugar like the wicked witch of the west, and her father will start turning lights on and off in her kitchen too.

"Okay, Mom, but I really can't stay long."

"Oh good, good. I'll tell your aunts. Why don't you bring the girls? Maybe the cousins have someone for Dana."

"Ma."

"Well, what's wrong with that? You never know. A nice Italian boy…"

"For one thing, she has a boyfriend." Rebecca nearly chokes over the words. "And she can't come…because she made plans with her friends already."

"I don't like that boy; he's no good for her. What nationality is he anyway?"

"Ma."

"One of those mixtures probably. *Amerigana?*"

"Ma!"

"Well, what about Lily then?"

The Forgotten Roses

"I don't know. Maybe. I'll ask her. I've got to go. I'll pick you up shortly."

"All right, that's okay. And wear something pretty, a nice dress. Fluff up your hair, lately it's been so flat on top. I don't know why you had to cut it. You really should get a perm. Joanie got highlights, why don't you try that? You should, Rebecca, you really should. I bet Drew would like it." Eva has started to wear Rebecca down. It's like being pecked to death by a baby bird. Rebecca closes her eyes, reaches up with her fingertips touching her eyelids where she is beginning to feel pressure.

"I've got to go, Mama. Bye."

19

Madonnas

Rebecca has heard the names all her life, Maverick Square, Mt. Carmel (the Italian church), Wood Island (now Logan Airport), Orient Heights where the "rich" lived. It wasn't that difficult to get there; if she hadn't been forced to take Joanie's van, which handles like a big old school bus, she would have arrived there sweat free. There wasn't nearly enough room in the Jeep; in addition to Eva and her sisters, Dahlia and Emma, cousin Rita came out of the woodwork. Plus multiple platters of food: sausage and peppers, *pizza dolce, cannelloni, biscottis, pizzelles*. And Lily.

Rebecca just couldn't leave her; couldn't bear to have another daughter floating around the universe unattached. When Lily got home from school, Rebecca thought she seemed tenuous, and somehow light as a snowflake, as if she could be lost to the next vagrant breeze. Lily shrugged her shoulders when Rebecca told her, "Okay, I don't care," she said. "I'll bring my homework." Thank God for Lily.

They were a rolling vessel of food and memories; essences of both swam through the interior, swirled about their heads, doped them up and made them giggle.

"Remember Bonzi's?" Aunt Dahlia says. Eva and her sisters, Dahlia and Emma look alike. Short and stocky now—when younger, wildly voluptuous—black hair poufed to perfection, stylishly dressed, they appear to march when together, three abreast as if on parade. Dahlia is the middle sister, the great beauty of the family; often compared to Liz

The Forgotten Roses

Taylor. Emma is the baby, she even looks the part still with her round face and pudgy fingers. Eva is the oldest, the boss. They all sigh a happy, sappy, breathy hum when Bonzi's is mentioned.

"Coffee rolls the size of my head," Aunt Dahlia continues, "and the icing...like no other!" Eva nods in encouragement. "Everything fresh! And the squares! Fig squares with about a pound of delicious fig in each square, no kidding. Lemon, pineapple, cherry. But the date and nut, out of this world! Us kids would go in and ask for the ends; they were just pennies."

"Sometimes they would *give* them to us," Eva announces to Lily. She reaches forward to Lily who is in the passenger seat in front nudging her around so she can talk to her face to face. Rebecca knows her mother is trying to impart an important lesson to Lily, but she's not sure which one that would be. Is it: the old days were better because the old ways were better, so being a product of that time, she knows best and we should do everything she says?

Emma takes the floor. "The summers, walking down Neptune Road to get to Wood Island and seeing the trees up ahead, running towards it." She turns to cousin Rita. "There it is, there it is, we'd be shouting, so happy to see the trees. It was the only place that was *green*."

Cousin Rita, sitting in the way-back next to Emma, is trying to blend into the upholstery so as not to be an intrusion. She holds her pocketbook on her lap, nods and murmurs agreements during the conversation in front of her like a Baptist lady at church calling out amens for the minister. It is her form of protocol; in this way she shows her gratitude for the ride.

"And the smell of hot dog stands," Dahlia continued, "not that we'd ever go to them because Mama had packed a big lunch, pepper and egg sandwiches, thick slices of fresh bread, salami, provolone. We thought peanut butter and jelly was for rich kids."

"Can you imagine they filled it in, and now there are planes on it;

huge, enormous airplanes! How did they do that?" Emma asks.

"Too bad Dana's not here, she could probably tell us. Why couldn't she come? " Eva demands.

Lily doesn't know that Dana left home today, but just knowing Dana is enough reason for Lily to cast a wide-eyed glance her mother's way.

Rebecca's voice rises a little, thins out into a flat ribbon, waves out of her mouth like a streamer, "She had other plans! I can't tell her what to do at her age! Teenagers aren't interested in sitting around with…"

Eva begins to talk over Rebecca. "It's good for the young people to spend time listening to their elders. In Italy the elders are revered," she declares.

"I think that's in China," Rebecca says, exchanges a look with Lily and they both laugh.

"Don't be so smart you two," Eva tells them. "You can learn a lot Lily!"

Aunt Dahlia elbows her sister, "Oh what's she gonna learn, how to make *baccala*? You'd rather be home with your friends, right Lily? Leave her alone, leave her alone," she tells Eva.

Rebecca remembers her grandmother using that same phrase when Eva scolded her for picking at her food, for being noisy, or messy. "*Lasciala!*" Nana told Eva. If Joe yelled at Rebecca, Nana's face would turn to brick, but she wouldn't utter a sound.

"You were always bossy, Eva," Dahlia tells her for the millionth time.

"That's because I was always taking care of you two. I remember running home from school in a panic so I could be there before you came home. Panic! Mama would be working and I was the only one with a key. If my teacher kept me after school, you and Em would be sitting on the steps crying when I got there, scared to death, all alone. I would get a stomach ache the minute the bell rang." She places her fist under her sternum, hunches her shoulders around it to demonstrate.

"When I went into first grade I couldn't speak English," she tells Lily.

The Forgotten Roses

"The teachers treated us as if we were stupid, stupid on purpose. They used to smack the boys, pull their hair. Of course you couldn't do that now."

Rebecca wonders if Eva thinks that's an improvement.

"There were no special classes, they just expected us to learn, to speak English. The teachers would call Mama and Papa and tell them, 'Look, you have to speak English so the children can learn. And they did, I don't know how."

"Then being kids, after we had learned we would kind of laugh at them whenever they made a mistake. Papa would get so mad, he would say, 'No, don't laugh, teach us how to say it right!'"

"Those goddamn teachers were so mean to us kids," Eva says angrily and leans toward Lily once again, giving lessons. "Because we were Italian," she says.

"They would pinch the boys, whack them, hit them with rulers, but the girls they would humiliate. You had to be really good so they wouldn't notice you. I knew just the way to act so the teachers wouldn't call on me," Eva announces proudly. "I sat really low in my chair and folded my hands on my desk and never looked at them. That way she forgot I was there," she says with satisfaction. "So I could go home."

❧

Aunt Josephine's house is in the "nice section" of East Boston. Orient Heights is a hill topped by a thirty-five foot tall statue of The Madonna of the Universe. Her arms are spread high and wide as she blesses the occupants below. Homes on the hill stand brick and tailored neat, outlined in bright white trim overlooking the more congested neighborhoods fanned out flat at the bottom. From up top, they can see the airport clearly and the way it interferes with the clean sweep of ocean on either side. Planes roar in their ears too close, like bullies.

Josephine's yard is surrounded by chain-link enclosing a small patch of lawn in front, and out back a recently prosperous vegetable garden; the beanpoles and grape lattice still in place, nothing left of the flowers except a row of shriveled brown knots that once were marigolds.

When they step up to the ornate wrought iron railing to the Colonial red front door, the older women grow nervous. They take turns holding overfull platters for each other as they straighten their clothes, smooth their perfectly done hair, and finally, eyes front and in unison, they take a deep breath and wait stiffly at attention. Once inside, they come undone, calling out noisy happy greetings, melting contentedly under the warm grasp of old friends and family.

The talk inside is gunfire rapid heavily laced with Italian–and explosions of laughter– the likes of which Rebecca hasn't heard in years. Lily is the only child there. Everyone touches her, hugs her, pats her, as if she were long lost, or some healing religious shrine. She flushes and giggles under the heat of their praise.

This could be Nana's dining room, Rebecca thinks. The relatives, the old friends and neighbors, are funny, and awful, and wonderful beyond belief. Still, it is a stunted group; the older generation, like Rebecca's grandmother, are gone. Except for Aunt Marie, known forever to this group, including Rebecca, as *Gooma Marie*. She is godmother to most of these cousins. As children, they heard the heavily accented version of Godmother, "Gomadda," and their tender ears phonetically fractured it further until it became *Gooma*. There are many godmothers in Rebecca's family, but only one Gooma, the most lovable one of all.

Gooma Marie looks the same as ever, tiny and sweet in a cornflower blue dress, with a halo of soft white fluff around her head. She sits daintily, her legs neatly crossed at the ankles dangling a foot off the floor. Her voice is high and raspy soft, as if she is talking through cotton, but it carries a weight none of the others can match; when she speaks they all stop to listen.

The Forgotten Roses

It comes back to Rebecca in a rush, this feeling of shared roots, of belonging. I wish Dana could have been here, she thinks and her heart sinks at the thought of her absence. It's been a long time and Rebecca realizes how much she'd missed this kind of connection, but for her it's only a nice place to visit—for most of them, it is their entire world.

Rebecca and Lily plunge in, they talk nonstop, laugh and gossip like the rest and it's only when the dishes are cleared and the smell of brewing coffee tries to find some space in the crammed full room that Rebecca remembers something is missing, something is so wrong with her life that she shouldn't be upright. Lily is the only thing keeping her in her seat— Lily on one side, Eva on the other, shoulder to shoulder. Rebecca can feel Lily's elbow resting on the table alongside hers, the weight of it feather light, but just enough to anchor her. Even so, her mind wanders to Dana; where she is, what she's doing, how to get her back, and back on track.

Eva is shaking Rebecca's shoulder, "Rebecca, didn't you hear me? I was just telling them about your real estate job and how you sold that man's house; the one who was at the girls' prison when Rose Gabrielli died." Rebecca comes to and glances across the table that looks like Christmas morning; the glitter of gold jangling on plump wrists, the boxes, mounds of confections laid out like a *Candy Land* game and grown women completely abandoned to the delight of this moment.

"Josephine, tell her what you just said about Rose," Eva says eagerly. Chairs scrape apart to observe from a better angle.

"Well...," Josephine sits up, lifting her ample chest, squaring her shoulders; she has the floor all to herself, a rare and relished moment. Her two daughters, Sharon and Jeanette, move up and down like silent pistons, clearing off the table so as not to disturb the performance. Josephine lays her hands flat on the table for emphasis, but tells her story barely above a whisper. Everyone leans forward straining to listen. "The Gabrielli's were a good family and all, but that Rose, she was a bad one.

Never listened, did as she pleased, hanging out at the corner with the boys, smoking, riding around in cars until all hours. Probably drinking went on, I don't know because I never saw it myself, I only heard. But it was well known, she was a real scandal. Her father used to beat her with the belt to get her to behave, but Rose didn't care. She was a big strong girl and she'd laugh in his face!

"Anyway, what put that poor family over the edge, was when she started sneaking around with Mr. Rocco who owned the meat market on Porter Street—you remember him Emma? That son-of-a-bitch had a wife and four kids! Well, the wife found out and went to Rose's parents screaming and yelling at them."

"That wife…she should'a killed the bahstad," Jeanette interjects.

"Maybe the wife loved him anyway," one of the aunts adds; Geraldine, who favors long square-tipped, black nails that, in keeping with the season, are decorated with tiny pumpkins. "Well…maybe he was good to the kids. Who knows? Life goes on, ya know?"

"Eh," Gooma Marie interrupts which sounds like the sneeze of a kitten, bringing her shoulders to her ears in a shrug. "Whadda ya gonna do?" And everyone shuts up because they know her husband was a drinker and when his liver finally gave out, she tended him like a baby until the day he died.

Josephine clears her throat and plows ahead. "The family couldn't take the shame of it. The mother and father had terrible fights about it; the mother was against it, but the father ruled the roost and finally he had her put in prison to straighten her out. They just wanted her to be good, that's all! I remember there was a terrible storm the night they took her away, flooded the streets and blew out all the lights. It was so dark, the rain so heavy, you couldn't see from house to house, we were all trapped inside. It was a bad sign. My own mother leaned out the window into the black and gave the sign to ward of *mal' occhio*; she demonstrates with her hand, three fingers folded into her palm, forefinger and pinky extended –the horns.

"Then before you knew it, Rose was dead. Just like that. Not only that, but the prison officials told the family that she had hung herself. Well, no one could believe it. I mean there was Rose, the strongest girl we knew. A fighter! Of all people, she would be the last one who would kill herself. We all knew that.

"After she was gone, it was kind of funny, everyone realized how much she meant to us. People cried and carried on like she was a martyred saint. She was such a part of the neighborhood, y'know? When we were walking down the street and she was hanging out, we'd whisper to each other, 'Look, there she is,' like she was a celebrity. Our mother's would tell us '*sta' zitto*' and squeeze our fingers. Truth is, us kids kind of admired her, we certainly didn't want to be like her, but down deep we thought she was something!"

"Yeah, 'cause it was the bad girls that were havin' all the fun," Jeanette pipes up and laughs but only the younger cousins snigger with her. They elbow each other, turn their heads away clamping their hands over their mouths to suppress the laughter that squeaks through their fingers.

Josephine shushes her daughter. "I remember the day that they told the family she was dead, you could hear the wails of the mother all up and down the streets from day to night, howling like a wounded dog. The father stayed drunk for days. They were broken people.

"The parents would never talk about it. But the father, when he got to drinking, would tell his buddies, his daughter knew something about that place and she was gonna tell. The father had told her to keep her mouth shut, '*non dieche niente*!' But Rose wouldn't listen.

"They say that when the prison sent the personal effects to the family, Rose's shoes were all bent and mangled and the parents believed she had been dragged to her death, struggling."

Rebecca butts in, "Did the Gabriellis complain, or tell anyone in authority? Wasn't there an investigation?" she asks.

175

Josephine looks at her as if she has three heads. "Who were they gonna tell? Who was going to believe them, the grieving parents, Italians just off the boat? Come on! No. They kept it to themselves, and we kept it to ourselves in the neighborhood. But we all knew the truth."

Rebecca puts her elbows on the table and presses forward to hear the rest, "And the truth is...*what?*" she asks.

Eva makes an exasperated noise and they all stare at Rebecca like she's thick-headed. Josephine explains, "That Rose was murdered because she knew a secret about that evil place and was going to tell. Rose was killed because she wouldn't be silenced." Josephine raises her head in the air as if she is as proud of Rose as her own child.

Rebecca keeps silent about the information Sully gave her. They would certainly relish the story, Rebecca can imagine them trading it up, telling it over and over; it would race through these tight streets like a nor'easter, growing to a monstrous size and might mow down people in its wake that don't deserve to be hurt again. No. *Non dieche niente*, she tells herself.

Besides, there are pieces of this puzzle that are missing from the box. Rebecca needs to find them, although she's not sure why it's so important to her. Tomorrow, while Rebecca is at the property on Farpath Road, waiting for Bud Grainger to finish excavating, she will step into the house and look around again, this time with fresh eyes. She will open all the blinds, windows and doors, letting in the light, the air, the sun—letting out the ghosts. She will look through papers stacked in drawers, poke her head into the attic, and... Oh, Noah's coming, she remembers. I'll have to get there ahead of him, she thinks, and begins to figure out what she will wear. The phone rings interrupting her.

It's Drew. Rebecca's heart begins a drum roll again. She excuses herself and steps into the parlor where it's cool and dark and quiet. The shades drawn during the day to save the upholstery from fading, the way Rebecca's mother does every afternoon when the sun makes its way around. She begins to pace in the little room—perfect as a museum—as she answers the phone.

"Hello?"

"Rebecca. I just got off the phone with Dana. She tells me that you and she had an argument and she's staying at the Connor's now. What did you two argue about this time?

"A lot of things… She skipped school yesterday…again," Rebecca says feeling a mealy twinge that Dana had called Drew instead of her.

"Why didn't you tell me?"

"Well, I'm telling you now. You've been…busy. I'm with my mother, Drew. We can talk about this later."

"I won't be home tonight."

There. He said it. She knew it was coming. "Oh? And where will you be?"

"I will be staying with a friend for a while."

"Oh for godsake, just say it Drew. You've got a girlfriend. Just say it for chrissake, you're leaving," Rebecca says thoroughly impatient with this dance.

Drew sighs, "*Girlfriend?* Don't be childish. It's more complicated than that…"

"No it's not!"

"All I'm saying is that I need some time to myself. To sort things out."

"What a load of crap. You just want to string me along. You think that I'll sit around hoping you'll come back. You would so enjoy that, picturing me at home, wringing my hands wondering what you're doing." Rebecca can picture it too. The way it's always been: a constant struggle to get something from him, chasing him for something he won't give, or can't give. She hates herself for it. He created this part for her and she's been playing it too long.

"That's absurd. I can see that it's not the best time for this conversation. I'll call you tomorrow and we can discuss it further." Now he's playing his part: withholding, condescending and beleaguered, Rebecca thinks. "My main concern is Dana right now," he says self-righteously.

That brings Rebecca up sharply, forcing her to struggle to put out the fire that he started, she smothers it until there is only the taste of ash left in her mouth. Gulping her anger down she replies, "Absolutely, Dana is the main concern now," she agrees because it happens to be true. Still she's furious that he cut her off that way, using Dana to hijack the conversation and put her in her place.

"I wanted to offer a solution. Something a friend of mine mentioned. It may be a tool we can use to bring Dana around."

A solution? There actually is such a thing. Thank God, Rebecca thinks at first, but is wary.

"I hope you can keep an open mind. It may sound drastic, but I think you'll agree that there are some definite benefits that can be achieved through the use of proven methods determined to be…"

"What *is* it Drew?" Rebecca butts in. She just can't stand his pontificating one more second.

"Well, my friend mentioned something called a CHINS petition. Which can be utilized to enlist agencies that specialize in intervention for troubled teens."

"Chins petition? What is chins? What agencies?"

"C-H-I-N-S" he spells out. "It stands for children in need of services. State agencies have expertise…"

"*State* agencies?"

"It's a perfectly reasonable avenue to explore. It's my understanding from a well respected source who deals with…"

"State agencies! Are you suggesting that we contact the state to oversee the raising of our child? To give them *control* of Dana?"

"Rebecca, let me finish please…"

The Forgotten Roses

Rebecca knows Drew is still talking, something about the administrator of some department who is a friend of a colleague... But she's no longer listening, she is too busy pacing, letting the scope of what he's suggesting filter all the way through her, into every corner, each hidden crevice, sinking down layer by layer. On its way, it opens unused passages, releases buried perceptions, clarifies. She finally comprehends all of what he is saying and stops in her tracks.

Rebecca assesses her feelings, notes how her body is arranged around her heart, the way she is standing at an awkward angle, in mid-step, with each shoulder reaching in different directions–almost twisted–like the game where you freeze when the music stops. Rebecca gathers herself together, frees up, plants her feet squarely–interrupts him.

"Drew? Have you contacted anyone about this 'avenue?' "

"No, not yet, but I do have some names that..."

"Who suggested this to you?"

"What? Oh, no one you'd know. But I can assure..."

"Where are you exactly, right now?"

"I'm in my office. Why?"

"I wanted to know, how quickly I could get to you if I wanted to." Rebecca presses the phone close to her lips and breathes these words into him, "You are done."

"What are you talking about?" He sounds confused.

Her voice is low now, heavy with rage, sharp as an ice pick. "Do not utter the words CHINS petition ever again. Do not contact any agency, or anyone connected to an agency. Do not discuss this with your friend; I *will* find out her name..."

"Are you *threatening* me Rebecca?"

"I would never threaten you Drew," Rebecca says evenly. "I'm simply delivering information. Do not come back. You won't like what you see. I'll mail you what's left of your things. I will call an attorney. The words that you said to me just now, will never be repeated. It will be as if they never came out of your mouth. They are gone, undone. Unthinkable. Are you understanding me, Drew?" Her words are dead calm, like the sea when there is not the slightest breeze, but her intentions are dark and ominous, building like thunderheads. Conditions like these portend lethal gales.

"Wait just a minute…"

"I'm done waiting," Rebecca cuts him off. "And done with you," she tells him with a finality that echoes inside the empty spot in her heart as she presses the End button on her phone.

❧

Rebecca stops at the hall mirror to check her face. Is this the first picture in my divorce album? Look, here I am in my Aunt Josephine's parlor peering into the mirror reflecting a large wooden crucifix on the wall behind me reminding me of my failure. Here I am in the next picture walking into the dining room feeling…determined? Rebecca shakes her head, wonders how it is she doesn't feel devastated, depressed? That will come later, she supposes. At this moment, mainly she feels as if she is in a hurry; as if she needs to get started on a long, arduous trip that is interrupting the flow of her life. Okay, but this reaction is not normal. Probably I should seek a mental health professional before getting started, she thinks with a dry little smile as she walks toward the dining room.

Rebecca ducks her head and looks around the table guiltily, not a divorce in sight. If she were to pass around the facts of her marriage here there would be consensus. "Men can be such jerks," they would say with resigned shrugs. "So what?" They would tell her. "The important thing is keeping the family together, for the children. Don't let that *putana* he's running around with break up your home. Stand up for yourself!" Rebecca has heard it all before. How could she explain that if Drew got his way, their family would suffer a cataclysmic break. Standing up for Dana, for her family, and–for the first time–herself, is exactly what she is doing.

Family is everything, Rebecca believes it too. These first and second generation Italian ladies whose overflowing passions have been firmly and safely channeled into their homes, cooking, children, they would shake their heads at her if they knew. First, they would call Drew names, laugh at him a little, diminish him. Then they would tsk at Rebecca, talk to her in low, encouraging tones, shooting arrows straight through her heart. "Well it's up to you, but think of the *children*."

That's all she can think about. Rebecca reflects on the way Drew's wintery and removed nature informs his relationship with Dana and Lily, how deeply it will impact their future choices. It is a worry that will gnaw at her as she monitors the way in which her daughters navigate through relationships as they grow. She will often reflect on how the past pushes on the future like ripples in a pond, connected, spreading outward touching others in an endless rhythm. She will try to read her daughter's tea leaves, but hope and fear will fog her view. There will be many signs– good and bad–dreams and premonitions. But the only sure thing, is that she will be there for them, watching closely as they choose their own paths; wondering, worrying, waiting, as ever, with each footfall as they move forward.

What Drew does and doesn't do, what he won't give or can't give will come to be of small significance to Rebecca. He will not be the opening sentence in the paragraph of her day. Eventually, he will be reduced to one chapter in her life, among others. She will stop trying to solve the puzzle of Drew, and the time that frees up will astonish her. It is time that will be spent helping her daughters write new chapters for themselves. Ones that will include Drew, but ones in which he will not be the central character. As soon as Dana is home, as soon as the three of us are together, I will pull them close and begin again, she resolves.

Lily yawns and Rebecca says loud enough to get Eva's attention, "Are you tired, honey?" It works, and they bundle themselves back into the van after many embraces and promises of getting together more often. There are tears too, because they see the aging in each other's eyes, reflecting their own, and the unspoken absence of others who have passed.

Eva makes an attempt to alter the pattern of their lives. "Next time, you come to my house," she tells them. They all promise they will, but know that they won't. These *paisans* will hop a plane to Naples or Florence, but any town west of the southeast expressway is foreign territory. As they leave, Eva and her sisters look back over their shoulders with sadness and longing. They wave as if they were leaving their one true home. They cry, just as Vincent and Gina once did when they left their homes in Italy long ago to come here, knowing they would never see their parents again.

Though Eva insists she saw her grandmother in a vision when she was a very young child. Eva was looking out their tenement window, barely big enough to clear the sill with her chin, when the grandmother that she'd never met, nor seen a photo of, smiled and waved at her from the street. Eva knew instantly who she was and waved back happily. The old woman blew her a kiss; Eva caught it and closed it inside her baby fist. She called her mother, excitedly, to the window, but Gina saw no one. The next day they got the news that Gina's mother had passed away. Eva swears her grandmother came to see her, the firstborn grandchild, to send her a message before she left—a message of love. No one here doubts it.

20

Saint

Rebecca loves babies. Fragrant as spring, every burp a miracle—sweet messengers from God. This baby appears to be a messenger from someone else. His face is as used as worry. His cheeks lack smoothness or color and, instead, have the look of wet sand, pasty and mottled. He sits in a box, Buddha-like with his legs crossed under him. Rebecca peers in closer. Taking the corners of each of the cardboard covers in her fingertips, she slowly pulls them apart to get a better look. He is naked and watching her. The worst part is that his baby hair has been combed over, parted on the side like an old man's and slicked down across his forehead. This strikes Rebecca hardest, like a last straw. It makes her want to cry and she starts to form the word, *Why?* when someone taps her on the shoulder and Rebecca turns to see her; disheveled, barefoot, smoldering like a damp fire. She assesses Rebecca calmly, sneers, blows some air through closed lips, almost a razz. She moves around Rebecca, steps over to the box and gestures to it with open offering hands. She is so…familiar. When she opens her mouth to speak, a terrible noise comes out.

It's only the phone ringing, and her own ragged breathing. Rebecca switches on the light and wipes the sweat from between her breasts with the loose fabric of her nightgown. "Hello?" It is a loaded question, bulging with others. Is this the dreaded call in the night from policemen? Hospitals? People trying to inform her of some terrible this or that?

There is something nagging and wrong, she can feel it, something bad, or missing, like a hole in the pit of...Oh, Dana's not home.

"Rebecca! How are you deeah? I apologize for calling so late, but of course it's morning here and I wanted to talk to you right away."

"Sophia?" Rebecca rubs her face, blinking at the phone trying to clear her eyes and the last fluttering wisps of nightmare lingering behind.

"We're in London; I've met the most wonderful man, but I'll tell you about that later. Right now I'm concerned because of what I'm hearing from Tandy about your sale of Dr. Deitzhoff's old place. What's going on Rebecca?" Sophia's voice sounds scratchy and diluted but it still has the power to bounce off the inside of Rebecca's skull and rattle its contents.

Rebecca's tongue is thick from sleep; she yawns into the phone and doesn't care if Sophia hears. Why couldn't she call at a normal hour when Rebecca has a clear head and could ask *her* a few pertinent questions, tie up a couple of those damned loose ends. No, she calls now because the world must spin around Sophia's schedule. "I could type it all up and send it to you in the morning," Rebecca offers.

"No, no. Tell me now. I don't know exactly where I'll be tomorrow and I've set aside this time to deal with the matter, so let's get on with it." Her voice is pleasant and chatty, but all business just the same.

So, Rebecca tells her. She tells Sophia about Eva's first warnings, and then about Sully's experiences growing up with Serena. She tells her about the conversation around the dining room table in East Boston yesterday, and now there is nothing on the other end of what is, most certainly, a very costly call.

"Sophia?" Rebecca asks, afraid that they've been disconnected and she has been talking to herself all along.

"I'm here... Now, listen to me carefully. That is an outrageous load of horse shit! I've lived in Havenwood for longer than I care to remember and I'll tell you exactly what happened. First of all my deeah,

The Forgotten Roses

Dr. Deitzhoff is a saint," Sophia announces emphatically.

"A *saint?*"

"Yes! He was the first person at that prison to treat those poor, unfortunate girls like regular people. And yes, he brought them out of that hellhole, but to *heal* them. Everyone in town knew that the girls were allowed out in his custody now and then, as kind of a little vacation for good behavior. And of course some people were appalled to think girls like that might be set loose among Havenwood's lily-white young. There were rumors, but they came from fear and ignorance.

"Harold Deitzhoff's biggest sin was that he was…unusual. A brilliant man; tall, handsome and carried himself with an aristocratic, bookish air," Sophia says with much drama, as if she were reading it out of an English novel. "He wouldn't mix with the townspeople, was downright unsociable, I'll give you that. He didn't give a fig about whether or not the town should give Constance Wauney a permit to sell cow manure out of her garage, or how to rein in business district expansion, or *whatevah!*" Rebecca thinks she hears a tinge of English accent creeping into this monologue.

"He kept to himself, he and his family, and he didn't bother anybody. Besides he had that crazy wife of his to deal with. And that daughter. Now, you know I'm fond of children, and ordinarily I wouldn't say anything against a child, but Serena–by God that child was peculiar. She looked strange for one thing, with those pale eyes and hair, like all the blood had been washed out of her. And I wouldn't say this to anyone else Rebecca, but whenever I saw her, I had the urge to make the sign of the cross. It doesn't surprise me one bit that your Mr. Sullivan was a cohort of hers. I mean, I like Francis and all, but let's face it, he doesn't have all his oars in the water either.

"And as for your family," Sophia finally takes a breath. "I feel bad for them; those poor people, the mother and father, no doubt overcome with guilt. It's no wonder they tried to blame others.

"Honestly, Rebecca," she says derisively. I don't know how you could have swallowed such stories. The real crime is that the girl was put in prison in the first place for just being stubborn. It was perfectly acceptable then, and let me tell you something else…"

Like I could stop her, Rebecca thinks.

"It's not so different now either. Years ago, I volunteered at the women's prison–there but for the Grace of God…! Women are imprisoned for things men are never jailed for, like prostitution, or petty crimes like kiting checks. Stupid things that have more to do with their economic situation than anything else. That's what comes from being overly dependent on men," she advises Rebecca.

"Things haven't changed all that much I'm afraid. But Dr. Deitzhoff at least tried to make a difference in the lives of the girls at that time and I don't want you spreading any rumors to the contrary. Of all people, Rebecca Griffin, I would never have suspected you of being so close-minded."

"Well, I'm sorry Sophia, it sounded plausible at the time." Why am I apologizing to her? It's an automatic reflex to the scolding, like she's my mother for godsake. Now Rebecca doesn't know what to think. She'll have to find out for herself what the real truth is. But one thing is certain, she doesn't need to sit in her own bed in the middle of the night and listen to admonitions delivered from halfway across the world. "Look, it's so late here and I've got to get up early. I'm glad you called, Sophia. It's good to hear from you." Rebecca actually means it on some level.

"All right, Rebecca. Take care. I hope I wasn't too hard on you, it's just that I don't like to see people treated unfairly. At one time people thought the worst of me as well. And, after all, you don't want any of that ancient history to get in the way of a sale do you?" Not waiting for an answer, she ratchets the decibels up a couple of notches and sings out, "It was good to talk to you too, give the family my love. See you all soon!

The Forgotten Roses

Ta-ta!" Delivered in tones that make dogs weep.

❧

"Lily, time to get up," Rebecca calls into the open doorway of Lily's bedroom.

"Isn't it Saturday?" Lily's muffled answer from under the covers.

"I told you last night, don't you remember? I have an appointment this morning and we made arrangements for you to go to Sammy's today."

"Why can't I stay home with Dad?"

Rebecca walks over to the bed, peels the quilt away from Lily's face. "Hello, is anybody home?" she says gently knocking on the top of Lily's head. "Don't you remember, Dad's away and Dana's at Amy's. I don't want you to be at home alone all day."

Lily glares at Rebecca, her eyes are as hard and round and steely as ball bearings. "I can take care of myself. I'm not moving," she says and slaps the covers back over her head.

Rebecca doesn't budge, doesn't speak. This is just a little glitch, it's nothing she tells herself. Lily is tired after a long day yesterday. Rebecca waits for her to recover, to turn back into Lily, but there is no movement from under the covers. Rebecca stands with her hands folded in front of her, waiting for a sign. She looks out the window; the sky is overcast with great swollen clouds ready to let go. Soon I'll be standing in the rain, slogging through the wet, watching mud holes open and close, she thinks. Perfect.

When Rebecca looks back at Lily, she sees eyes peering over the top edge of the quilt, watching her. "How long?" Lily asks with irritation.

"A few hours, maybe longer, I'm really not sure. Sammy's Mom mentioned a sleepover if you want."

Lily groans, throws her covers off, yawns and stretches. Rebecca backs up as if she might jump up from bed and knock her out of the way.

"Can we stop for doughnuts? I feel like a French crueler."

"That's funny, you don't look like a French crueler," Rebecca makes a lame joke and waits hesitantly for Lily's reaction.

"Ha ha," Lily says trying to sneer which she can't pull off because a smile is leaking out on one side. When she tucks her hair behind her ears, the face revealed is clear, light as air, and shines like a lucky penny and Rebecca can see that it really is Lily after all.

"Come on my own sweet Lily. My Lily-of-the-Valley, my Lily of the valley-girl," Rebecca tells her putting her arm around Lily's waist and pulling her towards the bathroom.

"Like, *whatever*," Lily says rolling her eyes pretending to resist Rebecca, dragging herself to the shower with exaggerated flops of her bare feet. Budding breasts behind the fabric of her camisole stand out like little meringue peaks and when she turns, her shoulder blades cut a path across the surface of her narrow back so exposed, so vulnerable and unfinished, Rebecca feels like an intruder and looks away.

❧

Dana has just woken up after sleeping all night in a car—someone's car, she's not sure whose. She groans as she unfolds herself; her stomach feels as if it's tied in a knot and inside-out. The smell of beer is overpowering and when she finally makes it to a sitting position, the car becomes airborne, spinning out of control until she's forced to open the car door and jump out to safety. She lands on her hands and knees, dry-heaving onto ground so solid she digs her nails into it for pure relief. She pulls up a fist full of grass and brings it to her nose inhaling its crisp, clean smell. That's better, she thinks rolling round to sit with her arms looped around her knees. She thinks maybe she should try eating grass the way dogs do to settle their stomachs and pulls out a sliver from its shaft. Dana examines its tender yellow core and snips at it with her front teeth–it is sweet and silvery on her tongue and tastes very…green. She makes an effort to take in large amounts of fresh air thick with dew. She chews on selected blades as she shivers in the damp and peers into the car trying to make out who its occupants are.

Dana's stomach has moved to a more convenient location and she feels better, but pissed. So pissed, she could eat dirt and grinds her teeth as if there is grit between them. Who are those fucking people anyway? Mangy-looking stinking losers, every single one of them. Luckily, she recognizes her surroundings; they are parked at the access road to the tracks where you turn in to get to the cliffs. But the asshole who parked here left the tail-end too exposed to the road and now she's going to have to wake one of these fuckers to move it. Or maybe she'll just do it herself.

She hauls herself up and trips over the ripped bottom of her pant leg. Fuck! She tries to remember how she got here, and who she's with when she recognizes one of the lumps in the back seat as a girl in her chemistry class. Corinne. That's right, she and Amy had hooked up with Corinne and some of her asshole friends while they were packy-hanging. After they'd found someone to buy for them, Corinne wanted to cruise Marlboro Street in Boston where she swore she knew about some Emerson College parties that she could get them into–that's when Amy bailed out. I hope she got home okay. Thank God I told her what to say to her parents, Dana thinks, Amy could never have thought up a good lie on her own. Amy was supposed to tell her mother that Dana decided to go back home. The Connors wouldn't have called her house in the middle of the night, so she was covered for a while, providing Amy doesn't screw up.

Dana remembers just wanting to *do* something, not just hang around with the same boring dick-heads. It felt like an all over electric itch: the wanting to move, to go, to get the fuck out of Havenwood. She remembers getting lost, picking a fight with Corinne, and needing to punch her, like a hunger; wanting to feel Corinne's bones mash under her knuckles and understanding with every cell, why boys beat each other up. Why they *like* to.

Finally, Dana remembers narrow hallways and small rooms, and the shoulder to elbow push of a noisy crowd, the sticky heat of bodies moving too fast inside too little air. She remembers doing keg stands, sinking down, warm and oozy like melted butter onto a soft pile of rumpled clothes, and of someone's hot breath on her face, the sour taste of sweat, the press of lips–someone's lips.

The keys are still hanging in the ignition and Dana pulls the car into the bushes gouging deep ruts into the soft earth; parking the car so the cops won't see it. She blows out of there fast, putting distance between herself and the others snoring their loser stink into the hidden car. She needs to get to a phone and find out how Amy's doing.

21

Storm

The clouds are so low and bulging, if Rebecca stood on her car in the parking lot, she could touch them and they would squeak like balloon skins against her fingers. They are so weighted, she might have felt rooted to her spot by their pressure. She might have wanted to go home and pull the covers over her head. Take a nap. But not today. Today she's moving on.

It's only eight a.m. and the office isn't open yet; she tiptoes through the rooms not wanting to disrupt the silence. As she heads for the key box, Rebecca can smell Tandy's perfume: sweet, spicy and expensive. It mixes with the odor of copy toner and new carpet.

She will have one hour to explore the Deitzhoff house before Bud Grainger arrives. If she finds something really interesting, she can linger in the house while Bud works, checking on his progress periodically until ten o'clock when Noah arrives.

Rebecca doesn't know what she hopes to find. What could be stowed away on shelves or tucked in eave space that can answer any of her questions? Was Harold Deitzhoff–*Dr.* Harold Deitzhoff according to Sophia–a saint or sinner? Did he abuse girls, take advantage of them, or help them? Was Rose a victim, cut down like a martyr, or a troublemaker, the bane of the parents who loved her.

Why have I been frozen in place for so long? Why is Dana so hateful? And those nightmares; why am I dreaming about babies? Rebecca asks herself over and over. These questions propel her forward like a hard push at the back. She is drawn to the shabby house as if it is the beginning of a circle, and the end; as if the answer to even one of the questions would solve them all, would make the puzzle whole.

Rebecca drives up the scarred driveway to Deitzhoff's house once again. It had rained a little, but now has stopped, leaving the trees studded with dull silver beads; if the sun broke through they would shine like diamonds, but in the grim, they look tarnished. She steps out of her car heading for the brick walkway and looks around at the plantings: beaten down, slumped over, surrendered to their fate. She needn't have bothered picking up the key, the door is unlocked again.

Rebecca feels overwhelmed with dread and stops short. The hairs at the back of her neck stand upright again; a message she ignores. Walk in fast, without looking up, just concentrate on your feet, she tells herself. Go straight to the windows and unhook the latch, push up the casing fast and hard, open each window wide; do that until you feel the rush of air swirling through your hair and circling your feet. Don't stop until you have replaced all the old air with new. Then you can begin, a voice from deep within tells her.

She starts the search with the dining room hutch, the one with the drawer whose contents had been emptied out onto the floor. There are check stubs from 1982, books of matches; she pricks a finger on a tack and sucks the blood, closes the drawer feeling let down. In the library, she tips books forward looking behind, takes a few out, shakes them, looks at inscriptions. The desk drawer is empty except for a desiccated silverfish in the corner and a stamp glued to the bottom. She glances at her watch, casts around looking for possible hiding places, resigns herself to moving on to Harold's bedroom.

She slides her hand between the mattress and box spring, catches a glimpse of her wild-eyed grimace in the mirror, and feels like a fool which doesn't deter her one bit. It smells in here still but not enough to make your eyes water, she observes as she steps over to the window and shoves it open. A raw gust rushes past, drops to the floor and forces the dust bunnies out of the way.

Dresser drawers, empty. Old shoes line the bottom of the closet, she kicks at them to see if they are stepping on anything interesting. Nothing. Someone's done more cleaning. Kitchen cabinet contents emptied into boxes wait for hauling to the dump. She looks into a few, shakes them to see if anything miraculous flies out.

Rebecca stands at the bottom of the stairway and looks up. She hears only the sound of the drapes fighting with the breeze and her own heavy breathing. It seems a long climb for nothing more than wire hangers and a rusting can of Comet. And the damned owl. Did someone pull the shade down before we left that room last time? Rebecca dreads having to see that ungodly stare. But she continues because she is on a mission, crazy or not. An answer is here, she knows it, feels it. She just has to find it before ten o'clock.

Rebecca opens closet doors to scan ceilings trying to remember which one had attic access. Shit, she thinks, I don't have a ladder. How the hell will I get up there? Finally she finds it. In Serena's closet there is a square cut out of the plaster in the ceiling and plywood covering the hole. Rebecca looks around for something to step on, pulls the flashlight out of her pocket then takes her raincoat off and throws it on the bed. She drags the desk chair into the closet and places it under the opening, climbs on top and pushes the plywood up with her fingertips, sliding it out of the way.

"Damn it!" she mutters, I'm too friggin' short.

She runs downstairs, gets an armload of Harold's books, stacks them carefully on the chair seat, side-by-side and one on top of another. It's wobbly, but it works. She hauls herself up and shines the light around. Eureka! Boxes of stuff; a promising cache. She looks around for bats hanging on the rafters but finds only cobwebs and the stuffy smell of old dust, dry wood and trapped air.

The rumble of a diesel engine: it's Bud. What if he comes in looking for me and finds me climbing down from this hole, Rebecca thinks. She takes a quick look around at the bonanza and eases herself back down, dusts off her hands, leaves the chair with the books piled on top in the closet and shuts the door. Before Rebecca leaves, she pulls the shade all the way down in front of the owl who watches its decent and glares its disapproval.

"Hi Bud! How's it going?"

"Pretty good, Mrs. G., except for this crummy weather; gonna be a messy deal this morning." Bud is the youngest of the Grainger sons, a nice lumbering kid with saggy pants and lumpy clothes. He always looks in need of a haircut and shave, like he's advertising for the kind of girl who'll want to clean him up, buy him jeans that fit and socks that match.

It's drizzling, an annoying driving mist that makes you blink to see and seeps relentlessly into your clothes. There is the distant growl of thunder. "If you don't mind, I'm going to go into the house to check on a few things. But, if you need me just give a holler, the door is open."

"Sure. No problem. I'm going to start right by the garage here."

"Okay. Let me know as soon as you find something," Rebecca calls back to him as she walks toward the house. He nods once, pulling his cap down so the ear-flaps stick straight out on the sides like a propeller.

Before Rebecca goes back upstairs, there is one more thing that she must do. She has to go down to the basement. There are metal file cabinets in one of the rooms and although she thinks they are empty, she needs to be sure—a testament to her obsession. She stands in the middle of the living room and swivels in her shoes, looking around for signs, signals, waiting for a presence to make itself known. But the interior is passive, devoid of color or life or mystery of any kind. She takes courage from the emptiness and heads downstairs. She will not look in the workshop; there is nothing hidden in there; everything in that room is exposed. And she won't look in the dark cave of the utility room either. She spent enough time there and knows its contents by heart: the oil burner, an old soapstone sink set in a bumpy fieldstone wall streaked with drip and seepage, rickety shelves with its *Little Shop of Horrors* display.

The only thing she must do down here is go straight to the file cabinets in the rec room. What form of recreation went on there is subject to interpretation, which strikes Rebecca as perversely funny and she almost laughs, except her throat gets all tight and nervous. Oh screw that, Rebecca! Suck it up, like Dana says.

The file cabinets are locked, but Rebecca shakes them and hears no rattle or shift of any kind inside, just the echo of metal knocking against itself. She places her hands flat on either side and rocks the whole thing back and forth just to be sure; it is empty.

Rebecca begins to leave and stops to listen. The house is silent as a dream, but down here there are no windows to force open, fresh air can't reach this level and so it is close and clingy like bad company. The hand she places on the rough pine banister is sweating. She clears her throat to hear her own sound and tosses her head back defiantly. She would whistle, but that's too corny, instead, she clomps noisily up the stairs, banging her foot down hard on each step deliberately, as if in warning, as if she's proving something. When Rebecca gets to the top, she closes the door and runs the latch across locking it, pulling at the doorknob hard to make sure it's secure.

When she gets outside, she calls to Bud and waves. He's too busy with the controls to wave back, so just nods in acknowledgement. It has stopped drizzling, but Rebecca sees a flash and counts the seconds until the bang. It's coming closer. The clouds hover expectantly, bunching up, rubbing their dark edges into purple blisters. Rebecca ducks into the house and gets back to work.

She wishes she'd worn jeans instead of this tight skirt. "Stupid!" she tells herself. There isn't much standing room in the attic; she must hunch over the boxes to rummage. Yellowed baby clothes, round boxes with woven handles containing fancy hats–the kind worn by the Queen Mother–now squashed and faded, boxes of ancient books. She takes out a few and realizes they are novels, prayer books, children's picture books; definitely not Harold's. She thinks these boxes belonged to Mrs. Deitzhoff, the first one.

Rebecca coughs and sneezes, her back is starting to cramp. She sits down and leans against a post. She looks around again, shines the flashlight up to the peak, the shadowed corners and edges. It's warm and dry, almost peaceful; she feels a tiredness into her bones. She can imagine taking a nap in here; it's cozy and private, like a tree house. She thinks she should close her eyes, just for a moment, just to get her energy back, and drops her head onto her knees. A heavy drowsy pull overtakes her, she cannot resist. There is a dream just ahead. It's as if she's underwater; if she could manage to break the surface she'd be there inside the dream. She stretches out her fingers reaching for it. The surface ripples and someone's face swims in and out of focus from above–it's Rose. Rebecca tries to call to her, but the words remain trapped underneath and merely bubble around her face. Rose scowls, she is exasperated, impatient, and finally pounds her fist cracking the surface as if it were glass, sending shards flying around Rebecca as silent as snowflakes. Rebecca jerks awake with a start–it's too quiet, the engine noise has stopped.

When Rebecca arrives outside, Bud is hauling something out of the depression he dug out by the garage. "I came across this thing," he tells her dropping a padlocked black metal box with a crushed lid at her feet. "I wonder what it is?" he says kneeling down to get a better look. "The cover is pretty well smashed, but I'll bet you could get it open with a crowbar." He brushes dirt off the top and examines the damage as Rebecca crouches down with him in the wet grass. It looks like a large safe deposit box, dented in the center and lifted at one corner wide enough to get two fingers in.

"Do you have a crowbar?" Rebecca asks.

"Nope."

"Would you mind looking in the garage to see if there's anything in there we can use to open it?" Rebecca asks Bud, handing him a key.

"Sure." Bud is as eager as a puppy. He disappears into the garage and Rebecca is alone with the box. She tips it on its side and hears things slide and clunk and her stomach does a little jump as if she's on a roller coaster. She remembers Sully saying that Serena saw her father bury something, she had followed him and watched him do it and it was important to her in some way. My God, is this it?

It has started to rain in earnest, big splotchy drops fall on the lid and roll into the opening. Rebecca picks it up protectively, cradles it under her raincoat. Bud lopes over. "This is all I could find," he says holding an assortment of rusty metal things in his big calloused hands: a trowel, a hammer, a screwdriver and a thing that looks like a wide spatula.

"I'm going to take this inside," Rebecca tells him and Bud follows, carrying the tools while she tries to decide what to do with him. She doesn't want him around when she opens the box, but she'll probably need some help doing it, and he looks as if this is the most fun he's had in a week, maybe longer; an honest-to-God treasure hunt. Rebecca sets the box down on the kitchen table and Bud dumps most of the stuff down looming over the box with the remaining tool.

"What is that?" Rebecca asks, hoping he'll succeed and hoping he won't.

"A wedge," he says, grunting with the force of trying to pry the metal cover off. He widens the opening, then picks up the hammer and bangs on the padlock until the hammerhead flies off hitting the wall so hard it makes a pockmark. "Whoa!" says Bud, who finds it funny. The lid is still tight on, but yawning wider on one side. He reaches to pick up the box and Rebecca beats him to it, saying, "Bud, I think we better put this aside for now and find that septic tank. The lawyer for the estate will be here soon expecting to see it and the inspector is waiting to hear from us too so let's get that done first, okay?" Bud looks crushed; Rebecca feels bad about disappointing him.

"Thanks so much for your help, Bud," she calls out to his sullen back.

After he shuffles off, Rebecca peers inside the box. There looks to be a leather-bound notebook, a ledger maybe, and another small one like the proverbial little black book. Also, there are some square packets, the size and shape of bricks wrapped in brown paper secured with elastics. Rebecca shakes the box, as if she could sift up some startling revelation to the surface. She tries prying some more around the edges of the cover using the trowel, then the wedge. It budges in infinitesimal increments, but she believes she could open it enough to see what's in there with more time. She looks at her watch. "*Shit,*" she swears under her breath; it's almost ten o'clock. She certainly doesn't want Noah to see this. She slides the box onto a shelf in the refrigerator and washes her hands, wiping them off on her raincoat before going outside to watch the dig and wait for Noah Hanes.

He's right on time, just as Rebecca knew he would be. There is a low rumble from above as he gets out of his BMW. Noah ducks his head and pulls his collar tighter around his neck when he steps out of the car engaging the security system. He pockets the keys and trots over to where she's standing. Rebecca wonders if he's worried about gangs and car thieves out here in the woods. Racoon Crips and squirrel Bloods. He shakes Rebecca's hand and nods over in Bud's direction. "Any success?" he asks smiling into her eyes, still holding her hand.

"Not yet," Rebecca answers and automatically smiles her optimistic real estate broker smile. She notices how sharp he looks; confident and well dressed. His skin fairly shines with well-being—or Elizabeth Grady facials, she can't tell which—he smells like the men's fragrance counter at Bloomingdale's, a little too strong for Rebecca's taste, but a welcome contrast to Bud's fuel oil and wet wool odor. Last time Rebecca saw Noah, he started out tense and all business; it took him a while to warm up. But today he appears relaxed and when he looks at her, he seems to be searching for something. In fact, he looks into her face a little too long, until she has to lower her eyes and look away, self-conscious and embarrassed.

The rain has let up again and Rebecca slips the raincoat hood off her head, aware all of a sudden of how flattened her hair must be. She looks down at her raincoat now muddy, her splattered tights, filthy shoes. She tries shaking her hair and pushing at it, brushing off her raincoat feeling rumpled and awkward. His shoes are spotless; boat shoes that appear right-out-of-the-box new and you could cut butter with the crease in his chinos.

It feels an intimate thing to do, standing shoulder to shoulder, hands in pockets watching Bud heave the metal claw into the soft give of earth, opening it wider and wider, cleaving the sod, pulling the ground up and spilling its contents carelessly aside. Noah has moved so close that they are actually touching but Rebecca doesn't move. "How is Mr. Deitzhoff?" Rebecca asks to break the tension she feels.

"Harold is doing well; very, very well," Noah declares. "He is really much better off where he is; taken complete care of 'round the clock." He turns to face Rebecca and puts his hand on her back as if to reassure her. "It's a marvelous facility you know. Birchview came with the highest recommendations."

"I've heard it's a lovely place," she replies. Rebecca knows exactly what kind of a place it is because she drove there to see it. She picked the last of her pink cosmos, put them in a glass vase, bought a jar of Wild Maine blueberry jam and a book of New England lighthouse photos, then made the thirty minute drive to Birchview to check it out. She saw Harold sitting by a window watching the activity at the birdfeeders. He looks clean, Rebecca thought, but barely there, almost transparent in the sunlight. Harold thanked her as she presented her gifts and asked her name. "I'm Rebecca, Rebecca Griffin...your real estate broker... remember?"

"Oh yes," Harold told her. He didn't seem very interested in the book, pushed the vase onto the window sill while examining the jar closely, bringing it up near his face to read the label. Rebecca asked how he was feeling, how he liked his new room. He told her he was "fit as a fiddle," and asked her name. "Rebecca," she told him again, but he had turned from her to watch the sparrows. "It's very nice here, isn't it," she said hoping to get an acknowledgment, a sense of his awareness. He turned and blinked at her blankly. "I hope you enjoy the jam," she said, patted his shoulder, and left. She was happy to know that Noah made a decent choice at least.

She smiles at Noah; this time it wasn't a real estate smile. He is so damned handsome and there is something very exciting about being here with him, no matter what the weather. Though she worries that the smile he returns is a lawyer smile rather than a genuine one, especially because he lacks the crow's feet that would normally signal at the corners of his eyes and, instead, they remain fixed, not pumping out anything discernible. He is so composed, so immaculately pulled together that he is missing anything you could term body language; all landmarks have been smoothed over. But his teeth gleam wholeheartedly; Rebecca takes that as a good sign.

"I found it," Bud calls out. He climbs out of the cab and into the crevice he's dug. He kicks way some fallen dirt and says, "There's your cover. You can call the septic guy to take a look inside now."

"Thanks, Bud. You've been a big help," Rebecca manages to get out before the sky cracks open, slashing a nearby pine in a scorching explosion sending blackened needles and bark flying through the air like confetti. Noah and Rebecca make a mad dash into the house and Bud takes off in his truck, leaving the backhoe where it sits, in the mud.

The Forgotten Roses

Rebecca's knees are trembling when they get inside, "My *God*!" is all she can say, breathless and shaken. Noah is brushing debris off his hair. "I'll be damned!" he says. They look out the front door at the top of the sizzling tree, another bolt lights up the sky, another ear-splitting crack reverberates throughout the house, vibrating into their feet and through their bones and they slam the door shut.

"It looks as if we're trapped in here for a while until this lets up," Noah says, surveying the room. "Let's try and get comfortable at least," he says, slamming down the living room windows. Rebecca quickly moves through the other rooms, fighting off whipping curtains and flapping shades, closing the others. When she comes back, windblown and out of breath, he's fiddling with the thermostat. "I guess they've already shut off the electricity." He hunches up his shoulders, rubs his hands together. "Brrr," he says looking at Rebecca smiling his bald-eyed smile. Not that it isn't a killer smile, Rebecca thinks, it's just disconcerting to be so unable to read what's behind someone's eyes. I think he's had them done, that would be an explanation.

"How about a fire," he says. Rebecca remembers the matches and retrieves them, bunches up newspapers, while Noah goes directly to the basement where there is a bit if kindling and firewood stored by the bulkhead door.

He makes a decent fire; Rebecca admires his competence. They make an unspoken and mutual pact not to sit on the sofa, but instead spread their coats onto the floor. Noah sits down first and holds his hand up to Rebecca in what she takes as a gentlemanly gesture to help her down.

Rebecca feels ill at ease again and struggles to make small talk, as if she's a teenager on a first date. "How did you and Mr. Deitzhoff meet?"

"Oh, he was a client of my father's from long ago. I took over his affairs when my father passed," he says into the fire and then turns to her and strokes her back. "Don't worry, this will let up soon."

His speech patterns remind Rebecca of someone much older,

although it's hard to tell how old he is exactly. His hair has a feather of white at the sides, just enough to look elegant, but not enough to date him. He fairly reeks of success and self-assurance.

It occurs to Rebecca that she has a golden opportunity here if she dares to take advantage of it. Besides, she feels as if she needs to keep talking for some reason. "Noah...what do you know about Mr. Deitzhoff's affairs? I mean, I realize you're constrained by client confidentiality and all, but I've heard some disturbing rumors lately, and I've been concerned...I mean my office has had some disclosure concerns."

"Disclosure concerns?"

"Well, yes. The rumors involve the former Mrs. Deitzhoff, Harold's first wife, committing suicide on the property. And also," Rebecca takes a deep breath, "it's been said that Mr. Deitzhoff may have been involved in some shady goings on with the inmates at the women's prison."

Noah turns away from Rebecca and stares into the fire again. "Regarding the suicide, that was before my time, however, if it's true, I would advise disclosing." He looks back at Rebecca quizzically, "Tell me more about these alleged 'shady goings on'."

Rebecca winces at the sound of driving hail pelting the house and says, "The story is, that he may have been running a prostitution ring with the girls at the prison."

Noah pauses, then asks, "Against their will?"

His question takes Rebecca aback. "Of course," she answers indignantly, and stops to reflect a bit. Pine branches are flailing, rubbing against each other, squeaking, beating on the roof, banging against the shingles. She squirms a little, irritably. "Well, who knows? But it was wrong in any case; he was in a position of ultimate authority and power. They had no free will! And there was a child living here at the time, his daughter. Did you know she disappeared?"

Noah ignores the last question and begins what sounds to Rebecca like a lecture. "Let's look at this logically, Rebecca. First, how would he have managed such an enterprise? He would have required a reasonable explanation for taking the women out of the prison. And precisely where would these illicit encounters have taken place? And to what possible end?" He regards Rebecca with a self-satisfied look that Rebecca finds deeply annoying.

"Well, looking at it *logically*, I'd say he was in a position to manage it quite well. He did have a plausible excuse for taking the girls out, he even published some papers on it, I think it was called "Respite Therapy" or something like that. Some people around here thought he was some kind of healer, that he was doing the girls a huge favor. But I've heard otherwise, that something really bad was going on and maybe he was going to be exposed." Rebecca looks sharply at Noah. "There was a murder at the prison around that same time." She wants to shock him, wants to see him caught off guard, knocked off his high horse.

Noah seems disinterested, shrugs. "Even if it were true, it was long ago, and it is irrelevant to your disclosure issue. I have no knowledge of a murder; as I said, it was before my time. But you have little to worry about. Unless your buyers are particularly skittish, I wouldn't think it would affect the sale."

Noah studies Rebecca, but his face remains annoyingly noncommittal. Rebecca doesn't think it's a deliberate façade, she thinks he really doesn't know anything about it. Still, she feels almost patronized. "Tell me something," she says pointedly, "if you were aware of Mr. Deitzhoff's involvement in some detestable wrongdoing, would you be so inclined to represent him in other matters?"

"On principle, yes," he answers, then laughs, "principal, interest and taxes." He sees the surprised look on Rebecca's face and says, "Come on Rebecca, I have to pay the mortgage too." And he does a strange thing. He reaches out and smoothes down her tousled hair then runs his hand across her shoulder to the back of her neck and squeezes. The warmth from his hand spreads, encircling her neck and making her face flush.

The room has become overly warm from the fire and Noah looks at Rebecca intently. It is a look that she feels hard pressed to turn away from; its intensity draws her in until she only wants to look at his lips as they slowly move towards hers. Noah still has his hand at the back of her neck and he applies only the slightest pressure, which is enough to keep her in place. Rebecca has time to study his mouth, the way it curves up promising sweetness, time to anticipate the weight of it on hers, its heat, consistency, firmness. All these things are worthy of deep consideration; in these few long moments, nothing else is. When he kisses her, it's too soft and she has to kiss him back to show him how. It's a thing she's always had to do because Rebecca can really kiss.

Most boys, and men, don't quite get it right; it's either mushy and too wet, or hard and stingy. They suck up your lips like a twister, or they roll their heads around like they're grinding corn. So when they're done, Rebecca moves back a little, assesses the situation, tips her head to the side and rubs her lips against theirs, coaxing their lips to part just a little, kissing them firmly, expertly, lingering until the pressure is just right and the timing; until they get it.

Rebecca teaches Noah Hanes how to kiss. It's so warm in here and he is so eager to learn. His hand moves to the back of her head. The other is on her back pulling her towards him. It's been a long time since Rebecca has been kissed, a very long time since someone has surprised her with his desire. She places her hands on the tops of his shoulders and his hands under her blouse along her ribcage. He slides one hand beside her breast running his thumb across the nipple under her bra. She draws her breath in sharply, shocked at how much she wants it. Whatever he wants to do, she's starving for it. It all seems so remarkably easy and she's savoring the thought of dropping back against the coats, looking forward to the push of him inside of her. I am a married woman she reminds herself, this is shameful, bad. She puts her arms around his shoulders, reaches her tongue between his lips as he slides his hands along her thighs, moving her skirt up, kissing her neck, unbuttoning her blouse. Noah mumbles something into her throat, and Rebecca reaches down and unzips him, needing to feel him hard in her hands.

Something nags at her, a voice in the background, a warning. She hears knocking coming from upstairs. It stops her cold.

"What's wrong," Noah breathes.

"Did you hear that?" Rebecca pulls back, listens carefully. Noah looks confused, his brows come together and his forehead develops beads of sweat. "There it is again," she tells him. A sound, like someone's banging on a door to get out. She stands up, tugs down her skirt, pulls her blouse together as she rushes off.

"Where are you going?" Noah calls after her, but Rebecca is already headed upstairs. She takes a sharp right at the top of the landing and charges down the hall and into the Deitzhoffs' old bedroom; rain and pine needles are pummeling the screen, the floor is puddled and the shade is knocking frantically against the sill. She steps around the puddle, a wet wind gusts into her face and across her chest as she leans forward to slam the window shut. She turns to find Noah standing in the doorway. Her blouse has nearly blown off, her bra is soaked through and Noah is standing in the doorway watching her breasts as she walks towards him. He is not very tall, she doesn't have to lean back to look him in the face and there is something both reassuring and compelling about that.

Noah doesn't say a word, but takes hold of her arms and kisses her hard, emboldened by the presence of the bed Rebecca guesses. She kisses him back but she's thinking, I'll never let him screw me on that bed. He puts his arms around her, she can feel him hard against her. He lowers his hands to her bottom and presses her to him, slides her skirt up and runs his hand around the front teasing the heat between her legs, rubbing and squeezing until she makes a little noise. He pushes down her bra strap, tugs down the fabric and kisses his way down her neck, his lips greedy for her breast. She begins to think maybe it wouldn't be so bad to get laid on Deitzhoff's bed, when there is another deafening crack, like the splitting of an atom, or the moon breaking in two. The house vibrates in protest sending the shade in Serena's room down the hall spiraling upward with a giant slap and there it sits, in plain view from the doorway–that goddamned owl, glaring at Rebecca–watching her not get laid.

Rebecca disentangles from Noah and tells him how sorry she is and "it's not a good time, not a good place." And, "I just can't right now." She apologizes while she buttons her blouse, pulls down her skirt. "I'm really sorry," she says brushing the hair away from her face, smoothing it down. Noah looks peeved, but nothing more; Rebecca is relieved.

He clears his throat and says, "No, you're right, you're right...of course," he says methodically tucking his shirt in all around.

"We should go. I think the storm is moving away, that bolt was probably a last hurrah." The light from the exposed window in Serena's room has illuminated the situation for Rebecca. She lets out a held breath and smiles ruefully at Noah's handsome face. She notices how sort of bland it is and too smooth, smooth as a boiled potato. Noah opens and closes his mouth a couple of times like a fish out of water, and Rebecca thinks maybe he's not as in command as she originally thought. She gives him time to buckle his belt before she turns her back and he trails her downstairs. She picks her coat off the floor and shakes it, wishing she could shake herself the same way, like a dog coming in from a swim, twisting her body until this close-call spirals off of her in a shower, evaporating like it never happened.

Yes, she can see him clearly now. He's Drew in a few years; colorless, odorless, tasteless like deadly gas–insidious. Rebecca wishes for invisibility but cannot feel the sheerness, the fading. She reaches for it, but it's gone.

The Forgotten Roses

Noah picks his coat up, brushes it off. "I'll call you," he says as if he's doing her a favor.

"I'm married." Rebecca replies, happy to have the excuse.

"You're not wearing a ring."

Rebecca's fingers fly to the spot where the ring should be and says, "Recently separated," because, after all it's true. He's standing there with his hands in his pockets and Rebecca nearly apologizes again, but stops herself. He looks uncertain, she feels remarkably solid. Rebecca begins to feel sorry for him.

I hope this is the one, Rebecca thinks, the "once burned, twice shy" one that she needed to get out of the way, because, God knows, I don't want another one like Drew. Probably the reason it was so easy to fall down with this one was that the two of them really are a lot alike.

We are attracted to the familiar. All we really own is our past. Good or bad, it is all ours and we return to it like a worn and accustomed path, no matter how rocky and filled with potholes. Rebecca feels like she just missed stepping into a pit, elated at the escape. The trick is to avoid tripping up again.

Rebecca opens the door to her Jeep and says, "I don't think I'm what you want," to poor, handsome Mr. Potato Head. "I am sorry," she tells him one last time because she really means it. She knows he is definitely not what she wants. As she starts the engine, she hears the beep of his alarm disengaging, but doesn't look back. The sky has cleared and she has a lot to do. Rebecca wonders where she can get her hands on a crowbar.

22

Journey

By the time Dana reaches the house on Farpath road, her blown-out, straightened-flat hair has sprung into a mass of curls; if she catches a glimpse of the corkscrews—fat as bananas—cascading down her back, she'll faint.

Fine wisps at her temples had begun to frizz in gentle fluffs like golden milkweed seeds when she'd left home this afternoon, the same way she got in, through the cellar window.

After she'd left that bunch of losers to sleep it off this morning, she had nowhere else to go. Luckily no one was at home, so she snuck in and fell asleep in the play corner in the basement. The easel was still there with broken nubs of pastel chalk left in the tray. So were the little table and chairs that Papa made where she and Lily used to sit molding clay into pretend food which Lily would feed to her dolls, or roll into long snakes that Dana would dangle from her nostrils and sneeze out onto the tea set with gusto. The beanbag chair smelled musty, but Dana immediately fell into a deep sleep. She never even knew there was a storm bearing down overhead.

When she woke up, she didn't want to go to Amy's, refused to go crawling back to her mother, and Corey...fuck him! So she began an odyssey which took her to several friends' houses and then out on her own again. She traced the quiet byways and winding side streets of Havenwood, avoiding the main road and its direct connections. And, she had avoided thinking about last night. It never once occurred to her to step outside Havenwood's borders; here you could be just as alone, just as hidden, just as lost as anywhere.

Dana hadn't had this much exercise since she quit field hockey and it felt good to stretch her muscles and push herself past cramps and fatigue. It felt great to be solitary and what was even better, what tasted as delicious as freedom, was that no one knew where she was. The back roads were quiet, peaceful. There were only a few times when an approaching car forced her to hide behind the bushes. She could have kept this up for days. Her mother thought she was at Amy's, the Connors thought she was back home; it couldn't have worked out better if she'd planned it. Although, there was one major problem approaching fast–the night.

She could hook up with one of her other friends and stay at their house, but it would be the same old shit: curfews, pain-in-the-ass parents, little brothers and sisters scurrying around like vermin. Unfortunately, the thought of dealing with her friends' parents made her think of her own.

Dana was crystal clear about what kind of an idiot her mother was, and didn't feel one bit remorseful about letting her know she could see right through all her bullshit, but whenever she thought about her father, she felt uncertain and irritable, like being put on the spot in class when you haven't got the answer. Dana thinks that her mother is, at best, a wimp. Going on and on about family and sticking together and blah, blah; constantly nagging and whining like a mosquito buzzing in your ear. Why can't she just shut the hell up? At least her father was quiet, or not around to bother her. At least he wasn't so fucking trite and stupid and hovering. He just thinks he's above it all, more important than God. Yeah, he's above it alright, a fucking space cadet, as far off as the man in the fucking moon, Dana thought, and if she'd had a mirror she would have seen that her face looked small and miserable as if someone had pinched her but she couldn't pinch back.

Dusk settled around her like a heavy heart. Keeping her eyes on the sky made it appear lighter longer, so she walked watching the cloud patterns and was shocked when the streets began to look unfamiliar, altered in the fading daylight. Dana felt, for the first time, afraid. She began to cast furtive, fretful glances behind her, startling at noises coming from the tangle of trees lining the road. The grass and weeds were clumped and plastered down, matted like the hair of witches and when another car passed, Dana didn't want to hide in the bushes with the scratchy, biting things that lived there.

She started to think about home and the story she could be concocting while heading for it. She wished she had just one friend with out of town parents this weekend. Why couldn't one of them be in the Bahamas, or the Berkshires or the Betty Ford Clinic? Then she remembered the empty house her mother just sold. Hadn't there been some old guy living there all alone? And didn't she hear her mother say that he was put in a nursing home? It was a house on Farpath Road, not too far from where she was standing with her options tightening around her neck. I'll bet it still has the For Sale sign out front, she thought.

Dana stopped to get her bearings; a hawk called from high above, circling, gliding, held aloft by the updraft of a thousand tremulous sighs from below. Dana added hers as she released all the uncertainty that had backed up into her lungs and, pivoting in her shoes, started towards Farpath Road. It's not perfect, but at least it's a plan, she thought. And that was enough to charge her up, quicken her steps and propel her forward like a good, stiff breeze at the back. She pulled an Almond Joy out of her pocket and took out one half, saving the other for later. It was so delicious that the hair over her forehead spiraled into ringlets that bounced to the steady rhythm of her steps.

❧

The Forgotten Roses

Over the past twenty-seven years, Honey Potts had been many things: a waitress, a housewife, an exotic dancer, and a bartender at a trendy Chicago bar. That's where she met Serena, on a day that was as hot and airless as only a summer day in Chicago can get. Serena came pouring through like quicksilver and drank two vodka tonics on the rocks in a row before she noticed Honey. Serena's scouring gaze lit on the tall lean girl with long hair the color of butterscotch and tits the size and shape of scud missiles.

The tits were compliments of Davie, Honey's former husband. If dumb was dirt, he'd cover about an acre. It was his life's ambition to own a couple of jugs like them provided they were attached to the right woman. Honey was the right woman until she slept with his sister and became the wrong woman. Honey felt really bad about that too, because even in Arkansas you shouldn't sleep with your husband's family members. But, Lord, she never planned it, it just happened, took her by surprise and turned her life inside out, which she guesses was probably a good thing.

After Davie threw her out, and her own family kind of disowned her, she found that the implants he'd bought her were as handy as a shirt pocket; way better than alimony or even a Ph.D. They were, in fact, *the* major factor in getting her a plum job as an exotic dancer for which she was paid better for dry humping a chrome pole four nights a week, twice on Saturdays, than she would've ever dreamed possible. She didn't even have to change her name like some of the girls did, although the manager suggested Roma Rockets, but she told him she liked her name just the fuck-ugly way it was. It was the only thing she owned at the time.

But, Honey got real tired of the unwanted attention of the club goers and her feet started to go bad from the spike heels. She took a day course in bartending, then flew as far north as she could get, landed in Chicago, and found *the* most perfect job. She could wear sneakers and had respect and friends and lovers all at once. Honey thought she was in heaven, but it was really a gay bar called Paris Dance located midway on Montrose between Broadway and Clark.

Then she met Serena who was on leave and Honey's life took another turn—which doesn't hardly feel one bit heavenly at the moment. On that day, which seems like ages ago, Serena came strolling in like a puma, all lazy and taut at the same time. The heat rising off her body filled the bar with the scent of cinnamon, and in the low light there her eyes glowed as she regarded the soft curve of Honey's hips, the charm of her long, shapely arms, the pulse at the base of her throat. Honey could barely breathe, as if all the oxygen had been replaced with the scent, the feel, and the want of Serena.

That was it. From that day on, Serena was Honey's obsession and she had been following Serena ever since from base to base and now here to Snottyville or Hatefulhood or some damn place. It's just a good goddamn thing that Serena put her up at the Marriott, because even obsession has its limits and if she had to bunk out on that godforsaken patch of scrub in that rotting outhouse one more second she would be g-o-n-e.

Truth be told, she couldn't say no to Serena—maybe she wouldn't dare. Serena's done a lot for her, taught her a lot, forgiven her a lot, and Honey would do anything for her in return, anything at all. That is why she parked the rental car, just as she was told, loaded up with a lot of smelly shit, about a mile down the creepy deserted street and is scrambling through wet bushes in the dark like a fucking possum, heading once again for the shack Serena refers to as the "little house." Honey thinks maybe she's embarking on yet another career, and fixing to turn another corner.

∾

The dusk is deepening, absorbing the day and replacing it with a cool, purple breeze that makes the leaves on the trees shiver as Dana walks up the brick path to Deitzhoff's. She stops to look up at the night sky; a ghostly ring circles the moon as if it's dissolving into the surrounding air. "Dog moon," Dana says recognizing the formation of ice crystals. That means it'll be cold tonight, and damp, she thinks. On nights like this, the woodland animals hold their breath and wait for what comes next.

Dana pushes the door open, feels along the wall for a light switch, and discovers the electricity has been cut off. There is just barely enough light left in the day to make out shapes and openings as she moves through the pressing silence of the living room and into the dining room where she finds candles and matches and a medieval looking candelabra that makes her think of Macbeth and of screwing her courage to it's sticking place. She lights the candles; long quivering shadows rise up along the walls and follow her upstairs. Dana is bone tired, too tired to pay attention to the creeps crawling up her back and relieved to find tidy beds and blankets waiting at each end of the hall even if the place has the overall stink of a public bathroom which reminds her that she has to pee. She opens a door in the middle of the hall and is grateful to find a bathroom there.

Afterwards, she steps into the bedroom with the pony lamp and, setting down the candelabra, examines the little desk, pulling each little drawer out and sliding it back in. She turns and peers into the darkened window, squinting, leaning forward to try and make out the odd shape see can just barely see. She moves closer and comes face to face with a pair of eyes as big and defiant as her own.

"What the f…who are *you*?" Dana asks out loud. She frowns hard at the bird and they glare at each other nose to nose through the glass for a while before Dana decides to open the window and invite the bird in. Once she gets the screen up, she leans through, puts her arms around the bird, and yanks. She feels it giving way, its resolve slipping. Dana yanks again and knows that it is hers, one more pull and it comes loose, the force of which propels them both backward on top of Serena Deitzhoff's old bed.

Dana sits up and pulls the bird towards her. She runs her hands along the cold surface, the sculpted feathers, the sharp beak. She shakes it, and something inside rattles. She examines the base, unscrews the bottom and a key falls out onto the bed. "Weird," Dana whispers and tucks the key into the pocket of her jeans.

The open window is letting the chill in; Dana tries to close it but it won't budge. "Oh, fuck it," she says and figures she and Big Bird will just close the door and move over to the other bedroom and take a little nap. She gets up, hugging Big Bird to her and notices the closet door in Serena's room is wide open. Inside there is a chair standing in the middle with books piled neatly onto the seat and a flashlight on top. "Weird as shit," she says and lays the heavy bird back down on the bed. She steps in, takes the flashlight and shines it up to the plywood covering. She wonders what could be up there that someone else wanted to get to and decides to see for herself. She pulls herself up into the opening easily and uses the flashlight to survey exactly what her mother had seen a few hours earlier. It's about twenty degrees warmer up in the attic and the air is dry, unlike the chilled, damp air streaming into the open window below. And it's cozy up here, Dana thinks; it reminds her of Nana Eva's attic, which was, before the yard sale, full of great old stuff. There was a chest, Nana called it a hope chest, that had Nana's satin wedding gown inside and her grandfather's scratchy wool army uniform pinned with cool looking medals. Dana asked him about the medals, she wanted him to tell her all about them and about the war and stuff, but he never did. Papa didn't like to talk much, Dana remembers. But he used to call her Papa's girl and buy her red licorice and popsicles and let her hand him his tools as he worked. Papa was always working. She liked the way he smelled of smoke, Ivory soap, and English Leather and the soft feel of worn flannel against her cheek. Dana misses him so much. She climbs back down to get the candelabra and matches just in case the flashlight batteries die, blows out the flames, then climbs back up, pulling the cover over the opening to keep out the cold. She leans—worn-out but warm at least—against the sagging boxes, matches in hand, props the flashlight so it shines a circle like yellow moonlight onto the rafters, while she nods off dreaming about her good old Papa.

❧

Serena is so mad all the color has drained from her face and she shines greenly like a glow-in-the-dark statue of the Blessed Virgin. She knows she has no one to blame but herself for this Mickey Mouse, half-assed job she and Honey are doing down in the basement of her childhood home.

"I'm getting this shit all over me," Honey whines and shakes her fingers, sending droplets of liquid splashing onto Serena.

"Will you watch what you're doing," Serena yells.

"Why don't you try filling the balloons; what I need is a funnel, this spout is too fucking big and I can't see what I'm doing. Shine the light over here more. Look, this isn't working, I can't tie off the ends, the balloons are too wet, and the ribbon is slippery now."

"For chrissakes, stop complaining and just do your fucking job! Christ! *Ribbon!* I told you to get string at the hardware store, can't you get anything right?"

"And *I* told *you* they were out of string, and it was getting late so I had to go the drug store and that was all they had." Honey wants to say more. She wants to tell Serena that she should be grateful for her help, and appreciative of her resourcefulness. If she says one more mean word to me, I'm out of here, Honey thinks. But when Serena keeps it up, Honey doesn't say anything, she just gets all closed down; her movements become slow and clumsy, and her eyes tear up which makes everything worse because she can't see how to fasten the balloons to the ceiling.

Serena doesn't notice Honey's distress because she's on a rip. Her eyes have flared phosphorescent making up for the inadequate glow of the flashlight. "Let me do that," Serena snaps at Honey. Serena gets up on a kitchen chair and begins tying gasoline-filled balloons to the metal grid that holds up the acoustical tiles across the ceiling. Serena heard from a firefighter friend that this was one of the ways arsonists do it: first, get some old tires and lay them on the floor, then tie balloons filled with gasoline to the ceiling over them. After you set the fire it will take a while to get going so you have time to get far away, the heat generated will eventually pop the balloons, accelerating the fire; the tires make it burn hotter. Serena wants the fire hot as damnation. She wants the house reduced to a fine ash that will blow over Havenwood and settle like snow onto the weathervanes, the sculpted lawns, the church steeples. And she wants to watch.

Honey waits as Serena finishes the job. And even though she's tired and nervous and her feelings are hurt, she stands there and sighs at the sight of Serena. With Serena's arms raised like that she looks like the Statue of Liberty, as solid and strong and as hard-headed too. Honey marvels at the way Serena always takes charge; it's one of the things Honey loves about her. Honey felt kind of drifty until she met Serena. Sometimes she feels like Serena's moon, kept in place in the Universe only by the gravitational force of Serena's will.

"There," Serena says climbing down, wiping her hands on her fatigues. "Now move the tires directly under the balloons. Get some more kindling under those logs in the corner before I light the fire. We should have plenty of time to get back up the hill to watch."

Just then, they both realize that they reek of gasoline, they have it on their clothes, and it has splashed onto their skin and hair. "Strip down," Serena commands, and the two peel off down to their shoes and throw their clothing into the corner over the firewood. They stand in the center of the workshop in the basement, their white flesh shimmering, illuminated by the glow of the flashlight at their feet. Serena looks Honey over and draws her fingertips down Honey's arm. Honey thinks it is a sad gesture. Then Serena strikes a match, takes one last look around the room, smiles at Honey and tosses the match onto their clothes. The fire catches with a hiss and Honey starts up the stairs.

Serena lingers to watch as the flames begin to consume the fabric and lick at the woodwork making black scorch marks and long snakes of smoke. Honey comes back down, grabs Serena's arm and pulls. "Come on, let's *go*," she pleads. Honey doesn't like the blank look in Serena's eyes; it frightens her and makes her mouth go dry. It's the same look Serena had when she burnt all the photos she could lay her hands on upstairs and then cleaned the fireplace out, washing the bricks down with a vengeance, as if even the soot was offensive. Serena is mesmerized by the sight of the fire gaining strength and Honey panics. "Come with me, Serena!" she shouts until Serena comes to, as if out of a dream, and allows Honey to lead her away. The two women run through the forest, wearing only their shoes, darting through the undergrowth like pale fish in a deep, dark sea, with only the night creatures as witness.

23

House

Living with that ice-cold prick all these years has driven me to commit foolish, heated deeds, Rebecca thinks. The whole day has been a mess from the very beginning. First, that close shave with Noah Hanes, the Drew clone, Rebecca shudders. Then the Green's offer on the Parker house didn't go as planned.

Rebecca was very close to closing the deal, but Mrs. Parker was peevish, dickering over minute portions of money and inconsequential terms. She just couldn't make a decision. And although Hannah's daughter had just been on the phone with Hannah begging her to come out to live with her, Rebecca could see that she wasn't convinced. Hannah had merely gone through the motions: did as she was advised, put the house on the market, let prospective buyers take a look, and agreed to the sale. But now, she was digging in her heels.

Sitting at Hannah's kitchen table, Rebecca smoothed the linen tablecloth in front of her. It was snow white, edged with embroidered cherries. Hannah served oatmeal cookies big enough for a meal and Earl Gray tea brewed from loose leaves. Her corgi, Tiggy, fat as a sausage, begged for crumbs at Hannah's feet and was obliged with cooing sounds and scratches under Tiggy's greyed muzzle. Rebecca rested her elbows on the table, her chin in her hands, and studied Hannah Parker as she went on about the geese that visit the frog pond out back and how as a little girl she wanted to fly like the geese, just fly away pointing south every winter and maybe that's finally what she should do after all. "Except Arizona isn't really south, although it is very hot and awfully dry, which would be good for the arthritis—that's what I've heard—but *terribly* far.

"I wish Mr. Parker were here because he always made the big decisions of course and Fridays are very inconvenient for the closing because I visit his grave every Friday after breakfast, just over the hill at Oak Grove cemetery. Isn't a lovely place! Who will plant the geraniums at his stone on Memorial Day if I'm not here? I love the pink but he favored the red; so red it is."

Her skin is translucent; bumpy blue veins snake up her arms like tributaries. A cloud of hair, the color of doves, is pulled into a loose knot on the top of her head, like a Gibson girl, Rebecca thinks. She must have been quite pretty once.

Hannah's voice was small but quite clear and firm, as was her stride around the kitchen reaching for honey, her favorite English bone china cups, the good napkins. Her hands trembled ever so slightly though, when she set down the saucers and Rebecca thought of her father's big rough hands. He was always annoyed and out of reach, but he built wonderful things for his family with his hands: entire additions, total household renovations for Eva, but also an enormous dollhouse including beds carved with tiny hearts, a kid-size table with four chairs, so sturdy you could dance on them—and they did. He fixed our bikes and later repaired our cars, Rebecca reminisced. If you asked Rebecca now, she would say, "of course he loved us kids." Back then they just tried to stay out of his way. When his hands started to tremble, like Mrs. Parkers, it broke Rebecca's heart.

"Hannah," Rebecca broke in finally, looking into her eyes. "We can always change the day of the closing. All of these other things…" Rebecca passed her hands over the pages of the agreement spread out on the table. "They are just minor details that can be ironed out. You are in charge here Hannah," Rebecca told her. "There is only one thing that you have to decide…not for the Greens, and not for your daughter–for *yourself*, Hannah. Do you want to sell your home?" Rebecca already knew the answer, but she wanted Hannah to declare it, to own it.

Hannah folded her wrinkled hands on the table and looked down at them for a long time. Rebecca placed her hand on Hannah's and met Hannah's gaze when she finally picked up her head and said, quite defiantly, "No, I'm just not ready."

Rebecca knew she could wear Hannah down. There were many rational reasons in favor of the move: her health, her daughter, the burden of home maintenance, the long winter months. Rebecca could have called on Hannah's daughter to press Hannah further, and she could have marched the specter of Josh, Jill and T.J.'s disappointed little faces before her. But, even before Rebecca decided to ask her the question outright, she had known what Hannah's answer would be. Because she had read Hannah's tealeaves too. Rebecca wanted Hannah to have the last word this time.

"Okay then, lets have another cup and I'll call the Greens and tell them they wouldn't want to live in Havenwood without Hannah Parker in it anyway. Don't worry, I'll find another house for them in no time. And you can always spend winters with your daughter in Arizona. How does that sound?"

If she were dead, Tandy would be spinning in her grave; in fact, that just might kill her. Probably Sophia was spinning in her seat on her layover in L.A. from bad vibes received through the psychic network. Maybe I'll be fired, she thought. Maybe I don't care.

And now, here I am stealing into this godforsaken house to retrieve that dirty old box as if it was a lifeline, Rebecca thinks. That is what comes from staying too long in a dead marriage. "I stayed too long," she says to the house as she enters and feels in her raincoat pocket for the flashlight. "Damn! Where the heck is it?" She decides to leave the door open and try to make her way to the refrigerator anyway when she suddenly remembers where she left the flashlight. Moonlight from the open door is lighting the stairwell, she might just as well go upstairs and get it, as go bumping and tripping through the living and dining rooms in the pitch black. She can still smell the smoke from the fire Noah lit this afternoon, it's probably smoldering a little.

Upstairs Rebecca stretches her arms out feeling along the hallway walls with her fingertips, staring ahead blindly until her eyes make out the open window in Serena's room. As she draws closer, she feels the air coming in, sees the moonlight through the empty open square, and... No bird! She steps to the window and leans out to see if it has fallen to the ground, steps back and tries to close the window but it's stuck. She bangs the sash with the heels of her hands; it won't budge. "Shit," she says, turns to the closet and startles when she sees the prostrate form of the gutted owl on the bed, its entrails hanging out on the coverlet. "*Jesus, Mary and Saint Joseph!*" she gasps.

Rebecca hears stirring from the attic and a tremulous "Mom?" causing Rebecca to suck in her breath and stumble back towards the window.

"Mom?" It's louder, and clattering is coming from the closet. Rebecca rushes up and flings the closet door open wide to see blue jeaned legs dangling from the opening above.

Dana drops down in front of her. "*Dana*" Rebecca shrieks. "What in God's name..."

"Listen Mom, we'd better get out of here," Dana whispers stepping hastily over books toppled from the chair. "I heard voices here just a little while ago. I think they were women, but they were arguing and it sounded bad."

Rebecca hears Dana talking but she's not registering a thing Dana is saying. "Why are you here Dana?" she shakes Dana by the shoulders. "What are you doing here?"

"*Mom*" Dana shouts. "Listen to me! There were people here yelling, they just left I think, did you see them... Wait a minute, did you hear that?"

They stop and holding each other by the elbows, listen with cocked heads. There is a loud pop, followed by another. "Was that a gunshot?" Dana asks.

"I don't think so. No of course not, but you're right. Let's get out." Then Rebecca remembers the box and tells Dana, "Get in the car and lock the doors, I just have to get something."

Dana looks at her mother wild-eyed, like she's lost her head, as they start down the hallway, but Rebecca pushes her on from behind. "Hurry, hurry," she tells Dana as they fly down the stairs—there is smoke everywhere.

"Oh God! Oh no!" The fire Noah lit this afternoon, it must have flared up, Rebecca thinks. "My cell's in the car. Call 911!" she tells Dana and pushes her out the front door before she runs into the kitchen to retrieve the box from the refrigerator. There is noise coming from below, a crackling roar, as if there's something angry down there. Black ribbons of smoke are squeezing out from all around the door to the basement and Rebecca begins to cough uncontrollably as she grabs for the box. An explosion shakes the bowels of the house and Rebecca drops the box and trips on it, stepping hard on the dent in the middle. The back hinge comes loose, a corner pops open and a few small things fall out; she drops to her knees fumbling with the box. As she gets up, to her horror more things drop out; something small and rectangular, the tinkle of keys hitting the floor. She is wheezing, her eyes sting and water, her nose is running; she manages to get to her feet hugging the box to her chest and with great effort makes for the open front door.

By the time she stumbles outside, she can barely breathe and realizes just what they mean on the news when they say someone succumbed to smoke inhalation. Her head hangs down like a sick dog's as she hacks and chokes, and when she picks it up again, wiping her nose on her sleeve, she finds Dana standing a few steps away with someone's arm locked around her neck.

Dana is tall but this woman dwarfs her, immobilizes her easily, casually almost. Dana tries to say something but the woman cinches in her arm and cuts her off. Rebecca steps forward reflexively, and the woman pulls back, dragging Dana with her. "What're you *doing?*" Rebecca asks in desperation, her mind spinning. "What do you *want?*" she shouts.

"What do you have there?" the giant woman asks.

Rebecca is confused for a second and follows the woman's gaze to the box in her arms.

"It looks like a safe deposit box to me. Toss it over."

The voice is sweet as candy. It drills fear into Rebecca; she looks around, casting about for familiar landmarks, something to ground her to reality. Is this a nightmare, another bizarre dream, she wonders? Dana's eyes flash from terror to rage and back again. Rebecca wonders what kind of struggle went on between the two of them before she came out.

"Let go of her, and I'll give it to you," Rebecca tells the woman, trying to keep her voice even, clenching her teeth so they don't chatter.

The woman raises her eyebrows and one side of her mouth curls up in a quasi-smile. "I'll keep both thanks," she says and snorts out a short laugh. "Honey, *honeee…*," she begins to call.

She's crazy. She's standing in the dark with electric hair rising off her head, gripping my daughter, my baby, calling for honey into the night sky. I will kill her. I'll bash her head in with this box and make bloody, clotted pools of those empty godforsaken eyes, she decides.

Someone steps out of the woods behind Dana and the crazy giant bitch. A beautiful young woman walks slowly towards the group. She stops to shake a stone out of her shoe then saunters closer, hesitantly. She is dressed only in a big, loose sweater; her bare legs are as long as a willow tree. Rebecca watches transfixed at the approach of this strange vision. The crazy woman senses the vision is close behind and says, "Take that fucking thing from her."

The vision moves shyly toward Rebecca and looks back at the crazy woman. "Go ahead," she commands. Honey reaches for the box but Rebecca sidesteps out of her way. "What the fuck," the crazy woman says infuriated. Honey shrugs apologetically and tries again.

Rebecca's head has cleared a bit. She has only one thought, getting Dana back. She has only one tool, one weapon. She glares at Honey and jerks away from her gripping the box closer; Honey gives up–as Rebecca thought she might–and slides off towards the crazy woman. Rebecca lowers her head, aims her eyes at the women, latches on, and moves off into a shadow pocket.

"Cut that shit out," the woman yells at Rebecca. "I don't have time for this bullshit!"

"There's a fire, we should call someone," Rebecca speaks up trying to sound reasonable, as if this is a perfectly normal evening and they should all behave logically. She's using the time that this woman doesn't have much of. If she wants what I've got, she'll have to let go of Dana to get it, she determines.

Serena throws her head back and forces out a laugh, hollow and mirthless. She elbows Honey and says, "That's funny isn't it." Honey doesn't look amused. "What do we do now," she whispers loudly.

"Let go of my daughter," Rebecca's hard, flat voice shoots out from the shadows pricking the woman like a splinter of ice.

"Humpf," Serena grunts. Your *daughter*…you mean this little trespasser?" Time ticks slowly by. Rebecca knows the woman is weighing her options, just as she is weighing hers. Neither one has many. Smoke fills the air, floating like a veil in front of Rebecca, fully concealing her. Her heart is beating hard, but steadily. She observes the woman shift her weight from one foot to the other, glance at Honey, kick the dirt. Rebecca waits.

The Forgotten Roses

"I'm running out of patience…" the woman calls out. But her voice is tentative now; she's running out of that time that she needs so much, Rebecca concludes.

"*Mom*," Dana cries out and Rebecca steps out of the shadow as Dana runs to her. Rebecca heaves the box towards the woman, but she doesn't stop to get it, instead she leaps over it to Rebecca and grabs her by the arm sneering. "Honey, get that fucking thing while I have a talk with *Mom*," she says derisively.

"We are going up the hill to a spot I have waiting," she tells Rebecca. Are you listening to me?" she says pulling then pushing Rebecca while Rebecca clutches Dana to her. "I will let you go, but not yet. This one," she tosses her head toward Dana, "better not cause me any trouble. I'm here to…finish a job," she says, "nothing more. Am I getting through to you?

"Honey," she calls.

Honey doubles back to them and falls behind, carrying the box under one arm trailing them: Rebecca and Dana hand in hand, and the crazy giant bitch dragging them through the forest. Rebecca is assessing her odds again; I'll be damned if I'll allow Dana to be taken to a remote location where there might be guns or other crazy people, she thinks grinding her teeth. I will pretend to twist an ankle, fall to the ground, pull the legs out from under that bitch, hold on, sink teeth down to bone; Dana could run. These women have the longest goddamn legs I've ever seen and they seem to know their way around these woods, but I'll take the chance she decides. Dana can make it.

"Hold up," the crazy woman tells them. Rebecca's muscles tense; this might be a good chance for Dana to get away, we are still close enough to the house, she could get to the road… The woman levels her eyes like shotguns at Rebecca, as if she can read Rebecca's mind and says, "Just relax, Mom. I'm only trying to buy time. I don't want to detain you two any longer than necessary, believe me."

Honey pipes up, "Don't worry, she won't hurt you."

Rebecca wonders if she should believe it. She thinks the only thing that might be true is that Honey wouldn't hurt them; she seems to be a reluctant accomplice to whatever this is. They don't appear to have any weapons; the most deadly weapon here is that damn strong box I brought them, she realizes glumly. They probably think it's full of valuables. Rebecca decides this is it; she will not allow Dana to be controlled by them any longer, and turns to Dana but before she can tell her to run, that son of a bitch woman pushes down on the tops of Dana's shoulders forcing her to sit, dragging Rebecca down with her. "Shit," Rebecca says angrily between gritted teeth.

"Do you have any idea who you're dealing with?" the woman says threateningly looming over them with her hands on her narrow hips.

"How would I know?" Rebecca snaps bitterly, but as soon as the words pass her lips, it hits her like a slap in the face. She'd been so muddled with fear, so occupied with Dana…stupid, stupid, she reprimands herself. Of course; the hair, the eyes…the *box*. "*Jesus*… you're Serena Deitzhoff."

Serena actually looks caught off guard, her mouth pops open and Rebecca seizes this upturn telling her, "I'm a good friend of Francis Sullivan's. He told me a lot about you."

"Sully?" she says almost dreamily. She squats down and asks Rebecca, "He told you about me? Why?"

Rebecca gets a glimpse of relief. She feels as if she stepped out of a boggy swamp onto a solid path. Still, there's no end in sight to this strange journey. "I'd heard rumors about the house, about your father and about…things…that might have happened there."

Serena stands back up. Peers out into the forest squinting in the direction of the house, and says, "Look, I'm not interested in causing you any discomfort. I only need time, a little more time. You can't go until I'm finished, can you understand that? Just let me finish," she says spreading her hands out, pleading.

"Finish what?"

Serena scowls down at her and says to Honey without taking her eyes off Rebecca, "Go back down and get...what's your name?"

"Rebecca."

"Get Rebecca's car and drive it around to where I showed you." She pulls car keys–wrestled from Dana earlier–out of her pocket and hands them to Honey. "Rebecca and I are going to talk. Take the girl with you."

"No," Rebecca shoots up face to face with Serena. "No, Dana's staying with me."

Serena hesitates and says, "Fine. But she better not give me any shit. I know her type," she says glaring at Dana. They all watch as Honey slips back into the brush muttering to herself disappearing into the dark ocean of night. "This way," Serena tells Rebecca gesturing to a path leading further into the forest.

They walk quickly, silently until they come to a dip in the hill; up ahead is a small log cabin. Dana and her mother are still holding hands as they walk through the door with Serena behind telling them to watch their step. Rebecca's foot bumps into something and when an oil lamp is lit, she sees that it is a tire. She looks around at the mix of ramshackle furniture and state-of-the-art camping gear packed into the cramped space.

"Have a seat," Serena nods towards a little iron bed and Dana and Rebecca sit down gingerly for fear of it collapsing under them. Rebecca sits close to Dana, with her side pressed against Dana's in reassurance.

Serena looks out the window and says triumphantly, "Flames!" She turns to Rebecca and announces, "It won't be long now." She seems lighthearted, energized, leans against the sill with her back to the window, crosses her legs at the ankle, and asks, "So what did Sully tell you exactly?"

"He said you were best friends as kids. He thinks about you, worries about you, wonders if he could've been a better friend. Prevented you from leaving maybe. He feels guilty."

Serena is crestfallen. "Sully was great. I think about him a lot. He couldn't have done anything. We were just kids…. Tell him…tell him you saw me, okay? But not about this. " She drops her voice. "You know you can't tell anyone about this," she says gesturing behind her, nailing Rebecca with her eyes in an unspoken threat.

"Tell him I'm…fine, and I think about him too, and he was…the best. Would you tell him that for me? Please?"

She's asking for a favor while she's keeping me and my daughter captive and burns down my listing. That's a good sign. "I'll tell him," she promises.

Serena actually appears grateful, somehow satisfied with the whole situation. "I've got to finish up, just sit there, it won't be much longer and we'll meet up with Honey and you can go. Understand? I couldn't let you call the fire department, obviously. I couldn't let you leave. You understand that don't you?"

Rebecca doesn't answer, still not trusting her completely. Dana, who has been silent as a stone, snaps "Just let us go then, we won't tell anyone," her voice a bit tremulous. Rebecca puts her arm around Dana, gives her a hug and tells her, "It's okay, a friend of Sully's wouldn't hurt you."

"That's right kid, listen to your mother. Now shut the fuck up." Serena begins to haul tires around the cabin and says to Rebecca, "Tell me what you've heard."

Rebecca begins hesitantly, "I heard that your mother committed suicide in the house." She stops, waiting for her reaction; there is none.

"Yeah, go ahead," Serena says as she keeps busy filling balloons from the gasoline can.

"Sully told me there were rumors that your father took the girls out of the prison to run some kind of prostitution ring…or something."

"Yeah…he took them here," she tells Rebecca distractedly, scanning the cabin. "Anything else?"

Rebecca pauses, takes in a big gulp of air and holds it as if she's about to dive, headlong, into a deep well, unchartered waters. "Someone died at the prison around that time; one of the inmates—a distant relative of mine. The official story was that she killed herself, but there were others who thought she was murdered because of something she was going to tell."

This last bit of information makes Serena stop hauling chairs around; she sits down on one and repeats, "One of the girl's killed herself."

"Or was murdered."

"Murdered," she repeats as if she's trying the word out. "Murdered," she chews on it, rolls it around her mouth, tasting it. Her face hardens all over and looks grim. She glares at Rebecca as if she were the one who may have murdered someone, and turns to climb back on the chair to finish attaching the gasoline bombs to the ceiling.

"Is it true?" Rebecca asks. Dana elbows Rebecca and whispers in her ear, "Mom, *don't*; you're making her mad."

Serena gets down from the chair and grabs binoculars off the table, looks out the window, waves Rebecca over and hands her the glasses. Rebecca looks through them to see fiery horns coming out of each of the second floor bedroom windows. Rebecca hands the binoculars back and Serena takes them telling her, "My father used everyone."

"I heard those girls late at night; he took them here. There were voices. Men's voices. I heard crying. Sometimes I heard laughter, sometimes the girls would laugh." She says, mostly to herself, drawing memories up to the surface, as she looks out the window.

"Someone else told me that your father was a saint. That he helped the girls, and that he was misunderstood."

"Really," she sneers. "Misunderstood," she repeats. Serena snaps her head around to Rebecca and says caustically, "I'll tell you what he was… arrogant and devious. A manipulator; twisting the truth to satisfy his own agenda." Serena turns back to the window. "And heartless."

Rebecca shivers, suddenly feeling dampness and gloom wrapping all around her, squeezing the warmth out of her flesh. "Sully was afraid your father may have hurt you when you were a child." How twilight zone to be standing shoulder to elbow with Serena Deitzhoff like sisters, chatting away about misery and destruction.

Serena knits her brows, "Molested you mean?" She looks out through the binoculars once again saying, "No, he never touched my body…in any way. Just screwed with my head…and my mother's. He might as well have been the one that pulled the trigger; it's his fault she killed herself. He may have had the same affect on others; the dead girl for instance."

Rebecca mulls over what Serena has been saying. "Serena, do you know for sure what happened here? Did you actually ever see any of the inmates? Do you have any evidence that your father did anything… *illegal* with the girls? Dana groans from the bed, shakes her head in disbelief at her mother, drops her head into her hands.

Serena glares at Rebecca, parts her lips over her teeth in what, on anyone else, might be considered a smile, on Serena it looked like a threat. There is no need for binoculars to see the flames down below, a red glow shines through the window and reflects onto Serena's face.

"It's time," she says. "Get out," she orders Dana.

Dana startles and looks to Rebecca. "Step outside the door sweetie. Wait there. I'll be right out," Rebecca tells her.

"Help me do this," Serena asks Rebecca quietly. It is a request, not a command. She waits for a reply and Rebecca tells her, "all right."

Rebecca pushes the last tire under the balloons. She throws whatever she can find into the knapsack, picks up the bedroll and tosses both out the door to Dana. She holds onto the oil lamp, while Serena begins to pour gasoline over the bed, the table, the woodpile, the walls. Serena's feet are sole deep in puddles, but she keeps pouring as Rebecca stands in the open doorway waiting for her to finish. Serena finally takes the oil lamp from Rebecca, backs through the doorway and flings it against the back wall with all her might. Rebecca sucks down the cold night air in shock, in satisfaction at the burst of flames that skitter across the floor in a blue streaked whoosh. For the possibility of it, she thinks. For the girls... For Rose.

Serena hesitates outside the door for only a moment before she turns, tears the backpack from Dana's hands, quickly looping it on, grabs the bedroll and takes off through the woods at a trot, with Dana and Rebecca frantically trying to keep up. Rebecca considers taking off with Dana in a different direction, but decides it would be too dangerous to try to find a way through what is rapidly becoming a forest fire.

They continue running, crouched down, fighting off whipping branches, ignoring stinging nettles and thorns that tear at their legs. They have lost sight of Serena and can only follow the fading sound of her crashing through the brush. Rebecca straightens up, turns back to Dana and takes her arm telling her, "It's okay, slow down. We don't have any reason to run."

Dana shoots her a look again like her mother has lost her mind and twists around frantically as if someone's chasing her.

"*Dana,*" Rebecca says sharply, then more softly, "Dana." Dana's eyes focus on Rebecca's and clear. Rebecca notices Dana's face is scratched and her hair fans out around her head, straightened and littered with leaves and bits of twigs. Rebecca loops her arm through Dana's and says, "Remember when you were very little and we were going to do something different, something we'd never done before, you'd climb into the car and announce, 'We're going on a bold a-benture!' You were always looking for adventure." Rebecca tells her and smiles encouragingly into her face.

"So that's what this is," Dana says sarcastically. She looks all around, through the trees, up at the sky, and back to Rebecca. "I think I can find the way out," she tells her mother and Rebecca lets her lead the way. They take deep, breaths, exhaling long and slow—just like Lily showed them—as they continue forward together.

24

Home

In the distance sirens wail. Rebecca and Dana stop and listen. Dana's eyes are large and luminous, absorbing the mysteries of the dark like the night creatures who watch them pass. Slowly, very carefully, they continue to pick their way through the undergrowth. These woods are laced with riding trails, if only they could stumble on one, they might make better time and be assured of arriving at civilization in the near future. Serena has abandoned them. But fear no longer accompanies them either. It's just the two of them; when Dana stops, Rebecca stops. When Rebecca listens, Dana listens; they look upward simultaneously at the leafy mesh of canopy, the sharp sparkle of stars across a coal black sky. Nearby, an owl swoops by on her way to a meal; its call ripples like nervous laughter and, as one, they move toward the sound.

The clouds have escaped. The air is autumn clear and sharply chilled; noises Rebecca and Dana make as they walk bounce against it vibrating through them like the tap of metal against glass. Each crunch of leaves under their feet sounds too loud; each call of a wild thing echoes. They make their way with great deliberation, noticing which way the breeze is blowing, which direction the scent of smoke is strongest, the change in smells, sometimes dense and pungent as droppings, or sweet and tentative as baby's breath. They close their eyes against the confusion of trees, try to sense the way out. They want to be certain not to double back to where they once were.

Rebecca knows where Serena was headed. Farpath Road leads to Old Farm Lane which curves around to Maidenfern Way; it is a circle. The Deitzhoff property, when viewed from assessor's maps, or from heaven above, forms a pie slice that cuts across the center up one side of the hill, down to the other. Rebecca feels certain they are heading for the narrow point that comes out on Old Farm Lane bordering neighboring Warington.

Mother and daughter arrive at the top of the hill at last; relieved to be at any destination intact and hoping it is a half-way point at least. When they look down, the Deitzhoff house is engulfed, nothing left but fuel for the flames. And a blazing path leading to what was once the little cabin. The clear night air carries the noise of commotion to their ears. There must be firefighters from five towns to help Havenwood's volunteer force. Row after row of pine burst into fiery beacons. Sparks fly into the sky like souls racing to heaven.

Rebecca and Dana worry together about the trees. They shake their heads, gasp and wince, but they watch, as Serena herself would, with admiration at the power of the fire. There will be little remaining of the two houses linked by a long black scar along the ground that will soon heal over. Falling leaves carried by autumn winds will drift onto the scorched earth. Soon the first snowflakes will flutter down, covering the wound, pressing secrets between the layers of each snowfall like dried flowers between pages of a book. And when spring comes, tender grass will emerge; by summer the forest will begin to reclaim the hill; as if the houses never existed at all.

The full moon lights their way, but it is a rocky climb down and Rebecca stumbles often; Dana seems to be perfectly at home in the lead, going at a brisk clip, head up. "Are you all right?" she asks Rebecca over her shoulder; then pauses and extends a hand. Rebecca tells her, "I'm fine," but takes her hand gratefully and presses it to her heart before letting go. She watches Dana march ahead, the determination of her walk, the confident swing of her arms. At this moment, Dana owns the forest. She is as sure as the owl winging through and this gives Rebecca some comfort as if this moment was a gift, a vision of Dana's future – a promise.

The trees are becoming smaller but more densely packed; young white-pine saplings with slender, pliant branches cause Rebecca and Dana to lift their arms in front of their faces like plow blades. They feel the brush of soft needles like a caress up and down the length of their bodies. They swim through this green sea; millions of tiny little fingers dust off their clothes, comb through their hair, scratching their skin like the nails of newborns, buffing their ears, their cheeks, until they shine and blush. And just as it becomes clinging, unbearable, they come to a little clearing. Serena is there.

Serena's hair gleams under the bright glow of the moon. She is sitting on her haunches, wearing fatigues and army boots. Honey is nowhere in sight.

"What took you?" Serena asks.

"I thought you'd be long gone. Where's Honey?"

"Honey is exactly where she's supposed to be. She's the only person on this earth I can count on," Serena replies.

Dana skirts the edge of the clearing warily, like a young wolf, pacing. Serena appears to ignore her, but Rebecca notices a flicker at the corner of Serena's eyes as she tracks Dana's movements. "Didn't you hear the sirens?" Rebecca asks. Suddenly she feels afraid for Serena. An unbearable irony, if she were sent to prison.

"I heard them. Don't worry *mother*, my escape is well planned." She says this sarcastically, like Dana would, but there is a note of something else, a fondness almost. "I need to show you something."

It must be the box, what's inside. Rebecca steps up to her eagerly, "Where is it?"

"Where's what?" Serena says still squatting.

"The box. I thought you were going to show me what's in it."

Serena's face tightens, "I can't get the fucking thing all the way open yet. I never found the key." Then she stands up and says, "Don't you notice anything?" gesturing with her arm out as if she's introducing the trees. Rebecca fears that Serena might be crazy after all.

"Look around you. Look at what you're stepping on," Serena shouts.

Rebecca looks down at her feet and under them is a little plaque. She hops off as if it might singe her toes and kneels down to look. It says, Grace 1951. That's all. She looks up at Serena, "What is it," she asks.

Serena spreads her arms, shrugs at the sky asking for help, then squats down beside Rebecca and touches the plaque with her fingertips. "It's a marker, a grave marker."

"We're near Old Farm Road," Rebecca tells her. "The old cemetery for the women's prison is close by, this must be part of it."

Serena pulls Rebecca up by the arm and drags her around the clearing. She uses her boot to move tall grass back from a tiny granite half-moon that says Ester Ann, 1948, then leads Rebecca to a small, worn and pitted cement headstone etched with several names underneath a single carved word – "Infants." "These are not women; they are *babies*. Babies who died during the years my father worked at the prison. Born in captivity, buried in secret."

The stars in the skies have dropped and dangle before Rebecca's eyes. *Not again*...Christ, if I see a bright light, I just might walk towards it, she thinks. But in a moment the stars fade and she hears a deep sigh coming from the young pines as they nod in the breeze. Something unravels inside her, like a great knot slipping loose, breaking apart into tiny particles drifting away like a puff of dandelion seeds. Rebecca thinks about Rose, and dreams, and secrets turned to ash, and knows with a certainty why she is here.

"I'm sure there are other explanations," Dana blurts out and Serena looks like she could pound the girl into the ground until she's reduced to a blot the size of the markers that dot the little clearing.

"You tell me then, why are these babies here? Why aren't they part of the prison cemetery? I'll tell you what my *explanation* is. My father used those girls, some got pregnant. Babies died, were disposed of. I've lived inside the walls of that knowledge all my life; it tied me to this place, and now…now I'm free of it."

Dana steps close to Rebecca and leans heavily against her for support. "You don't know anything," she shouts at Serena vengefully, too tired to be afraid. "They were probably pregnant when they were locked up. Probably they lost the babies." Rebecca clutches a fistful of Dana's shirt and tugs hard to make her shut up as Serena steps up and pushes her face into Dana's. They stand, chin to chin, glaring at each other. Then Serena's gaze shifts, she peers into the woods beyond them, her face softening in recognition. Rebecca swirls around to see Honey stepping into the clearing cradling the box in her arms. They all watch, stock still, frozen in time as Honey walks shyly toward them, her long legs still bare, pale blue in the moonlight, tossing her hair over her shoulder with a flick of her head. These few moments seem in slow motion as Honey glides forward; they wait with held breaths as if she brings them their future. She comes straight to Serena and places the box at her feet like an offering. They form a circle around the box and all at once, kneel down to take a look. Serena holds Honey with her eyes, questioning until Dana's arm stretches out between them. She opens her palm and in the center is a little key. Serena snatches it as if it might disappear, as if it was never meant to be in Dana's hand at all, though not surprised that it is.

Once the lock falls away, they must hold the box down together while Serena pries the top loose with her fingers until it gives way with a grudging screech. She reaches her hand in but Rebecca places hers on Serena's arm. "Wait. I have to tell you. Some things fell out, I couldn't get them. The smoke, I couldn't breathe... I'm sorry."

Serena lifts packets squeezed together with thick darkened elastics, hands them to Honey. Serena scratches around at the few loose papers that remain at the bottom of the box, takes them out and looks them over.

"What are they?" Rebecca asks.

"I've seen this stuff before. Just some shit about his goddamn "Respite Therapy." There's nothing here for me. Nothing."

"What did you expect to find?" Rebecca questions softly.

"Answers," Serena says curling her lips into a sneer. "Get some of that 'closure' you hear so much about," she huffs derisively.

"You know, Rebecca, like 'The End' in a storybook," she says finally, in weary resignation. Serena stands up abruptly and the rest follow. She turns her back and walks off while the bewildered trio exchanges wide eyed looks. Suddenly, she turns and sprints forward, raises her arms straight out on each side like a football player and kicks the empty box high into the air. They watch it land on the far side of the clearing, the way the metal glints in the moonlight as it rolls, tumbling away, enveloped finally by the forest. "The end," she says.

Honey puts her arm around Serena's shoulder and they touch their foreheads together briefly before walking away. After a few steps, they turn back around as if a single unit. Serena takes one last look at Dana and shakes her head. "Don't blow it," she warns Dana, and in a few long strides, they vanish like moonbeams at dawn.

The Forgotten Roses

Rebecca and Dana stand hunched together, disheveled, looking around like a couple of immigrants who have finally stepped off the boat onto a foreign land after a long, treacherous voyage. Dana plucks at her mother's sleeve. "Do you believe her Mom? What she said I mean, about this being a baby cemetery and all?"

Rebecca scans the little clearing, closes her eyes a moment before speaking. "I think I do. I do." What she doesn't say and will keep to herself, is that she believes Rose led them here.

Dana is disgruntled, stoops down to look at a marker, picks up a rock and throws it as she gets up. "I can't. There must be some way to find out, investigate, dig up the truth somehow."

Rebecca nods, acknowledging Dana's feelings, and tells her, "We can try if you want. But sometimes it's not always possible to know a thing without a doubt. Sometimes all you're left with is getting beyond the uncertainty and moving forward. Trusting yourself... your instincts... Sometimes your head can't explain what your heart already knows." Rebecca tells these things to Dana, but she also hears the echo of her own decisions ring in her ears and likes the way it sounds.

Dana's eyebrows come together swift as arrows. Rebecca knows her answer was too foggy for Dana. At this stage, Dana's life is full of hard edges and sharp angles. They jab her like barbs, until she grows her own in self-defense. For now, Dana prefers it this way; she feels their point, tastes the blood that spills, gratified by its sure path. Maybe it's what keeps her from becoming invisible. Some day Dana may learn to surrender, but not today.

Dana sits down again in front of a granite square no bigger than a child's fist. Her hair falls forward covering her face, concealing her feelings. Rebecca sits down next to her. She touches the soft bend of Dana's head, following the curve with her hand the way she used to when Dana was little, when she'd let Rebecca do that sort of thing

– when she liked it. It's funny what happens to girls once they close childhood's door. Some fold their wings down tight to fit in the small spaces provided for them, others get mad and grow thorns. Some girls go bad, get even.

Rebecca rubs Dana's back, pats her own sweet baby and says, "If you want to, we can try to find out," knowing that sometimes it's not the answer you need after all, it's the search. Rebecca tucks Dana's hair behind her ear and Dana turns her gaze, unclouded as the night's sky, toward Rebecca.

"Maybe," she shrugs. "I don't know," Dana says rubbing the dirt off the stone with the cuff of her shirt, pulling at the surrounding grass.

They stand up and walk over to the papers Serena tossed onto the ground. The pages begin to tremble and skim along a breeze, scampering toward the forest. Dana bends to pick up one sheet, chases another, and squints at a page trying to make sense of what's there. She raises her eyebrows and hands it to her mother.

Names. Long rows of names written in meticulous, deliberate, Palmer perfect hand. Rebecca drops to her hands and knees, scrambling to gather the rest of the papers escaping over the grass into the dark. Dana hunts for others picked up by gusts tossed to murky outer edges. Rebecca sits back cross-legged with the crumpled pile in her lap and scans other lists, other names. She smoothes out the pages, bends down, tilting her head angling for moonlight. Her face is so close to the paper she can smell the oldness and confinement on them, running her fingers along the names as if they were embossed. Rebecca finally finds her. *Rose M. Gabrielli.*

"Look at this!" Rebecca hands the page to Dana.

"What is it?"

Rebecca stands up. "It's a list of women's names, inmates…

The Forgotten Roses

Look at this one," she jabs her finger at the page. "Rose M. Gabrielli," she tells Dana.

"Who's she?"

"She's family."

Rebecca grabs Dana's hand and explains as they explore the clearing together. The grave sites are random, small and forgotten. Rebecca tells Dana the story she'd heard about Rose as they brush away leaves from a smattering of tiny granite stones and squares pressed into the earth like silent messages. "They said that Rose was a strong girl, fearless. Tough. Did whatever she pleased," Rebecca tells Dana. "She didn't know how to use her strengths, didn't know where to put feelings that were big and raw and new: anger, frustration, impatience. Her only release was defiance and risk." Dana kicks a clump of dirt at her feet irritably, but becomes quiet and pensive. Someday Dana may learn to compromise and give in, Rebecca considers but feels a prickly ambivalence at the thought.

A shy, unlikely glow winks at them from under a thorny bower across the far edge of the clearing. They lift the branches to discover a carved stone, very different from the rest – raised on a pedestal, an alabaster angel blows kisses from above. Here the ground is carpeted with moss, soft as a baby's smile. The trees begin to whisper "Hush" as their branches sweep down like arms to comfort, and sway rocking back and forth.

Rebecca and Dana lock elbows, tipping their faces up to the moonlight. The wind rises billowing their hair, their shirttails, into fluttering wings. They spin once around, like children, catching the currents, filling their lungs with the cool night air as if it were nourishment, grateful, as if it could sustain them forever.

They notice a narrow path nearby, but as they begin to leave they stumble over a rounded outcropping, like stone bubbles blown up from below. In the middle, on the largest stone, "In Memoriam" is printed in uneven black lettering, faded now and worn off in spots. Long dry reeds quiver as they stoop to bend them back, clear the weeds away from the face of the rock. It is a thing Rebecca knows they will do again.

They will return, Dana and Lily and Rebecca; they will bring pruning shears, and rakes. Together they will clear away leaves and dirt and broken twigs from the little markers, pull overgrown grass from their edges. They will cut back overhanging branches, unveiling the guardian angel waiting behind. And they will talk about Rose, not in whispers, but in clear voices that will ring inside the circle.

Sometimes when it is very warm and the wind rustles the tops of the tallest trees, Rebecca will swear she can smell smoke, but it's probably only the sun beating on dried leaves she will tell herself.

And when Dana and Lily get to squabbling while working, they will suddenly cock their heads to listen, each asking the other in low urgent voices "What? Did you say something?" Their brows will furrow as they sidle closer together pressed side-by-side until the warmth of their skin flows into one another like blood. Dana will reassure her sister, bending her head towards the smaller girl, speaking softly. "It's only the buzzing of bees," she will explain, or the shushing of meadow grass as hot air whisks through and not someone murmuring in their ears.

Early next spring, when snowdrops and crocus begin to push through the moist earth as winter loses its grip, Rebecca and her daughters will move into the little farmhouse near the town center sold by Constance Wauney. Rebecca will add window boxes out front overflowing with annuals for the pleasure of everyone who passes by, and a porch out back under the crabapple tree that protects a ring of Lily-of-the-Valley at its feet.

She will strip and polish the wide pine floors, paint the inside pure white, the outside butter yellow and the door a lighthearted spring green, the color of new beginnings. She will surround her half acre with an old-fashioned privet hedge just like her Nana's, tall enough for little children–or a puppy–to hide under, but low enough to limit its shade. Her perennial bed will be too small and haphazard to attract Floyd Eames' goats but big enough for all of Rebecca's favorites: tall white phlox and bright blue delphinium, pink coneflower, lavender, coralbells, Japanese iris, bee balm, Oriental poppy – some transplanted from her old house before the move; a covert operation. And the luxurious heirloom roses – the ones that looked most like Nana's – imported from England; a very costly operation.

Danny Jalinski will send his Dad, long widowed, to help with the planting. "Give him something to do on the weekends," he'll implore Rebecca. She'll be grateful for his help, amused by his resemblance to Danny – an older, stockier version with the same appealing shaggy curl of hair at the back of his neck. When she shakes Mike Jalinski's hand she'll see that his eyes are such a clear blue, nothing could ever hide behind them. Rebecca will bring him fresh lemonade when he works and he'll bring her peony clumps from his garden, planting them securely in hers. She'll be pleased to see that he knows which plants are shade loving, which require full sun. On his own, he'll sprinkle lime under her hydrangeas to deepen the blue, add peat moss to her perennial beds and pinch the dead heads off of annuals. Something comfortable and sunny will grow between the two, along with her new garden.

Eventually, Rebecca will tell her mother about the secret place. Eva will insist that Father Capasso bless the grounds – *"Pace e bene."* All four women – three generations – will gather there together in an unspoken sacred covenant. Their footsteps will tamp down a soft trail. Their laughter will light the way, lifting the spirits that reside there, releasing them.

Maybe someday Rebecca will move beyond Havenwood's borders. Most likely Dana will, Lily too. Even so, one thing is certain, their family will know this place and keep this place, always. For the babies. For the girls.

Hidden within the shelter of pines, they will plant some hardy pansies for hope, forget-me-nots on the cool shady edge where the hemlock greets the sunrise, and where the path opens to the clearing, a flame red rose.

Glossary

Alla mia famiglia	To my family.
Amerigana	American*
Baccala	Salt Cod
Bella! Bellisima bambini!	Beautiful! Beautiful babies!
Cafone	Crude - a crude or low class person
Cin-Cin	A toast: the sound of glasses clinking together.
Lasciala.	Leave her alone.
Mala femmina.	Bad woman.
Mal 'occhio.	Evil eye.
Mangia, mangia. Bello giovane.	Eat, eat. Nice youngster. **
Non dichia niente.	Say nothing.
Pace e bene.	Peace and goodness – a blessing.
Paisans	Fellow countrymen.
Piglia in culo!	Stick it up your ass!
Povera figlia.	Poor girl.
Putana	Whore.
Sta' zitto!	Be quiet!
Sugo	Gravy (spaghetti sauce)
Zia	Aunt
Zio	Uncle

*This was a term used to differentiate those that were privileged to be born in America between those who fought to get here and earn the prize of citizenship.

**The phrase "bello giovane" suffers from being "lost in the translation." The precise translation is nice (bello) and giovane (young). However, the phrase is used as a term of endearment whose meaning is closer to "such a nice young girl" or boy as the case may be.

Acknowledgments

First, I would like to thank Gene Hayworth for his enthusiasm and expertise, and Jeanne Haskins for her encouragement and belief in my work. I am indebted to my readers: my dear friend, Meg Randa, my poodle pal, Nicole Picard Kelly and my beautiful daughter Sabra Dudman as well as my very early readers, Jack Kutner, Loretta Lee and Brett Frechette. My author friends C. Anthony Martignetti, Barbara Walsh and Kim Triedman, have been a cherished source of help, support and wisdom. An additional bouquet of thanks goes to my daughter, Sabra, for her advice and assistance in all manner of computer snafus. Flavia Laviosa, Senior Lecturer in Italian Studies at Wellesley College, generously offered invaluable assistance with Italian translations. And I want to remember here, Miss Mahaney, my seventh grade English teacher, who took the bus from her home, then walked a mile in high-heeled shoes to tell my mother that I was a writer.

Finally, as always, I am grateful to my family – my Italian heritage – for all the boundless riches and blessings that have been bestowed upon me. I can only aspire to pass them forward and hope this book, in some small way, helps achieve that goal.

Deborah Doucette began her writing career as a free-lance journalist subsequently writing a non-fiction book, Raising Our Children's Children: Room In The Heart. She is a blogger for the Huffington Post, an artist, and mother of four. She lives in a small town west of Boston with her red standard poodle Fiamma (Italian for flame) surrounded by her art and enjoying the comings and goings of her twin grandchildren. She is currently working on a new novel.